BEYOND ABSOLUTION

BEYOND ABSOLUTION

Cora Harrison

For my sister Eleanor, who is very fond of my Reverend Mother.

This first world edition published 2017
in Great Britain and the USA by
SEVERN HOUSE PUBLISHERS LTD of
Eardley House, 4 Uxbridge Street, London W8 7SY.
Trade paperback edition first published
in Great Britain and the USA 2018 by
SEVERN HOUSE PUBLISHERS LTD

British Library Cataloguing in Publication Data
A CIP catalogue record for this title is available from the British Library.

ISBN-13: 978-0-7278-8713-9 (cased)
ISBN-13: 978-1-84751-821-7 (trade paper)
ISBN-13: 978-1-78010-885-8 (e-book)

Typeset by Palimpsest Book Production Ltd.,
Falkirk, Stirlingshire, Scotland.

ONE

St Thomas Aquinas:
Poenitentia non sit virtus.
(Repentance may not be a virtue)

I t was very dark at the back of the Holy Trinity Church and Father Dominic's confessional stall was in the darkest and most remote corner. There had been a long line of penitents during the Novena prayers, but now all had left to join other queues. And yet, the small, dim light above the stall still signalled the presence of the friar.

The Reverend Mother watched anxiously as Prior Lawrence strode down the church and wrenched open the central door. Father Dominic was still there: his tall, broad-shouldered frame wedged into the narrow, centre cubicle of the confessional, bare sandal-clad feet, long brown robe, waist circled with white rope, crucifix on the breast, bushy iron-grey beard protruding. But the head had fallen to one side, the listening ear was now slumped upon his shoulder and the dead orbs stared sightlessly ahead. The Reverend Mother got to her feet and went across. One glance at those eyes had told her that he was dead.

She could do nothing for Father Dominic; she knew that, but she could be there for his brother. Father Lawrence was not just a brother in Christ, but also a brother by blood. She knew how close they were. Lawrence and Dominic Alleyn had grown up in a lovely old Queen Anne house outside Cork city, had both attended the prestigious St Columba School in Dublin, had together converted from Protestantism to the Roman Catholic faith of their pious mother and both had joined the Capuchin Friars in the same year.

'Lawrence,' she said now.

He did not look at her, but reached out to feel his brother's face. She hesitated for a moment, standing behind the prior, but then touched his shoulder. She could feel him shudder. He turned and held his own hand towards her, palm upwards, the viscous red gleaming in the light from the lamp above them.

'Blood,' he said. 'He's bleeding.'

The Capuchin order of friars are always bearded and she had noticed nothing initially. But now she saw that the whole of the right side of Father Dominic's face was sticky with coagulated blood. A fly descended and she waved it away with her free hand, her forefinger steady on the dead pulse.

'What's wrong?' It was Judge Gamble, yet another elderly man who had once been part of her youth, she thought fleetingly as she saw the white beard and the drooping white eyebrows. 'Is he dead?' he asked.

She nodded and wished that he remained in his seat.

'Should we send for the police?' The judge had a tentative note in his voice and she thought that she could probably ignore him. She wanted as little fuss as possible for the sake of the living brother.

'Brother Martin,' she said authoritatively to one of the friars who stood helplessly around, 'would you please telephone Dr Scher of South Terrace. The exchange will know his number. Tell him to come quickly.'

Dr Scher was the police doctor as well the doctor for her convent. He would know whether the police should be sent for. But the news that a doctor was coming was always reassuring. Her old friend, Father Lawrence, would want to know that everything had been done for Dominic, though she had little doubt about the verdict.

The prior turned a bewildered face towards her and she said quietly, 'Lawrence, I think he is dead.'

'Dead.' He dropped to his knees and she knelt beside him as he prayed aloud. The judge stood around awkwardly for a moment and then walked towards the door. Let him be the first to spot the doctor. She murmured the Latin words under her breath, '*Profiscere, anima Christiani, de hoc mundo, in nomine Dei Patris omnipotentis . . .*'

The belief that the soul remained within the body for half an hour after clinical death was, she thought, a consolation to all of the Roman Catholic faith. As she listened now to

Father Lawrence praying that his brother's Christian soul would go forth out of this world in the name of God the Father, she puzzled over the mystery of what or who had struck down the gentle priest. Why was he bleeding from the ear? She didn't know, but she had an uneasy feeling that the dead face wore a startled, terrified expression as though in his last moment Father Dominic had seen something menacing.

A young friar appeared carrying the holy oils but Father Lawrence made no move to take them, almost as though he feared to interrupt his passionate petition. Dr Scher arrived, ushered in by Judge Gamble, but the elderly priest continued to bombard the Mother of God, her spouse, St Joseph, the apostles and the saints. He did not cease while the doctor made a quick examination, shook his head sadly at the Reverend Mother and then stood back with bowed head until the prayer was finished and extreme unction was given.

By now, the prior was joined by most of the other friars, all kneeling around the dead body and reciting *Dies Irae*. So the Reverend Mother moved away and stood beside Dr Scher, wishing that Judge Gamble would take himself off. It was a surprise to see him there, she thought fleetingly. She had never considered him a religious man. Perhaps, ever since the death of his Protestant wife he might have reverted to a more fervent practice of the religion of his youth. The Reverend Mother tried the effect of a cold stare and was glad when he went and sat beside Sister Mary Immaculate and began a whispered conversation about St Aloysius, a sixteenth-century saint, renowned mainly for having taken a vow of purity at the age of nine. Since, in her experience, nine-year-old boys mostly loathed and despised girls that vow did not in the least impress the Reverend Mother and so St Aloysius was not a favourite of hers. However, some predecessor had appointed him, with the support of the bishop, as patron saint of the school. And so, despite having already honoured the saint this morning in the convent chapel, she had allowed herself to be persuaded by Sister Mary Immaculate to attend the evening Novena in his honour in the church of the Holy Trinity.

Now she turned her back on the nun and the judge, and

gave her attention to Dr Scher. His face was troubled and she guessed what he was going to say.

'Not a natural death, Reverend Mother. I think someone stabbed him through the ear,' he muttered. 'This is a police affair now. Show me where there is a telephone and I'll call Patrick Cashman. Poor old man,' he added compassionately as she summoned a friar with a lifted finger.

Through the ear! But Dr Scher had already departed so she went back towards her seat where Sister Mary Immaculate, wimple and veil now neatly in place, rosary beads moving, awaited her superior.

'Sister, could you return to the convent now and take my place at supper,' she said. 'I will be back later but I want to stay with Father Lawrence now.' The woman had been a nuisance all through the service, suddenly rising in the middle of it to join the queue to confess to Father Dominic and then fidgeting with her veil and wimple for the rest of the time until her superior had produced a spare hat pin. She would, of course, make a fuss about walking alone through the streets of Cork. The Reverend Mother had a sudden inspiration.

'I wonder, Judge Gamble, whether you would be good enough to see Sister Mary Immaculate back to the convent.' He probably had his car with him, she thought. She had seldom seen him on foot for the past few years. If not, then he could easily fetch it. His house was less than five minutes from the church. Or else he could escort the nun along the quays. Without waiting for questions from either of them, she walked swiftly back to Dr Scher.

'Let me tell him,' she said. And without waiting for an answer, she went and knelt down beside the man who had been a friend of her youth. Time enough to talk to him when the police inspector arrived and when the verdict of unlawful death had been pronounced. In the meantime, she could pray with him for the repose of Dominic's soul.

'Someone killed him, Lawrence; the police will want to ask some questions,' she said just as soon as she heard the heavy boots of the policemen replace the whisper of sandals on the tiled floor. She touched his stone cold hand and then withdrew it. He was a very private man and she did not want to intrude too far into his grief, just to be there for him if he needed her. She could rely on Patrick to be courteous and sensitive towards an elderly priest.

Inspector Patrick Cashman had been a pupil at the Reverend Mother's convent school, moving on to the Christian Brothers' School in his eighth year. It was hard to recognize the skinny, bare-footed boy from this well-dressed, quietly authoritative policeman. He had a low-voiced conversation with Dr Scher and then with the bursar of the friary. He assigned his sergeant to talk with the few members of the public who were still in the church – and she had a moment's compunction when she thought how unceremoniously she had dismissed Judge Gamble and Sister Mary Immaculate, both of whom might be potential witnesses. Still, Patrick could always contact either later on.

A nice boy, she thought appreciatively as he waited respectfully, cap in hand, for Prior Lawrence to finish his prayers. No boy, though, perhaps. A man with a very responsible job. He had acknowledged her presence with a quick glance and a polite nod. His eyes, though, were on another young policeman who, after a whispered order, went to the confessional stall, unobtrusively checking everything, taking out a small slide rule from his pocket and measuring the screen between penitent and confessor. From time to time, the young man made a note and then came to show them to his superior.

Still the same Patrick, thought the Reverend Mother, still making sure to garner all the facts. Slow and patient, she had thought him at the age of six, but this steady patience had brought him a scholarship to the Christian Brothers Secondary School, and then, in his early twenties, to the great achievement of being selected to join the newly formed Irish police corps. The Civic Guards – *Garda Siochána*, 'Guardians of the Peace' they were to be called to distinguish them from the greatly hated Royal Irish Constabulary – were an unarmed force and the quietly spoken Patrick had done well within their ranks, had passed his examinations by dint of very hard work and was now an inspector.

She waited while Patrick spoke briefly with the prior; she heard the comforting word 'hospital' and then the body was carried away and Patrick and his policemen left the church, followed by Dr Scher. She had not approached him. If he wanted any information from her, then he would come to see her.

Father Lawrence began to walk up the aisle, but then, as though his legs had failed him, he sank down upon a seat in the nearest pew. She went to join him, but said nothing, just sat and waited for him to speak. He should be in bed with a cup of tea and a hot water bottle, she thought, but understood that for now he could not bear to leave the church.

'I don't understand why that young policeman thinks that Dom was murdered,' he said. His voice sounded cracked as though he had not spoken for weeks.

She said nothing. Let him talk, she thought. An autocrat like Lawrence could not readily show his feelings to the brotherhood within the friary. Funny how he had reverted to the childhood name, Dom, for his brother. Once they had gone to boarding school, Dominic had told her, his brother would never allow anyone to use the names Laurie and Dom. They were always, even to her, Lawrence and Dominic from then on. She had seen a lot of them when she was growing up. Her father had been a very prosperous wine merchant and numbered as friends most of those Anglo-Irish, in their big houses, each owning thousands of acres of the fertile land of Cork. The brothers had attended the same parties as her cousin Lucy and herself. No one, then, could have predicted that three out of the four would have ended up in religious orders in the city.

'Would it have been anything to do with those republicans, with the IRA,' he said breaking the silence.

She thought about this, not so much because she considered that there was any truth in that idea, but more to give the question due consideration.

'No, I don't think so,' she said after a moment. 'I think he was reverenced by the Republicans. Do you remember how he visited the men on hunger strike in the gaol, despite what the bishop said? And set up a first aid centre in the Father Matthew Hall to deal with wounds? He said someone had to look after these men as they did not dare go to the hospitals in case they would be handed over to the RIC – no, the Republicans would be the last people to injure Dominic.'

He nodded sadly and stared stonily ahead. She was half-sorry not to have discussed the question more; not to have encouraged him to talk.

'Was there anything worrying him, do you think?' She tried this question and was glad to see that he immediately turned back towards her.

'Do you know; it's funny that you said that? He came to me on Tuesday, not yesterday, the day before . . .' He seemed to be thinking hard, and so she did not say anything, just waited quietly. After a few seconds, he gave a heavy sigh.

'I suppose that there is no harm in saying this, because I am giving no details, just as he gave me no details, but he said, talking to me as his prior, not as his brother, he said that he was worried about something told to him under the shield of confession. He said that a man had confessed to him that he had been involved in some sinful crimes and that further crimes were planned by . . . by the gang, he said and Dom wondered whether without betraying the penitent . . . he was asking me whether he could take action to prevent such a crime. He would not betray anyone – that was what he said, but he could prevent robbery and perhaps a death.'

The Reverend Mother kept her silence for a long minute, but Lawrence did not appear to have anything else to say.

'What did you say to him?' she said eventually. He was staring at the altar, his face white and strained.

'I said that I would have to think about it,' he said and there was a note of bitterness, of self-hatred, perhaps, in his voice.

She reflected upon this. The seal of confession was a serious matter and she had often thanked God that this burden was not placed upon the shoulders of nuns.

'I wouldn't be sure what to say, either.' She hoped that her voice held a matter-of-fact note. Lawrence needed comforting. He had been a deeply sensitive and almost morbid boy, lacking the happy assurance of his younger brother. She guessed that he would suffer over his apparent refusal to give advice to Dominic. So Dominic held a dangerous secret. Could this be connected with that strange death? Murder it must be; Dr Scher was a clever man. He had looked at the body, seen enough to have the strongest of suspicions and had immediately requested the presence of the police.

'You can't blame yourself in any way,' she said as decisively as she could manage. 'I'm sure he would have been happy to wait for your decision.' Even as she said those words, she wondered whether they were true. Dominic was a man at peace with himself and did what he felt was right. He thought it right to minister to the wounded and to the dying whatever their politics and he went ahead and did it, without asking permission of anyone, not even of the prior at that time. The interdict of the bishop had meant nothing to Dominic. He had done what he felt was right to do.

Still Lawrence needed comforting and she did her best to reassure him. 'Lawrence, you were right to say that, right to give yourself time to think about it,' she said earnestly. 'If you had advocated action, then Dominic might have been placed in danger, but you told him to wait while you thought about it, prayed about it. I'm sure that you did the correct thing. Don't blame yourself.'

'I hope you are right,' he said, but his voice was dull. She sat for a while wondering what else she could say, but then she saw that his eyes were closed and his head was drooping. He needed to rest now. He had suffered a bad shock and she half wished that Dr Scher were still here. The bursar, Father Francis, was peeping in from the sanctuary and she summoned him with a nod.

'I think the prior needs to rest now,' she said and was pleased to see how gently he took the old man's arm and conducted him up the aisle. She waited for a moment after they had both disappeared. She needed, she thought, to gather her strength. Oddly, she, too, felt weak. Another tie with the past has been broken, she thought, as the door opened and a figure, carefully removing his hat, came in through the door.

'Thought you might like a lift back to the convent,' said Dr Scher. 'Of course, I know that you are going to tell me that you could walk across the bridge as quickly as I could drive, but think of my scintillating conversation on the way.'

'Well, perhaps that might tip the balance,' she said getting to her feet. Normally she made a habit of rising straight up, but this time she clung to the top of the kneeling rail for support as she levered herself up and she knew that his keen eyes had noted the fact.

'Today, I've lost a very dear friend, someone that I've known for all of my life,' she said, excusing herself. And then, hurriedly, she added, 'How did he die, Dr Scher?'

'Can tell you more tomorrow, once I've had a chance to do the autopsy,' he replied, holding the door open for her and waited as she dipped her finger into the holy water and crossed herself, her lips moving in a prayer for Dominic and for his desolate brother.

'He was a good man,' said Dr Scher as they went down the steps. 'He'll be very much missed. A nice man, too,' he went on and then when she looked at him, he said, 'I met him once. In that antiques shop over there. We had a little chat. I liked him. Who, on earth, could have wanted to kill him.'

TWO

History of the Civic Guards
*In February 1922 the Royal Irish Constabulary began to
be replaced by a new body to be named 'The Civic
Guards'. The general election of 10th June 1922 returned
a majority in favour of the treaty at national level with
Griffith's and Collins' pro-treaty Sinn Féin winning
fifty-eight seats. De Valera's anti-treaty Sinn Féin won just
thirty-six seats. The civic guards had to keep the peace
between the newly elected and the anti-treaty rebels.*

Inspector Patrick Cashman looked across his meticulously neat desk at Dr Scher who was idly drawing a spider's web on a police notebook. The elderly man looked puzzled, he thought. 'And the cause of death, Dr Scher?' he prompted gently.

Dr Scher rapidly added an extra set of lines to the network in front of him, joined them up carefully and looked up. 'The cause of death is easy,' he said. 'I could see that instantly. Someone stuck something sharp through the man's ear. It pierced the brain. He would have died instantly. The complicated thing is *what* killed him. Something very narrow . . .'

'I had someone measure the holes in the screen,' said Patrick. 'Very small – about the width of your first finger – no bigger.'

'And so you want me to wave a magic wand and tell you what killed him? Not a bullet anyway.'

'No, that would have been ruled out, anyway. Too much noise. There were still plenty of people in the church.'

'Including Reverend Mother Aquinas. He was a friend of her youth, you know. You should go and have a chat with her. She might give you some information. All I know about the dead man is that a sharp, very thin instrument pierced his brain sometime within the hour before I was called to examine the body. Oh, and that he was interested in ceramic antiques.'

'Ceramic antiques!' Patrick thought through the vast numbers of priests that he had met in the city of Cork. Many of them were interested in football teams, quite a few were fanatical fishermen and he had known several who frequented horse meetings, but he had never known any to be attracted by antiques. It seemed an odd interest for a friar. 'Are you sure?' he questioned.

'Yes, met him in the antiques shop on Morrison's Island, Morrison's Island Antiques, quite near to his church, of course.'

'But the Capuchins take a vow of poverty,' said Patrick. 'He wouldn't be buying anything for himself. They don't have any money.'

'Well, I like looking at some rare pieces of antique silver, but I know that I can't buy all that I see,' said Dr Scher. 'Perhaps he just liked looking at it.'

'Perhaps.' It seemed somehow unlikely to Patrick. You didn't see priests doing that sort of thing. 'And the owner of that shop is a Protestant,' he said aloud.

'Perhaps he hoped to convert him,' suggested Dr Scher. 'He asked to see the manager, anyway. I heard him ask the young lady there, pretty little Rose Burke, Rose O'Reilly, now, of course, if he could have a word with the manager.'

'He just wasn't that sort of priest. He was very tolerant. Too tolerant, some thought him. There were rumours that the bishop didn't care for him. But most of the people in the city thought that he was a bit of a saint.'

'Saints sometimes get murdered, not that I know a lot about them,' said Dr Scher. 'But I have seen a picture of St Sebastien, and he had a lot of arrows stuck into him. It wasn't an arrow that killed our man, though. Something thin and sharp penetrated through the ear and all the way into the brain. An arrow broadens too quickly for what I have in my mind.'

'And no one could have killed him for his possessions; he had no money, no power, nothing really that anyone would want.' Patrick was still musing and then he roused himself. 'He was definitely killed while sitting within the confessional box. Your evidence would point to it and we have a few witnesses who came forward to say that he was alive earlier when they confessed to him. We are posting notices everywhere asking people to get in touch if they saw or heard him, or didn't get any response from him, but we've had very few volunteers so far. People are reluctant to come forward. Confession is a very private affair. You still see lots of women who hide their faces in their shawls and men who turn up their collars or wear a scarf around their face while they are waiting. And, of course, there are some in this city who don't like talking to the police under any circumstances. Father Dominic had a name for being lenient towards Republicans. That's why he always used that confessional stall in that darkest corner. I wouldn't expect a Republican to come forward. Some of their leaders don't like the idea of confession.'

'Well, there you are, a Republican atrocity – no one will expect you to solve that, so you don't need to look so worried. Perhaps the good priest gave one of the brotherhood such a hefty penance that he whipped out—'

'Whipped out what?'

'A stiletto,' suggested Dr Scher. 'A narrow, fine-bladed stiletto.'

Patrick shook his head. 'Never seen or heard of one of them in Cork. Too expensive for our murderers. They stick to the ordinary knives, or guns. There are still plenty of guns knocking around the city of Cork ever since the days of the British Army and the Black and Tans. They had no care for their equipment, so people said.' He got to his feet. Dr Scher had done his part; had told him the cause of death; had hazarded an opinion as to the cause of death. He could do no more. It was now up to him to sift through the evidence and to list opportunities and motives.

'I'll see you out, Dr Scher,' he said, 'I want to check if Tommy has any messages for me at the desk.'

Tommy was not at his desk as usual when they came to the front hallway of the barracks. He seemed to be barring the front door to someone as they came out. There was a tall thin man with his hand on the doorknob, shaking his head as Tommy pleaded, 'Just wait another minute, sir. He won't be long.' And then with a note of relief, 'Here he comes! A gentleman to see you, inspector.'

'I can't wait,' said the man impatiently. 'I've already told

this man all that I know. I went to confession to Father Dominic
last night and he was in very good form. Wished me good
night when I left and told me to say a prayer for him.'
   Patrick nodded. Father Dominic was famous for asking
people to say a prayer for him. One of the reasons why he
was so popular in the city. Everyone felt at ease with a man
who was so cheerful about being a sinner and needing prayers
said for him. He glanced quickly at Tommy's note. This man
had gone into the right-hand stall, though, and that was of
interest.
   'And who went into the box after you?' he asked.
   'A chap from the bank, O'Reilly, I think is his name. That's
right. Mr James O'Reilly.'
   'And after him, did you see anyone else?' With luck, the
man had knelt in one of the pews at the back of the church
in order to say his penance before leaving the church. It
would not be long. Father Dominic was famous for short
penances, but it might have been long enough. The man
nodded reluctantly.
   'I think it was a woman with a shawl,' he said shortly.
   'What did she look like?' Patrick was busily writing.
   'Didn't really notice her. Just an ordinary shawlie. Not a
black shawl. One of those old ones. A big long one, covered
her right down to her boots. Now can I go?'
   'Of course,' said Patrick easily. 'We'll just need to take
your name and address in case I need any further information
from you, though I don't suppose that I will.'
   Now that he was free to go, there appeared to be a slight
hesitation about the man. After all, Patrick thought rapidly,
why had he waited? Why not just give this information to
Tommy and then depart?
   'Oh, Dr Scher, Tommy wants to have a word with you about
his rheumatism,' he said. He prided himself that he had done
it in a nonchalant way, but saw Dr Scher give him what his
mother would have called an old-fashioned look. Nevertheless,
it was a good excuse. Tommy always wanted to have a word
with someone about his rheumatism. Like most Cork people
of that age, the damp had got into his bones.
   'Come with me, sir, and I'll just jot down your details,' he

said hastily. He picked up Tommy's notebook and steered the man down the corridor and into his own room. He allowed the man to relax while he slowly and painstakingly took his name and address.

'You didn't happen to notice anything else of interest when you were in the church, Mr Heffernan,' he enquired nonchalantly as he wrote out the Morrison's Island address.

The man hesitated. 'Well, it's probably nothing to do with it, but I thought it was a bit odd,' he said cautiously.

'Yes.' Patrick went as slowly as he could with writing down the address: 1c Queen Street.

'It's just this English fellow that runs the antique shop, Mr Doyle; I thought it was a bit odd to see him. Him being a Protestant and all.'

'In the church? At the confessional?'

'Not at the confessional!' Mr Heffernan sounded shocked. 'No, Protestants don't go to confession, but he was standing at the back of the church, just beside the bell rope. Before the Novena began.'

'Beside the bell rope, where the sacristan would stand, is that right?'

'That's right.'

'You're sure that it was Mr Doyle?'

'I'm quite sure. I work at the garage on Morrison's Island. Often fill up that old lorry of theirs, and the cans; either he or his partner, Mr Power, drop in once or twice in the month. We used to call them Mutt and Jeff, just like the cartoon in the *Evening Echo*. Mr Power was such a big fellow, just like Mutt, and Mr Doyle such a little fellow. I couldn't mistake him. Little fellow with a black moustache. Dressed the same as always, three-piece black suit. Very nattily dressed always, pinstripe, just like Jeff.'

'And he was definitely inside the church, standing beside the bell rope.'

'That's right,' said the man. He was more relaxed now, seeing that his story was of interest. 'Had his hat in his hand, too, so he knew that much, but he's a Protestant, all right. I've seen him often passing the Holy Trinity Church and never once did he bless himself. Now, I'd better be going, inspector.

Got just an apprentice at the garage today and God only knows what he's been up to while my back was turned.'

Well, thought Patrick after he had left, Protestant or not, it's my duty to interview everyone who was in the church at that time. Joe had drawn out a placard asking for information and had gone down to Morrison's Island with it and the *Examiner* had a note appealing for witnesses at the bottom of an article, entitled, rather sensationally, 'AN ATROCITY BEYOND ABSOLUTION'. Meditatively he took down his cap from the hook behind the door and after a glance through the window, added a raincoat.

'I'm going out, Tommy,' he said.

'The superintendent has the car,' warned Tommy.

'I'll walk; I won't melt,' said Patrick. As he strode down the hill and along quays, he racked his brains. The superintendent had told him how lucky he was to be getting so much experience in such a short time and that there were more murders in the city of Cork than in any other place in, what he still called, the British Isles. He wasn't sure whether that was true or not, but it was a fact that he had dealt with quite a few murders since he had joined the Civic Guards. And had solved them. Now he was grimly determined that this particular murderer would not escape justice. Father Dominic was a very nice man and a very good priest. Who on earth would want to kill him? He had no money, never would have money; the man had neither power, nor desire to have power; no complicated human relationships, just a brotherhood of friars; no likelihood of arousing anger, the whole city spoke well of Father Dominic. Already there was talk of a great funeral for the man, a funeral that would be bigger than that of a bishop. As he walked down along the quays, he mentally mapped out the route that funeral would take from Morrison's Island to St Finbar's Cemetery and decided on which roads to close.

Morrison's Island was a small triangular portion of land, less than a third of a square mile in size, its longest edge backing on to the South Mall and the two shorter sides jutting out to a point into the south channel of the River Lee. The Holy Trinity Church and the friary fronted onto the Father Mathew Quay and the antiques shop was on Morrison's Quay.

The owner of the shop was inside by the counter, serving a customer who was watching the wrapping up of her small silver bell and chatting happily about her collection of bells. The other Englishman, Jonathon Power, was carefully cleaning an oil painting. Patrick walked over to him.

'A skilled job, that, Mr Power,' he said.

He looked up and grinned. 'Less dangerous than your job, inspector,' he said. 'These pictures never kick or punch no matter what I do to them.' He was an affable fellow. Very tall and blond-haired with a ready smile.

'It's the smoke is the problem,' he said, 'dims all the colours.' Then he changed rapidly to an exaggeratedly Irish accent. 'Sure, it's the ole turf, it do be smoky when the sods are a bit damp, like.' As he spoke, a portion of the girl's dress showed brilliantly blue under his rag and he bent his attention back to the picture, working with light, circular strokes, gradually exposing the full beauty of the original painting. 'The work of one of your Cork artists, Daniel Maclise,' he said. 'Lovely man with colour. Knew just how to use it. It's a pleasure to work on his paintings.'

'Well, good luck with it,' said Patrick. Peter Doyle had now finished with his customer and so he went across to the counter. This man also smiled in a friendly way.

'It's a fair cop,' he said in an exaggeratedly cockney accent. 'I never meant to do it, h'inspector. It just fell off the counter and into my hand and I puts it into my pocket before I knowed wot I did. Didn't even know I 'ad a knife in my pocket.'

Patrick eyed him uncertainly.

'Oh, my dear sir, don't look so serious.' Once again, Peter Doyle had changed his accent and now was exaggeratedly upper class, English. Suddenly he leaped on top of the counter, struck a pose and began to sing: 'When constabulary duty's to be done, to be done/A policeman's lot is not a happy one, a happy one.'

And then he jumped down from the counter and beamed at Patrick.

'Inspector Patrick Cashman, sir,' said Patrick stiffly. The murder of a priest was nothing to be funny about, he thought, but decided not to make that remark. He would just doggedly follow his usual procedure. He produced his warrant card. 'I'm investigating the death of Father Dominic of the Capuchin Friars. I just wanted to ask you a few questions, sir.' To his annoyance, the man lifted his voice again, singing the same silly refrain.

Our feelings we with difficulty smother, with difficulty smother,
When constabulary duty's to be done, to be done,
Ah, take one consideration with another, with another,
A policeman's lot is not a happy one.

He finished his song with a flourish and beamed at Patrick. 'Gilbert and Sullivan, you know,' he said.

'You may have heard that Father Dominic was murdered, on Thursday evening, in the nearby Holy Trinity Church,' said Patrick even more stiffly.

'Murdered, goodness, that's terrible! I didn't know that. I'm very sorry to hear of it.' The shop owner seemed to go without hesitation from comedy to an air of shocked seriousness.

'You don't read the *Cork Examiner*,' stated Patrick.

'Not often,' said Peter Doyle with a smile.

Unlikely, thought Patrick. Everyone in Cork read the *Cork Examiner*. And this man ran a musical opera group, put on performances in the nearby Father Matthew Hall. Surely he would read the *Cork Examiner* if only to read the reviews and the letters page. Everyone read the letters page. It was the first thing that the superintendent read in the morning, while he was waiting for his tea to cool.

'But you knew Father Dominic, didn't you?' He watched the man closely.

'I don't think so.' Was it his imagination or did Peter Doyle give a quick, wary glance at his assistant?

'We have a witness who saw him in here; looking at some . . .' Patrick took out his notebook. Although he remembered Dr Scher's words very well and did not really need this notebook, he was slightly afraid that the man would start singing again unless dealt with on a very formal basis. '. . . some ceramics,' he finished.

'Ceramics,' echoed Peter Doyle. 'Did you see a priest in here examining the ceramic jugs, Jonathon?'

'Saw a man in a black suit,' responded Jonathon, 'looking at those vases over there. Might have been a priest, don't know too much about priests.'

'He was a friar,' said Patrick and waited.

'Or a friar, whatever that might be,' said Peter Doyle. 'Though come to think of it, I do know about Friar Tuck and Robin Hood – used to love those stories when I was ten years old.'

'Neither of us are of the Church of Rome, inspector,' said Jonathon Power apologetically.

'I see,' said Patrick, but he was unimpressed by the explanation. Both of these men ran a shop only a few hundred yards away from Holy Trinity Church and they had done so for over two years. Surely, they would recognize a friar, dressed in the floor-length habit of rough brown wool, girdled with a white rope. Apart from anything else, the full beards and bare, sandaled feet would attract attention. They must know the difference between a friar and a priest.

'So you don't recall speaking to any priest or friar,' he said.

'I'll think very hard, inspector,' promised Peter Doyle. Patrick allowed a silence to fall for a minute while he scrutinized the bland face in front of him before looking back into his notebook, again.

'And there is another matter, sir. A witness, another witness, observed you in the church of the Holy Trinity sometime yesterday evening. You were standing at the back of the church beside the bell rope. Do you think that you could tell me what you were doing there?'

This time there was an astonished look on the man's face. 'Me, inspector! In a Roman Catholic Church! You must have made a mistake!'

Was he really astonished? Or was this another piece of acting? If so, he was good. He did, genuinely, appear to be astonished.

'The witness described you very accurately, sir. He described you as of medium height, wearing a dark suit and with a black moustache.'

'Well, I'm not too unusual. There must be loads of people in the city who look like me. Anyway, I'd have called myself small, rather than medium. Who was it anyway, who recognized me?'

Patrick tactfully passed over the height question. 'I can't divulge the name of the witness, sir, but I was satisfied that this person would know your personal appearance.'

'A customer, I suppose.' Peter Doyle seemed to muse for a while, fairly obviously astonished. Then he shrugged his shoulders. 'People make mischief, do things for a laugh,' he said rather unconvincingly.

Patrick wrote for a while in his notebook, very conscious that Peter Doyle was going through a pantomime of disbelief, scratching his head, grimacing, rubbing his chin. Playacting, thought Patrick, but then there had been a genuine appearance to that first look of astonishment. This exaggerated acting was probably second nature to him.

'And there is nothing that you can tell me about Father Dominic?' he asked.

'Nothing,' said Peter Doyle. 'Very sorry to hear about his death and all that.'

'And your own movements yesterday evening?'

'I was here in the shop, I tend to keep it open a bit late in case someone wants to pop in after work, and, of course, I was expecting the rest of the cast for the performance of *The Mikado* that evening. We have a habit of all meeting here, run through a few songs etc., have a cup of tea and a few sandwiches, and then all go out to supper after the performance.'

'And who makes the sandwiches?' Patrick was reluctant to leave. There was something odd about this. Why had Father Dominic visited the place? And if the garage man spoke the truth, why had Peter Doyle so vehemently denied being in the church?

'Oh, it's usually the women. Miss Gamble, she's the headmistress of Rochelle School for Girls, or else it's her assistant Miss Anne Morgan, or perhaps Rose, Mrs O'Reilly. They do the sandwiches and the men take care of the supper bill. We're all great friends. Sorry I can't be of more assistance to you, inspector.'

Patrick went on writing for one long minute after this. It was, he thought, only right that he asserted his position as inspector and made it clear that he would be the one to end the interview.

'Well, thank you, sir,' he said, putting away his notebook and pencil. 'Please get in touch with me in the barracks if either of you remember anything further that could be of use to us. Don't stir. I'll see myself out.'

It was now automatic with Patrick to stride briskly away, open the door with a flourish, shut it with a firm click, and then to pause just outside and to listen intently. He did that this time, but he heard nothing.

And that, he thought as he walked away, was quite significant.

There were two men left behind. What did they do after he had left? Did one man look at the other with a measure of suspicion? Or did they both hold their breath until his footsteps died away. Suspect everyone in the first place, his superintendent had said to him when he was in the early months of his job. Suspect everyone and gradually, one by one, clear each suspect and then see who is left.

But why on earth should one of these men murder someone like Father Dominic? Jonathon Power had an honest look about him. Instinctively he had liked him. But Peter Doyle, well, he wasn't sure about him. Something about that man that he had disliked.

Still, this was speculation, not something that he encouraged in Joe at this early stage and it was something that he should not indulge in, himself. There was solid police work to be done and he would see that it was done. Only when he had traced and interviewed everyone who had confessed to Father Dominic yesterday evening, should he begin to speculate upon a possible murderer.

It took Patrick five minutes to walk from Morrison's Island and down the South Mall towards Lapps Quay. The Savings Bank loomed up, facing up the length of the South Mall, magnificent in the June sunshine, its well-cut silver limestone blocks sparkling white. Patrick eyed it with satisfaction. One of the first things that he had done when he had obtained the coveted position of a civic guard had been to open a bank account there and to deposit a small weekly sum. His promotion to sergeant had doubled that amount. When he had passed the examination that confirmed him as inspector, his savings had begun to look exciting. One day, he hoped, he would be able to buy a house. With that happy thought in mind, he leaped up the limestone entrance steps and marched through the double-leaf, panelled front door.

'Inspector Patrick Cashman,' he said briskly to the man at the desk. 'I'd like to have a word with Mr James O'Reilly.'

'One moment, inspector.' The clerk had a wary look and he sidled off through an unmarked door with a backward glance over his shoulder at Patrick as he slid through it. He was back before long.

'This way, inspector,' he said briskly and Patrick followed him down a carpeted corridor and after a brief knock, flung open a door to a sumptuously furnished room, heavy desk, revolving chair, thick carpet and velvet curtains. Patrick instantly knew that he had been shown into the manager, a Mr Broadford, judging by his desk sign. He sat quietly on a chair indicated and resolved that he would not be bullied. A new manager, he remembered. Younger than he would have imagined. Had grown that moustache to make himself look more impressive. Cleared his throat before speaking, just like an elderly man. They modelled themselves on a predecessor, he supposed.

'Yes, inspector. Perhaps you would let me know why you need to see Mr O'Reilly.' The tone was hostile.

Patrick looked at him woodenly. It had been a mistake to come here, he thought, but he had not wanted to wait until the evening.

'I'm investigating the murder of Father Dominic of the Holy Trinity Church and we wish to speak to everyone who attended Father Dominic's confessional on that evening,' he said quietly. 'Mr James O'Reilly's name was given to us and I wish to verify that he did indeed see the priest.'

'I'd have preferred if you had seen him out-of-hours,' said the manager. 'He has his work to do, you know.'

'Indeed, but murder has to take precedence,' said Patrick boldly. There goes any hope of a loan towards a house, he thought.

'Are you insinuating that one of my clerks had something to do with that abominable crime?'

Pompous idiot, thought Patrick, but he knew that his face would show nothing of his thoughts.

'Every tiny piece of evidence is of importance, sir,' he said woodenly.

'Very well.' The manager tinkled a small brass bell on his desk and waited. Patrick waited also, feeling very tense.

'Send Mr James O'Reilly into me,' said the manager when his summons was answered and Patrick braced himself. He rehearsed the words and the instant a rather scared looking young man entered the room, he was on his feet.

'Thank you, sir, now is there somewhere that we can be private while I put a few routine questions to Mr O'Reilly? That,' he added hastily, 'will save him having to miss an hour's work by coming back with me to the barracks. I would hate,' he said looking steadily at the bank manager, 'to inconvenience the bank in any way, but . . .'

'You can use my secretary's office.' The offer was made abruptly, but it was a surprise. Patrick had expected to be banished to some distant cloakroom, or underground vault. There was a look of alarm on James O'Reilly's narrow face. He looked even more like a scared rabbit. Did he fear to be overheard? It was a reasonable offer, though, and Patrick nodded.

'Thank you, sir,' he said and decided to leave it at that. No point in being too obsequious. He wondered whether the manager had noticed the look on O'Reilly's face. One might almost think that it was a look of guilt. Patrick felt a rush of slight excitement and kept an eye on the bank clerk as he politely held the door open for the flustered secretary.

'Let's sit over here by the window, Mr O'Reilly,' he said as soon as they had the room to themselves. He pulled two chairs near to the window and sat down. The door had felt reasonably heavy and he was confident that if they kept their voices down they could not possibly be overheard. Why did O'Reilly look so terrified though? 'You've heard about the death of Father Dominic yesterday evening in the Holy Trinity Church?'

'N . . . n . . . o . . . no, I . . . I d . . . d . . . didn't know.'
The words came out with a pronounced stammer. Surreptitiously,
O'Reilly wiped his hands on the padded surface of the chair
seat.

Unlikely, thought Patrick, writing busily, unlikely, and a
silly lie. Everyone in Cork would have been talking about the
murder of the priest. The instant that James O'Reilly arrived
at the bank he would have heard the news, if not earlier. He
decided to allow the matter to pass and continued, 'I understand
that you went to confession to Father Dominic yesterday
evening in the Holy Trinity Church.'

'No, no, you are mistaken.' The bank clerk had risen. He
cast a terrified look at the communicating door and then
lowered his voice. 'No, I don't think so,' he said very quietly.
Even his lips were white.

'You were seen going into the right-hand cubicle,' said
Patrick evenly. 'By a business man who lives near to this bank,'
he added.

O'Reilly's face turned even paler. He seemed to be thinking
hard. 'Perhaps I did,' he said after a few seconds. 'I . . . I
didn't take much notice. One priest is so like another priest.'

Patrick allowed a silence to ensue. There was no sound from
the other room. Either the door was completely soundproof
or no one was speaking. He wondered whether the secretary
had been sent off. It would have been easy to despatch her to
get a cup of tea. Perhaps even now the manager was standing
with his ear to the door. Patrick got to his feet and walked
across the room as silently as he could. The lock was a little
stiff and by the time that he pulled open the door, the manager
was standing in front of a bookcase beside the door, taking
down a book. There was no sign of the secretary.

'Finished?' he enquired, but Patrick was pleased to see that
he looked a little flustered.

'Almost,' he said coolly. 'But it just suddenly occurred to
me that I might consult you about the shutting of roads for
Father Dominic's funeral. Would it be an inconvenience if we
blocked off this end of the South Mall against traffic?'

'No, no, in fact I think that we might close as the funeral
leaves the Holy Trinity Church, as a mark of respect, you

know. Just for an hour or so.' He seemed to hesitate, looking beyond Patrick and into the small room where his clerk sat. 'Perhaps we could have a word about it after you have finished, inspector.'

'Certainly,' said Patrick. Decisively he closed the door. And went back over towards the window seat. The clerk was looking drearily out at the morning shoppers. Something odd about him, thought Patrick. He made an effort to sound reassuring.

'Father Dominic was a very popular confessor,' he stated, his eyes on the young man's downcast face. 'There is nothing wrong with going to confession to him. We just want to pinpoint the time of death.' He said the words as casually as possible. The young man opposite, probably only about his own age, looked terrified. But why? People went to Father Dominic week after week. Everyone found him so approachable and so comforting. Patrick knew that. He remembered from his own school days how the most scrupulous and most worried of the boys from the North Monastery School made a point of going down to Morrison's Quay for their weekly confession. Father Dominic, kind and reassuring, he reckoned now, had saved many of those very hard-working, neurotic boys from a nervous breakdown. He looked back at the address given. Pope's Quay. So that was where he lived. It was surprising that the man hadn't gone to confession at St Mary's Church, on his way home from work.

'I suppose you always go to confession in the Holy Trinity Church, nice and near to your work place,' he hazarded.

'That's right.' O'Reilly seemed relieved at that explanation. 'Yes, I think it might have been Father Dominic,' he said with more confidence. 'It was an old man, anyway.'

'And did he say anything?' Patrick began to write again.

'Just the usual. Now can I go? I have a lot to do, today?'

Patrick made a quick decision. Let him go now. He could always question him afterwards, perhaps at home where he would be more relaxed. There was something odd about the man, though. He was sure of that.

'Thank you for your time, sir,' he said without raising his eyes from his notebook. He was aware, though, of how quickly the bank clerk scuttled across the floor and slid out of the door leading to the corridor, opening it with care and closing it with hardly a click to betray him. Patrick finished writing, then stood up and with a perfunctory knock went into the manager's room.

James O'Reilly was guilty of something. Every instinct within him told him that. But of what?

He found the bank manager standing at the window, gazing down at a team of horses dragging a cartload of beer barrels. The city was awash with beer, he thought. Half the crime in the city was beer-related. It took the sting from poverty, but was no solution and he was impatient of those who sought comfort from it.

'You wanted to see me, sir,' he said politely.

'It's about that young man, James O'Reilly.' The bank manager turned so abruptly that he took Patrick by surprise. 'I'm worried about him and I want you to tell me what brought you here today.'

Patrick thought rapidly. By the book, there was no reason why he should tell the manager anything, but for O'Reilly's sake, it might be best to tell the truth.

'Oh, we're just interviewing everyone who went to confession to Father Dominic yesterday evening,' he said casually. 'One name leads to another and then we build up a picture of what was happening in that church around that time. Hopefully it will lead us to pinpoint the time of death and perhaps lead us to find the man who murdered him.'

'Oh, was that it.' The manager, Patrick noticed, had certainly heard all about Father Dominic's death, had even begun to make plans to close the bank for the funeral. It made it even more unlikely that James O'Reilly had heard nothing of the matter.

'I'm worried about that young man, inspector.' The manager had taken another long look out through the window and then seemed to make up his mind. Decisively he pulled down the blind, shutting out the unusual sunshine and lending an air of secrecy to his next words.

'Something's wrong,' he said emphatically. 'I know how much money James O'Reilly earns; I know where he went to

school; I know his father's job; his mother's maiden name;
what his uncles do for a living; I know who he married,
nice little nurse, she used to be, apparently; related to Judge
Gamble's wife on the distaff side, but no money on her
side of the family. Her father, they tell me, is a shop manager
in the Queen's Old Castle. No rich uncles on the father's side,
either . . .'

That's Cork for you, thought Patrick. No doubt, the bank
manager knew all about him also. Knew that he was a boy
from the slums, who had managed to get a scholarship to the
North Monastery School. Knew that he had got his school
certificate, had managed to get into the newly formed Civic
Guards. Knew that he had entered for one of their competitive
examinations for the post of inspector. And, perhaps the
manager even knew of his midnight hours studying until his
head felt about to explode . . . *used to see his light on all
hours of the night and then he'd walk up to the top of Barrack
Street and he'd just stand there looking down at the city* . . .
He imagined how some native Cork person would explain to
a newly appointed bank manager, how it came about that this
fellow with a low-class accent had been appointed as a police
inspector.

'Yes?' He looked a polite query at the man.

'How on earth does he afford that place of his on Pope's
Quay? And that car of theirs? And how does he afford to go
drinking, night after night in the Imperial Hotel with Tom
Gamble and his friends, that fellow Beamish and those two
English men that have a shop on Morrison's Island. That pair
might be able to afford it – the shop is doing well. Tom Gamble
mightn't be making much as a barrister, but there's money in
that family, and of course, we all know about the Beamish
family, but I can tell you one thing, inspector, James O'Reilly
can't afford that sort of company, not on the money that I pay
him. I tell you, I'm worried about that young man.'

Patrick concealed his impatience. Everything is relevant to
a murder enquiry, he reminded himself.

'You think he might have helped himself to some of the
bank's money, sir,' he asked.

'I know that he hasn't,' said the man bluntly. 'I'm not one

to trust blindly, inspector. I run checks from time to time and I've run quite a few on young James. No, wherever he's getting the money, it's not from the Savings Bank. In fact, he's brought in a few accounts from his friends in that musical society. Used to be golf, where I come from; they used to advise the clerks to take up golf, but in Cork, apparently, it's singing.' He gave a short laugh but his sharp eyes keenly scrutinized Patrick's face.

Patrick said nothing. This was the way to deal with this matter. Stand very still, listen very respectfully, do not be trapped or surprised into any remark that might be regretted afterwards. He had found James O'Reilly's account of his visit to the confessional to be slightly suspicious, but that was nothing to do with his employer.

'I'll bear in mind what you said, sir,' he said when he judged the appropriate amount of time had elapsed. 'Thank you for your time. And I'll send one of the Garda around to let you know if we are closing off this end of the South Mall for Father Dominic's funeral. Now, if you'll excuse me, I'd better get on. I'm trying to interview everyone who was in the church yesterday evening.'

THREE

St Thomas Aquinas:
*Praeterea, docere nihil aliud est quam scientiam in
alio aliquo modo causare.*
(To teach, therefore, is nothing other than, in some
way, to give rise to knowledge in another person.)

'Thank you, sister,' said the Reverend Mother, 'and could you send Jimmy to me. I want to send a note to Dr Scher. Sister Assumpta was complaining of a pain in her ribs this morning and I would like him to see her if he has time during the evening.'

The very elderly Sister Assumpta, who had taken to her bed several years ago, was always complaining of something. Nevertheless, she reminded her conscience, which was telling her that she should not waste the time of a busy doctor, that it was only right that the woman should have all possible medical attention. And, of course, Sister Bernadette would insist on serving the kind Dr Scher with tea and cake and that would provide an opportunity to discuss Father Dominic's visit to the antiques shop. She had been still in a state of shock when he had mentioned it, so she had not questioned him, but afterwards she said to herself, *What on earth was Dominic doing in an antiques shop?* Quickly she wrote a note, popped it in its envelope and then wrote another. Jimmy could deliver the two at the same time.

Jimmy was a new member of staff in the convent. Traditionally lay sisters did all the errands. However, at this time – perhaps because of a big intake in the 1860s and 1870s – it was a fact that almost all of them were quite elderly and reluctant to go out on winter days through the chilly fogs and almost continual showers of rain and to get their feet wet in the constantly flooded gutters as they crossed roads. So the Reverend Mother had an inspiration and in came Jimmy to the life of the convent.

Jimmy had been a pupil at the convent school until the age of seven years and then had been moved on to the Christian Brothers. The Reverend Mother had worried about him at the time. Jimmy appeared to be a bright child with a great interest in any oral facts or stories, but not one of the three teachers that he had during his time at the convent school had managed to teach him even the elements of how to read and write. He approached his speller every morning as though he had never seen it before. The whole business was a sealed mystery to him. Even the Reverend Mother herself had taken a hand in the process, but for Jimmy, words and sounds were like marks in the sand. No matter how firmly they were etched on his mind one day, by the next the sea of oblivion had swept across and erased them. The Reverend Mother had been so worried about him when he reached the age of seven that she had personally visited the Christian Brothers National School and had talked about the child's problems, emphasizing that Jimmy was neither lazy nor stubborn, but just could not retain letters nor numbers. She had been listened to politely, but had been full of apprehension and her worst fears were realized when Jimmy turned up one day with bruised hands and legs black and blue from constant beatings and had begged to come back to the convent school. Jimmy's mother said that she didn't think school was any use to him, but when she kept him at home, the school attendance officer had threatened her with prison.

'None of my sister's children are like that, Reverend Mother,' she wept. 'They all do her credit at school. They live over on Morrison's Island and they go to the Model School.'

She stopped, obviously embarrassed and perhaps thinking that the Reverend Mother would be offended at the implication that the Model School was better than the convent school. Unlikely, thought the Reverend Mother. They had huge classes there in the Model School and everything was learned by rote. The sound of hundreds of children chanting in loud sing-song voices was a permanent accompaniment to the traffic noises on Anglesea Street. No, she was inclined to think that Jimmy's lack of progress was due to some quirk within his brain, intelligent though he was. Not the child's fault, nor the teacher's – just one of the many unknowns in the teaching of children.

'Perhaps it is because he is the only one that lived and I spoilt him,' continued Mrs O'Sullivan tearfully. 'I've tried everything, slapping him, everything, but he's just a dunce. And, of course, his father just skipped off to England, but my sister's husband stayed and queues up every morning for some work on the docks. It makes a difference for a boy to have a father. I don't know what to do about him at all. I wish they'd just let him sit at the back of the class and ignore him, but the Brothers say that he's clever, but just doesn't concentrate and he needs to be punished. But the poor little fellow, Reverend Mother, he sicks up his breakfast on a Monday morning and he cries and cries and begs me to let him stay at home. I wish I could help but the Brothers say that he is just stubborn.'

The school attendance officer was of the same opinion, but the Reverend Mother soon disposed of him, startling him with a few long words and bombarding him with names like Montessori, Piaget and Steiner, crisply summing up their educational theories. Very quickly, she got agreement that Jimmy would return to the convent and would work as a messenger and get private lessons from the Reverend Mother herself. He was to be paid a penny a week for running messages, she decreed. He was also to help Sister Philomena with the babies in the Reception class. When he was not needed there, and when the Reverend Mother had a moment, she was to give him a lesson in reading. They had started with a map of the Cork streets; he had learned to read the names of the streets that he was sent to – perhaps not as useful for early reading progress as the regulation speller starting with words like 'cat' and 'rat' and progressing to 'rattled' and 'cattle', by-passing all irregular, frequently used words like 'said' and 'come'. However, she was hopeful that once some words were got into his head, once they were seen by him to be useful, that the whole process would suddenly become clear to him. In the meantime, she equipped him with a pair of rubber boots, a mackintosh, a warm jumper from the last jumble sale and directed Sister Bernadette to see that he had some hot cocoa whenever he came back from those chilly damp streets. And from time to time, they tackled the alphabet together.

'I went to a bonfire last night, Reverend Mother, with my cousins at Morrison's Island.' Jimmy's little pale face was lit up with excitement when he burst into her room.

'Yes, of course, Midsummer's Eve,' she said. The midsummer bonfire was always a great event. She had forgotten about it in the tragic affair of poor Dominic's death, otherwise she would have made a point of going around the classrooms and hearing the stories. The children would have been keeping woodworm-rotted pieces of wood dry inside hallways of the tall Georgian tenements and begged old newspapers from the surrounding shops. It was always great fun for the children especially when some kindly roadman donated some tar in order to keep the fire going in the heavy mist.

'We got some rotten old wood from that old warehouse 'n Morrison's Island, the one with no roof and we had a fire and it burned the floor down and there was a road under the floor and my cousin's little dog Patch went down there and he chased a million rats!' Jimmy was beside himself with excitement.

'Goodness,' said the Reverend Mother, doing her best to sound impressed. Morrison's Island, she thought, had been abandoned by the wealthy Gamble family. Someone should be checking on the safety of those old warehouses. And then she thought of the busy morning ahead of her and her duty to educate Jimmy.

'This letter is for somewhere beginning with an S,' she said, holding it concealed from his view and focussing attention on her hand-drawn map of Cork city streets.

'South Terrace,' he guessed triumphantly pointing to the spot by the river. 'Where Dr Scher lives.' Jimmy loved delivering letters to Dr Scher who often came up with a sixpenny piece on delivery and who usually handed him over to his housekeeper for a slice of cake and a glass of milk while he waited for the reply to the letter.

'Well, done,' said the Reverend Mother, thinking with dismay that although South and Scher began with the same letter, their sounds were completely different. Jimmy had made her realize the complexities of the English language. 'Yes,' she said aloud, 'and this letter is for Dr Scher, but the second letter is for someone else. It's for someone who works in a little lane off South Terrace, just around the corner from Dr Scher. Ask for the Lee Printing Works. Look, I've made a large L for Lee here and now I'm going to write in the name of our river, it's the Lee, isn't it – do you hear the sound of the two ees? And the letter is for a lady who works in the Lee Printing Works, Miss MacSweeney. They've got the same first letters, Miss and Mac; can you see that? It's the letter M, isn't it?'

'And M is for Mam,' said Jimmy.

Heartened by this she gave him a sweet. Her conscience sometimes pricked her when she included sweets under 'sundries' on the convent grocery list, so that the bishop's secretary, who audited the convent accounts, would not discover such a frivolous item amongst her expenses. Sweets might be a luxury, but she did find them invaluable for encouraging learning and the thin, undernourished children did love them.

'My mam said to ask you to pray for me that I learn to read,' said Jimmy diffidently as he paused at the door on his way out. 'She said you were a very holy woman . . . nun, I mean,' he added with an apologetic expression.

'I will, Jimmy,' she promised.

Not too holy, she thought when he was gone. Her days and half her nights seemed to be spent worrying about practical affairs, working out solutions instead of praying for them. Jesus would definitely class her as a Martha, rather than a Mary, she guessed, remembering the biblical story of the two sisters. She hauled up her watch from her pocket and pressed it open. It was time for the senior class's English lesson and after that was finished, she wanted to supervise a lesson given by a newly professed nun who had an unpleasant habit of shouting at the children. And after lunch she needed to answer a letter from the bishop, write her thanks for a donation from the Architects and Surveyors Society, start on her six-monthly accounts and . . . and think about that murder, she added. This was a very strange business and might involve the Church in some scandal.

It was, she thought with exasperation, just like Sister Mary

Immaculate to choose to go to confession in the middle of the Novena prayers. She would have to tell Patrick about this and the nun, no doubt, would have to be interviewed. And before she did all of this, she would indeed say a prayer for poor Jimmy. Not to St Aloysius, she decided, there was a self-satisfied look about the boyish face, framed in the Renaissance ruff, and according to his life-story, he was a brilliant student. No, she would pray to humble old St Joseph, who, surely, had taught many boys the dangerous and difficult arts of handling saws, hammers and knives without injuring themselves. Perhaps he could do something for a boy so eager to learn as Jimmy O'Sullivan.

And then her mind turned from Jimmy and back to Father Dominic. Someone had gone into that confessional cubicle, under the eyes of more than a hundred people and had murdered him. She remembered the blood on Dominic's face and shuddered. It seemed to be an extraordinary affair. Why murder a priest? And, especially, why murder a good and gentle man like Dominic?

With a sigh, the Reverend Mother picked up her copy of *Jane Eyre*, and went off to her class of senior girls.

She was inspecting the publisher's list of text books with Sister Mary Immaculate when she heard Dr Scher's voice. Leaving the nun to do the addition, she went rapidly out to the hallway and interrupted the banter between him and Sister Bernadette.

'Met your little lad,' said Dr Scher as soon as she came into view. 'Saw him down on the quay and he waved the note at me.'

'He'll be disappointed not to have gone to your house,' she said.

'Well, as a matter of fact, I drove him over there,' said Dr Scher apologetically. 'It's that housekeeper of mine, she loves having someone young to feed. He said that he had another letter to deliver over there, anyway.'

'That was very kind of you, Dr Scher. Now you simply must come and see my potatoes,' said the Reverend Mother quickly. Dr Scher was very indiscreet and she did not want the name on the second envelope mentioned.

'It's raining,' said Dr Scher, with a longing look into Sister

Bernadette's kitchen where the range glowed and a kettle was already at singing point.

'You won't melt.' She got him outside and walked him over to the potato patch. They would be quite private here. Hopefully, Sister Mary Immaculate would have finished the tally by the time they returned.

'Look at that mist. Very bad weather for moulds. Those potatoes will get the blight. You'll have to spray them with Bordeaux mixture,' said Dr Scher giving a disparaging look at the dripping foliage.

'I'll tell the gardener,' she said absent-mindedly. 'Any news about Father Dominic's murder?'

'Bit early in the day for that. Patrick is trying to get a statement from everyone who went to confession to the poor man, trying to pinpoint the moment when he died, I suppose. Funny place to commit a murder. Father Dominic walked the streets and went down the lanes. You'd think that someone could have murdered him somewhere like that. What's it like in those cubicles?'

'Very dark,' said the Reverend Mother, 'and, of course, there are people who keep their eyes shut. It's considered holy to shut your eyes.' And then she remembered.

'One of the people who confessed to him was Sister Mary Immaculate,' she said.

'Still, I don't suppose that she drove a stiletto into Father Dominic's ear,' he said.

'A stiletto?'

'Something sharp and narrow. Went through his ear and into his brain. He would have been dead within moments.'

'Is that how he was killed? I was wondering. A stiletto, are you sure?'

'Well, Patrick tells me that they don't have stilettoes in Cork, so it will be something else. A knitting needle, perhaps. How sharp are knitting needles?'

'I have no idea,' said the Reverend Mother. She was brooding on that death. 'He knew that he was about to be killed,' she said. 'He knew his murderer and he knew why. I could tell by his face. It's no use you looking dubious. I knew Dominic and you didn't.'

'He was well-known in the city,' said Dr Scher thoughtfully. 'I often heard people speak of him. A very nice man.'

'He was,' said the Reverend Mother sadly. 'Dominic and I have been friends since we were in our cradles. I knew him very well. I'll miss him, though I might only see once in every few months. The whole of Cork will miss him. He was a man of great warmth.'

'Yes, indeed. Great warmth. That shone out.' He nodded his head in agreement.

'You met him, you said, didn't you?'

'That's right. I met him. A very nice man. It must have been Wednesday evening that I met him, over on the other side of Morrison's Island, in the antiques shop run by those English men.'

'An antiques shop!' So she had recollected correctly. She was quite startled. 'But what was a priest doing in an antique shop?'

'Don't know.' He looked a little surprised at her exclamation. 'I know what I was doing, bought some lovely silver, old Cork silver, a Queen Anne tea set. Cost me a month's wages from the university, but I don't regret it. A beautiful set and in lovely condition. Pretty rare, I'd say.'

'But what was Father Dominic doing there?'

'Looking at a ceramic. A beautiful Japanese hawk, a blue Arita hawk,' said Dr Scher.

'A Japanese hawk!'

'That's right, looking quite upset too.'

'Upset?' She seized upon the word.

He looked at her with surprise. 'Well, there's normally two of them,' he explained. 'They lose about three-quarters of the value if one is gone. I spoke to him, nice man, knew me straight away; called me by my name. And I said to him, "Well, it will happen, you know, Father. There's always one gets broken."'

'And what did he say in reply?' asked the Reverend Mother.

'He looked even more upset. He was peering at it, you see. "There's a chip out of the beak, too," he said, sort of talking to himself, and then he turned away and went down the stairs and asked the young woman if could see the manager. He was still wandering around when I left. Exchanged a few

words with people. Everyone seemed to know him. More
returning their greetings, than talking, but he seemed to be
examining all the goods on sale. He looked very troubled,
though.'

The Reverend Mother brooded on this after Dr Scher had
left to check on the elderly nun. It didn't make sense. Why
on earth should Dominic worry about a damaged Japanese
hawk? He had been the most unworldly of men. And yet at
the back of her mind there was something about an Arita
Japanese hawk. Where had she heard the expression before?
And then she roused herself. It was recreation hour for the
nuns and she made a habit of appearing for the first five or
ten minutes of this.

But for a long moment she stared down at her potatoes.
How awful if they were stricken by blight. She was relying
on them to feed some of the poorest and thinnest of the children. Perhaps a lump of butter in the centre of each one if she
could persuade the manager of the Savings Bank to extend
her credit a little. One of the butter stalls in the market might
be persuaded to donate unsalted butter that was nearing the
end of its storage life. That, she thought, would be worth
trying. She paced the length of her potato patch. One half of her
brain was anxiously scrutinizing them for signs of the dreaded
blight, but the other half was busy with the spectacle of Dominic,
on his last full day of life, wandering around the antiques shop
and looking distressed.

And where had she heard of a Japanese ceramic hawk, a
blue Arita hawk?

FOUR

W.B. Yeats:
'Hearts with one purpose alone
Through winter and summer
Seem enchanted to a stone.'

Eileen stared in a puzzled way at the letter from the Reverend Mother. She had been glancing at it from time to time throughout the afternoon, but it did not enlighten her. A summons from her former headmistress was probably of significance. The convent was always available to a past pupil like herself for advice and even as a place of refuge, but Reverend Mother Aquinas, while she might have sympathy with the Republican aims to form a united Ireland, firmly deprecated the methods of the rebels. She would not summon her unless she had some purpose. She had made it very clear that she thought Eileen should sever all connections with an illegal organization. Was this going to be another attempt to persuade her to change her mind?

But Eileen found it impossible to give up the connection with the Irish Republican Army. It was, she thought sometimes, as though she were frozen in time by a spell, like one of the fairy princesses whose stories her mother used to relate to her. She could not plan for the future, could not move on until the whole island of Ireland was a republic. It seemed to her that the treaty, allowing England to retain six northern counties of Ireland, was a disaster. Every right-minded patriot had a duty to fight against those who supported that treaty. There could be no softening, no yielding, until the whole of Ireland was a republic. Outwardly, she was a respectable office girl, working for a printing works, but night after night, she penned articles passionately arguing for a united Ireland and then turned them into pamphlets or even sold them to newspapers. I'm now eighteen years old, she said to herself rebelliously, as she redrafted an auctioneer's leaflet, hammering away efficiently on the battered typewriter. I can make up my own mind what I do with my life. In any case, the Reverend Mother, in giving her a choice between Saturday at nine in the evening, or Sunday at the same time, had not given her much of a choice. Saturday night was impossible, as there was a late-night performance of *The Mikado* musical. The Sunday performance was earlier, but on Sunday her Republican friend, Eamonn, was coming into the city to see the show and then to spend the night in Eileen's mother's house.

'You're looking very serious. Not worrying about your stage performance, are you?' said Jack coming in for his last task of the day. Jack was a compositor, very skilled, and totally oblivious to whatever he printed. Words that sang to Eileen were just a series of letters to him as he worked with astonishing speed, picking up the individual letters from a type case with his right hand, and setting them into a composing stick held in the left hand. When Eileen had first arrived, she had been bemused by his skill and had spent any spare moments watching him as he set the letters from left to right, and upside down. From time to time, when business was slack, Jack had shown her how to do it, and now, slowly and painfully, she had learned to compose a page.

'Never know, you might want to set up an underground press,' Jack had said with a wink and Eileen had even managed to print out a few poems that she had written and presented them to her mother as a birthday present. Now she took up the letter from the Reverend Mother again. What did the woman want? *Your advice,* it said. That seemed somewhat unlikely. There was no way in which Eileen would dare to give advice to the Reverend Mother. It was normally the other way around. And yet, this was a woman who did not prevaricate. If she said that she needed Eileen, then she did need her. Perhaps she would go after all.

'It's Sunday,' she said to Jack, frowning. 'I just need to be in two places at once. The show doesn't end until nine o'clock and someone wants to see me at that time.'

'Well then, they'll just have to wait, won't they?' said Jack. 'But you told me that your boyfriend with the motorcycle is coming to see the show on Sunday. Why don't you get him to give you a lift? It's just as well to be careful, you know. A lot of funny people around these days. Wouldn't like a daughter or a granddaughter of mine to be meeting someone at nine o'clock on her own.' He cast a suspicious glance at the envelope on her desk.

Eileen giggled for a while after he left. It seemed very funny that the elderly compositor thought that Eamonn, a member of the IRA, would form a good protection for her against Reverend Mother Aquinas. It was a good idea, though. Eamonn on his motorbike would be across the bridge and down to St Mary's of the Isle in under five minutes. It would give a good excuse to the other members of the cast for her to rush away so quickly after the performance. She had only to say, 'my boyfriend is waiting' and all would be explained. 'Would you be able to come to the show on Monday as well as Sunday?' she asked when they met at the entrance to South Terrace for her lunch break. 'I'll have to rush off on Sunday. The Reverend Mother wants to see me. But on Monday we'd have plenty of time to ourselves. Peter Doyle gave me another ticket the other day. I think that he was probing a bit, wanting to know who my friends are.' She frowned a little when she thought about Peter Doyle, but said no more until they had finished lunch in nearby Pembroke Street and were walking along beside the river. By this time, the early edition of the *Evening Standard* was selling on the streets, with paperboys shouting out the news about a murdered priest. '*A Scandalous Atrocity*'; '*Beyond Absolution*'; '*Priest Murdered*'; '*IRA Involvement Suspected*'.

Eamonn gave a disgusted exclamation, but she hushed him. One never knew who was listening. She could understand his anger, though. It was true that most crimes these days were automatically blamed on the Republicans. When a murder was committed, it was assumed that the Republicans were guilty.

'Do you know anything about the killing of Father Dominic?' asked Eamonn when they were alone together, walking along Lapps Quay. He had not said anything other than idle chat right through their lunch – Eamonn was always very careful – but she had known that there was something on his mind.

'They're blaming us for it, as usual, but that's not true,' he added.

'I just read the article in the *Cork Examiner* blaming the Republicans, but they are always blaming the Republicans for every crime. No one would really believe something like that.' Eileen looked at him anxiously.

'I'm not so sure.' His dark eyebrows were knotted and his grey eyes were fixed on a ship coming slowly up the river to where a line of would-be dockworkers, all hoping to get a few hours' work in unloading the grain, stretched back down the quay. 'Every story like that loses us ten supporters. Bet it's the Anti-Sinn Féin Society. They might have done it purely to discredit us.'

'Not likely,' said Eileen. 'Why Father Dominic? Much more likely that they would murder someone that the Republicans have condemned. Like the Bishop of Cork. Anyway, I'll keep an ear out tonight. I'm not sure that you're right, though. I haven't heard anything yet that would say these musical society people belong to the Anti-Sinn Féin Society, although I've been listening as hard as I can ever since you got me to join.'

'They must do. That girl on the exchange was positive that it was that English fellow, Peter Doyle, who rang the *Examiner* to say that the Republicans burned down Shanbally House. She said she knew him well, because she works three days a week in the bar in the Imperial Hotel on the South Mall and Peter Doyle and his friend have lunch there nearly every day. They're all Protestants, aren't they? They'd be very likely to belong to the Anti-Sinn Féin Society. You just watch yourself and take care. We want evidence, but we don't want anything to happen to you. Remember that.'

The intensity of his dark gaze was almost frightening. Eileen felt that a lot depended upon her. It was easy to plot against people who were just names on a sheet of paper. Not so easy to spy upon people who had been kind and welcoming to her, who had praised her singing voice, who had taken care to dress her in flattering clothes, and who had shown trust towards her. She nodded solemnly at Eamonn's words, but hoped, with all sincerity, that he was wrong and that she would not be the cause of any executions.

'I'd better be getting back,' she said aloud. 'I don't want to be late. It's always busy at the printers on Friday afternoon.'

Eileen examined her face in the mirror behind the stage of the Father Matthew Hall before the rehearsal. Friday night was an important night, always a full house and they usually had a quick run-through of the more important songs before the main performance. Although it was not yet seven o'clock, the room faced east and already was evening-dim. It was a good place to lurk. No one, she hoped, could suspect her of listening into conversations, as she slowly removed her small, head-hugging hat and patted into shape the sharp lines of her newly bobbed hair. She wasn't sure whether they had heard her come in or not, but she thought that they had not. She had recently invested some of her precious salary in a pair of rubber and canvas shoes. Sneakers, they were called and although they were not very suitable for the wet and often flooded streets of Cork city, they did allow her to move noiselessly and to overhear things that might confirm the suspicions of her friends in the Republican Army.

'No one will suspect you,' Eamonn had said when he persuaded her to go for the audition. 'And they do need another soprano. Didn't you read all that stuff in the *Evening Echo*? That letter from the clergyman's wife saying that she was taking her daughter away from Rochelle School because the headmistress had wanted to put her on the stage? And there were loads of other letters from parents, most of them saying that it was all right to have them in the chorus with their friends, but they shouldn't be in one of the principal parts. You just practise that song 'Three Little Maids from School', turn up, give them a performance and they'll have to take you on, no matter what they are up to. They should be delighted to have you and if they're not, if they refuse you, well then it means that I'm right about them.'

They had taken her on; the show was opening in three days' time, but whether they were as delighted as they said was a question that she had not solved. Sometimes, when she paused to tie a shoelace, or deliberately dropped something on the floor, Eileen felt that they were getting suspicious and she began to feel a little uncomfortable.

'I think that Peter Doyle might suspect me,' she said to
Eamonn on one of their evening meetings. 'He jokes with me,
just like he does with everyone else; but I can see his eyes
examining me.'

'Probably fancies you,' said Eamonn, but she could see
that he was worried. 'But if he does suspect you, it shows that
we're right and that this musical society is part of the anti-Sinn
Féin movement. I might be able to get hold of a pistol for you,'
he added.

'No, they won't do anything to me. They're just a pack of
play actors; I'm a match for them any day,' said Eileen disdain-
fully. 'And I certainly don't want to arouse any suspicions by
going around with a pistol. One of the women or the girls
would be bound to catch sight of it when we are changing
into our costumes. I just have to be careful when I am trying to
listen in.'

She was thinking about Eamonn's suspicions while she hung
up her coat and lingered for a while in front of the mirror.
Despite her brave words, she felt slightly nervous. The Anti-Sinn
Féin Society were reputed to be ruthless. A young republican,
a boy of only seventeen years old, was tortured until he revealed
the names of those who had taken part in a recent raid. Still,
others ran greater risks. She couldn't back out now.

And then she heard her name. Said quite softly, but said in
a voice that did not belong to any of her fellow actors and
actresses who all spoke with what she called 'posh' accents.
This was a singsong Cork accent, southside of Cork, she
thought. Gently and carefully, she prised the door open, just
an inch and peered cautiously through it. Now she could hear
the voices of the two men standing beside the window.

'I understand that you've been making an enquiry, sir, that
you left a photograph of a young lady at our station. The
inspector asked me to call and to say that we do recognize
the girl, the lady in question, but there is no actual criminal
conviction, no reason for us to involve ourselves.'

Eileen moved a little further out from the ladies' cloakroom.
Station, inspector, what was going on? And *photograph*? They
had taken a photograph of her the other day that had puzzled
her. Jonathon Power, the man who acted the part of Ko-Ko,

had taken it. She had wanted to dress in her Pitti-Sing costume, but he had insisted on her wearing her ordinary street clothes, just removing her stylish cloche hat. All the rest of the cast had their photographs in the window of the hall, but they were dressed for their parts in *The Mikado*. He had come up with some nonsense about her being a new member of the cast, and so they wanted one for their records, but now she understood and she froze with apprehension. There had been a time when the police had suspected her; when there had been a wanted poster with a blurred photograph on it displayed on lampposts and in post offices. No one could recognize her with a degree of certainty from it, but after that daring jailbreak, the name 'Eileen MacSweeney' had been in the paper as one of the suspects. What a fool she had been not to change her name, not to realize that first thing everyone in Cork did, on meeting a new acquaintance, was to find out who their parents were and where they came from. 'Breed, seed and generation' as her mother would say.

'Well, that's all right, then, sergeant. Very good of you to come around. Very grateful.' Peter Doyle's voice held its usual affable, easy-going tone. 'Must say goodbye now. We are just going to do a quick rehearsal, just run through a few songs, you know.'

'Perhaps I could stay and listen, sir. I'm very fond of these shows, especially Gilbert and Sullivan.'

Peter's laugh was a little forced as he and the policeman walked together down the hall. 'Stay if you like, but this won't be too interesting. We don't even have the orchestra; just manage with a gramophone for rehearsals. Come on everyone, I just want a quick run through of the main songs. There were a few hesitations last night and it ruins a song if you miss a beat.'

There was a note of tension in his voice. Perhaps it was the presence of a member of the Civic Guards had put him out. He had not reckoned on this public appearance, probably thought there would be a discreet visit to his shop, at some time when Eileen would not be around. Now he seemed to be looking for a quick distraction.

'Anne, my darling, let's go through the duet, will we?' He

placed a kiss on Anne's cheek, deliberately making a loud, smacking sound with his lips as he did so.

He was overdoing everything tonight. Eileen's eyes went to Robert Beamish. He and Anne Morgan were supposed to be engaged. She wore his splendid ring, but now Peter Doyle was fondling and holding her much more tightly than usual and when it came to the lines: 'And, to mark my admiration, I would kiss you fondly thus—', the stage embrace turned into a passionate kiss. Anne Morgan's colour rose. She was blushing, her cheeks turning a bright crimson. Robert Beamish took one step forward, the Garda turned towards him, his attention caught by the sudden movement. Robert stepped back again, his mouth tightened into a thin line. His colour was as high as Anne's as he watched. The pair fell into each other's arms, singing: 'This, oh, this, He'll/I'll never do'. The second embrace lasted a long minute. Eileen looked on with interest. She thought that it was only the presence of the Garda which stopped Robert Beamish from punching Peter Doyle. Anne was behaving like a fool, in her opinion. Robert Beamish was a much better looking man than Peter Doyle, very tall and very handsome. And everyone in Cork knew that the Beamish family were very rich. Robert, when he gave up this rowing business that now occupied most of his time, would be found a good job at the brewery. Peter Doyle, well, no one knew much about him. An Englishman who owned a shop. Not in the same league as Robert Beamish. If Anne Morgan really wanted to give up teaching, then she was going the wrong way about it.

'I'll go through mine, now, Peter.' Miss Gamble's cool, commanding voice made both her assistant teacher and Peter Doyle stand back from each other abruptly. Anne Morgan made a half movement towards Robert, but then took a step backwards as she noted his eyes fixed on Peter Doyle and his hands clenched into fists.

Eileen looked at the size of those hands. One punch from Robert Beamish and a small man like Peter Doyle would be stretched on the floor. Robert Beamish spent hours every day of the week rowing up and down the River Lee, right into Cork harbour. Those hands were enormous and the flimsy silk

of the Japanese robe did nothing to hide the size of the muscles
in his upper arms. Marjorie Gamble had done the right thing
to intervene. A fight between two such unequally matched
men would have been most unpleasant and would have caused
a scandal. Anne would be in trouble from her headmistress if
she played fast and loose. Miss Gamble, like Robert Beamish,
was a member of the upper class in Cork. Peter Doyle, though
amusing and talented, would be a nothing in their eyes. Still,
a flirtation with Anne might distract him from Rose O'Reilly,
who was, after all, a married woman. Eileen speculated
on that while Marjorie Gamble's contralto throbbed through
the song.

> My hallowed joys!
> Oh blind, that seest
> No equipoise!

Peter seemed to have his eye on the policeman watching
silently; there was no more flirting with any of the girls and the
rehearsals were brief and to the point. Peter contented himself
with a pat on the shoulder of each and a whispered few words
in an ear. When he came to James O'Reilly, the bank clerk,
the man's face went quite white. He gave a hunted glance at
the sergeant and then turned back to Peter, biting his bottom
lip. His clean-shaven face had gone so pale that the black dots
of the hair roots stood out almost like freckles. Peter Doyle
frowned at him and seemed to hiss a few words into the bank
clerk's ear before he moved on to have a word with Tom
Gamble, the barrister. James O'Reilly looked around in a
strangely hunted fashion and then went to stand beside his
wife. Rose O'Reilly looked pale, also. She gave one swift
upward glance at her husband's ashen face and then, not at
the policeman, but at Peter Doyle. It was strange to see her
look so worried as she was normally such a competent, assured
sort of person.

'Peter's in a bit of mood, isn't he?' Eileen thought that she
could venture that remark to Anne Morgan. Together they had
giggled about Marjorie Gamble's old-fashioned ways, and the
manner in which she treated the young teacher as though she

were one of her pupils. But today Anne Morgan did not reply and moved away. Interesting, thought Eileen. Deliberately, she moved after her in order to continue the conversation. 'That's a gorgeous dress you have on. You must have come into a legacy. I saw it in Dowdens a couple of weeks ago.' The bold design of stripes had taken her eye but she had almost fainted when a bored assistant had told her the price, adding condescendingly that it was a model.

Anne looked a bit uneasy, even a little alarmed.

'Oh, payday, you know,' she said brushing the matter aside.

'And you blew it all on one dress.' Eileen tried to sound interested and friendly, and not betray any scorn. There was no way that a young music teacher would be paid that much money. Oddly, Anne Morgan seemed almost as though she were trying to snub Eileen.

And yet, up to today, she had seemed very friendly.

When the rehearsal was over, Peter Doyle presented a couple of free tickets to the policeman, insisted on him accepting them, managed adroitly to manoeuvre the man through the front door, locking it firmly behind him. And then, instead of lingering, fetched the key of the hall from the small office and stood by the stage door, twirling it until all went through. Eileen made sure that she was one of the first to go out, then she quickly turned the corner onto Morrison's Quay and lurked in a doorway there until the rest came out. Instead of dispersing, they all went into the antiques shop. Perhaps it was to have a quiet place to talk without either Eileen or the policeman to listen into them. For a moment, she half thought of endeavouring to follow them, but she had a meeting arranged with Eamonn and she did not want to be late. In any case, there was probably no way that she would be able to get into the shop without them spotting her.

Her mind went back to the mission that she had undertaken. There was no doubt in her mind that something fishy was going on with this crowd of Merrymen. They all seemed to have more money than one would imagine they could possess. Flashy cars, expensive clothes and, from their conversation, they usually dined out in expensive places like the Imperial Hotel. And then there was the way in which they had taken

such alarm at her presence that they had summoned a
policeman, hoping to find out about her background. She
frowned impatiently. There was still no evidence one way or
the other. Suspicions were not enough.

Eamonn was waiting for her at 'The Statue'. Most people in
Cork who wanted to assign a meeting place named The Statue.
It couldn't be missed. An enormous pedestal and an enormous
statue of Father Matthew right at the top of Patrick Street, just
before the bridge. Eamonn was leaning against a nearby lamppost, keeping a sharp lookout, but otherwise, with his college
scarf, looked just like the university student that he had been
before he threw up his studies to join in the armed struggle
to ensure that Ireland should regain the whole of its thirty-two
counties from England and not be content with the twenty-six.
As soon as she saw him, Eileen felt a pang of loneliness. She
had left the Republicans in a moment of anger against Tom
Hurley and his treachery towards herself and the boy that she
had been in love with then. But now that boy had gone to
England; she rarely heard from him and she wished that she
were back hiding out in the remote farmhouse with the rest
of the dedicated nationalists. When Eamonn had asked her to
do this job of surveillance, she had agreed with such eagerness
that he had been surprised. He would like her to come back;
she knew that.
    'How's things?'
    His voice was casual. He dropped a kiss on her cheek, but
she wasn't sure whether that was a cloak to the serious purpose
of their meeting, or whether he really wanted to kiss her. He
had never done that when they had all shared a house, but
then she had been going out with Sam for most of that time.
    'Interesting,' she replied and said no more while they strolled
across the bridge, looking down at the northern channel of the
River Lee that periodically flooded their city. When they
reached the other side of the bridge, they both turned automatically to stroll along the riverside of Camden Quay. There
was no pavement here, only an iron chain and very few people
walked on this side of the road. They could talk in safety, with
no chance of being overheard, as long as they glanced over

their shoulder from time to time. It was the moment to give her report.

'I think you are dead right about that place, Eamonn,' she said. 'There's something going on with them; they're all in on it and they don't want me to find out; they're dying to get rid of me. Wait till you hear what they did! They took my photograph around to the barracks.' She told him all about the arrival of the policeman and the low-voiced conversation. 'The sergeant said that I wasn't wanted for any crime at the moment, but that they were *aware* of me.'

He frowned a little at that and she was warmed by the look of concern in his eyes. He seemed more worried about her than pleased at being proved right.

'I couldn't believe that they would do that, take my photograph to the police station. And they always pretend to be so friendly and so nice, praising my voice and everything. So you must be right; they are up to something. But why all the great fuss about me? Except that they are now scared that I would get my machine gun out and hold them all up.' She was exaggerating, trying to make him laugh, but he frowned and looked serious.

'You're not scared, are you?' asked Eamonn.

'No, of course not,' said Eileen stoutly. 'I've taken on the job, so I'll finish the job. There's definitely something going on. Why should they do that? If they thought that I was stealing or something, then they would say so. No, they're guilty of something. I'm sure that you are right that they belong to the Anti-Sinn Féin Society, but they are keeping it quiet as it might be bad for business.'

'Perhaps they use the premises of the shop for evening meetings of the Anti-Sinn Féin crowd. We've never been able to find out where they meet. Most hotels or public houses wouldn't like to have them because of the risk to their premises if we found out. Could you get any clues about that?'

Eileen shook her head. 'It's difficult. I've never been invited to the shop that the two of them, Peter Doyle and Jonathon Power, run. They do invite the others. Tom Gamble is always there, do you know him? He's a barrister.'

'I know him,' said Eamonn with a grin. 'He's having an

affair with a girl out our way, has her tucked into a little cottage just near to our place. I've seen him go there a few times. Got a baby, too. If his rich wife finds out, then he's for it.'

'Why would someone like Tom Gamble, a rich barrister, want to be mixed up with anything dodgy like the Anti-Sinn Féin Society?' Eileen stopped and waited. A man on a bicycle was approaching, cycling slowly along looking over his shoulder at the river. She and Eamonn drew back and watched him warily. It was second nature to both of them to scrutinize faces, to remain always on the alert. He passed them without a glance but Eamonn waited until he was out of sight.

'Most of these sort want the British back again; better for business,' he said briefly. 'But as for rich, well, he mightn't be that rich. I wonder if they are up to something shady. Easy to do things like raiding shops and then telling the *Examiner* that the Republicans did it. These young barristers don't earn much. My mother wanted me to go in for the law, but I persuaded her that she and my father would be supporting me until I was in my middle thirties; that I'd be better off being a doctor. Tom Gamble has got a rich wife, but he can't exactly ask her for money to fund his little love nest, can he?'

'I wonder he risks it,' said Eileen.

'You should see the girl! She's gorgeous, really, really, gorgeous! I've seen her out walking the lanes with the baby in a very stylish baby carriage, and the house looks nice, too. Even got a servant. But, of course, it is a risk, and, of course, he has to have extra money.'

'And the lark, perhaps, too. He's that type of man.' She decided not to tell Eamonn that Tom Gamble had made a pass at her. Perfectly gentlemanly, had held his hands up and apologized, but with a twinkle in his eye that showed he was quite a ladies' man.

'They're all the same kind,' she said. 'They're all the type to be in it for the fun and risk, just as much as for the money. Peter Doyle is that type. He takes risks with people. I thought that there would be a fight between him and Tom Gamble one day. He was saying something to him, in a very low tone, something about Tulligmore and Tom Gamble went a dark red, turned around and grabbed him by the collar.'

'That's interesting; looks like this Peter Doyle has got hold of his little secret. That's the place. Don't you remember Tulligmore, Eileen? You must remember the bridge where my motorbike always lurched, almost tipped you into the air one day, well, that's the townland where this girl is living; just along a lane near to the bridge. I noticed his fancy car going slowly up that lane quite a few times and once I followed it, just on foot and going by the fields. It's a small cottage about half a mile up the lane. He's had it done up, though. Looks all fancy, painted and the garden dug, and flowers planted in it, lots of roses. Very romantic,' finished Eamonn, with a grin down at her. 'Let's walk back there,' he said suddenly. 'I'd like to have a look at that crowd before they get dressed up. You can introduce me. I can be your young man. No one will suspect anything. They've got rid of the policeman, haven't they?'

'Yes, but they've probably all gone home now for their suppers. I don't suppose they hung around too long once people started coming into the church. There'll be loads of people milling around, they'll all be coming out of the church by now. It's the second day of the Novena, a saint a night for nine nights. St Aloysius last night, St Paulinus tomorrow, St John on Sunday, then some old martyrs and then Mary Magdalene and then . . . and so it goes on. My mam is very keen on these Novenas. Goes if she gets a chance, but she's working tonight.'

It was very nice walking around with Eamonn. She realized that she had been quite lonely for some time since she had left the farmhouse where they had a hideout. She tucked her arm in his. They bought a couple of cakes from a shop on Cook Street and munched them happily, as they went along.

And then a policeman passed them. He looked very intently, first at Eileen and then gave Eamonn a long and lingering look. When she glanced back over her shoulder, she could see that he had stopped at the inside edge of the pavement, his back to a shop window and that he was still looking at them.

'Don't come. It may not be safe. Trust to me. I'll keep an eye on them. I don't want them to start asking questions about you at the barracks,' said Eileen when they came onto the

South Mall. Eamonn still looked like a university student, but Cork was a small city and a most inquisitive one. There was a continual effort to identify everyone and she thought it probable that, now that she was identified from that old poster, one of the Civic Guards might start to wonder about him. 'You go now,' she said firmly, standing very still and slightly apart from him. 'I'll be early; we don't start until 9 on a Friday, but I'll wait. Peter Doyle will probably be along in a while. He's always the first to arrive. Usually he comes before the caretaker. Here's your ticket for the show. Don't come too early. Wait until the queue starts moving in and then slip in and sit at the back.' She watched him go with a twinge of regret. For a moment, she almost ran after him and asked him to take her with him. It had been such fun in that remote farmhouse hideout, living with people who shared her ideals and who were prepared to lay down their lives for the freedom of a united Ireland. She still helped with the propaganda, drafting and designing leaflets and posters, but it wasn't the same thing.

FIVE

St Thomas Aquinas:
Nam alia animalia memorantur tantum, homines autem
et memorantur et reminiscuntur
(For other animals only remember, but men both
remember and can recall to mind at will)

'Montenotte, two three,' said the Reverend Mother into the phone. It was fairly early on Saturday morning and she hoped that her cousin Lucy would be out of bed. She was impatient to see her. Lucy had been away on a visit that week and only returned the previous night. She was the only one who could confirm her suspicions.

There was something very strange about the story of the priest's visit to the antiques shop. And of his reaction. Dr Scher had seemed to find Father Dominic's distress at the chipped ceramic hawk perfectly natural, but then Dr Scher was a dedicated collector, with a cabinet full of antique silver. He might be upset if he found a prize piece badly damaged, but why should a friar like Dominic worry? The Capuchins had taken a vow of poverty, so what was Dominic doing in that shop in the first place, and secondly why was he so worried about the damage to a Japanese hawk. An *Arita hawk*, she repeated to herself. There was something in the back of her mind about a Japanese hawk; but try as she might, she could not resurrect it. Arita was the name of a Japanese town, so the word probably referred to the type of clay used for the ceramics.

After pondering over it for some time, she decided to make the phone call. Her cousin Lucy was the only one left now who shared her memories. And, of course, Lucy, married to a prosperous solicitor, and the owner of a beautiful house, would know all about this antique shop. In any case, she needed to tell her about the death of poor Dominic, if she had not already heard the news. So she got up from her chair, disregarding her pile of correspondence, went down the corridor, lifted the phone and gave the number.

'Yes, of course, Reverend Mother, you'll be wanting to speak to Mrs Murphy, of course. I'll have her on the line in a minute, that's if she's up out of bed at this hour on such a terrible day. And, of course, they would have been late home last night. Away visiting relations in Kerry, weren't they?'

The Reverend Mother, despite herself, found her face relaxing into a smile. There were, she supposed, other countries where the exchange operators took a number in silence and put you through, preserving an air of total anonymity about the process, but here in the city of Cork, that would have been considered discourteous. In Cork, it was assumed that everyone knew everyone else's business. And the telephone exchange women did their best to add to that common pool of knowledge. Sensible people, keeping this in mind, spent the first minutes exchanging remarks about the weather and the state of the streets before moving on to matters that were more private. And the Reverend Mother, trained in discretion, never uttered a word on the telephone that she would not have been happy to shout from the spire of Shandon Cathedral.

'Terrible weather,' said Lucy when she arrived at the phone. She had probably been still in bed when the call came, but she sounded alert and interested. Lucy, as the telephone exchange woman had informed her, would have been late home. Nevertheless, the news of the murder in the confessional at the Holy Trinity Church on St Matthew's Quay would have been relayed to her the instant she was inside the door. Lucy, she would take a bet, had already heard that her cousin, Reverend Mother Aquinas, had been present when the door of the confessional had been pulled open and the dead man revealed. She would be dying to know what had happened.

. 'I have some bad news. There was a priest killed in the Holy Trinity Church. It was Father Dominic, Dominic Alleyn,' she said soberly.

'Dominic Alleyn!'

There had been a sharp intake of breath. That had surprised

Lucy. She had probably heard the story, but not the name. 'But why?'

'Terrible news, isn't it?' The Reverend Mother didn't reply. That had been an involuntary question from Lucy. She would not expect an answer or any attempt at speculation from her cousin. There was a sound of a sneeze in the background. This damp air in June made moulds grow in buildings and the telephonists all seemed to have colds.

'Well, thank goodness the fog has lifted a little.' Lucy immediately changed tack. 'I was thinking of paying you a visit. Are you all right on St Mary's Isle?'

'We're fine,' said the Reverend Mother. 'The fog has lifted here, also.'

'That's good,' said Lucy. 'Well, I'll pop in this afternoon and pay you a visit. I've got a few books for your library. Shall we say half past three? Would that suit you?'

'That would be perfect,' said the Reverend Mother sedately.

'And get someone to light a fire in your study,' ordered Lucy. 'I know it's June, but it's damp and cold after that fortnight of heavy rain and old ladies like yourself need pampering.' With a chuckle, Lucy rang off and the Reverend Mother returned to her room and pulled the bell to the kitchen.

'Mrs Murphy is coming this afternoon to have tea with me,' she said as Sister Bernadette came bustling in.

'We'll need a fire in here, then,' said Sister Bernadette instantly. 'And it wouldn't do any harm to light it now. This place is terrible damp. Look at the glass on those photographs. You can hardly see the pictures for the haze on them.'

What would Lucy make of the story of Dominic visiting the antiques shop on Morrison's Island? This question kept recurring to her mind during the morning as the Reverend Mother tackled correspondence and accounts, and listened in a discouraging silence to the chaplain's request for some new vestments. She had, she thought, better things to do with her scarce resources.

'You can take off your fur coat,' she said when her cousin arrived. 'This place is as warm as toast now. And it is June, you know.' And then, as Lucy took off her coat and sank gracefully into the chair beside the fire, she said, 'Can you remember a blue ceramic hawk, Lucy, a Japanese Arita hawk? I have something in the back of my mind about a ceramic hawk.' 'Shanbally House,' said Lucy instantly. 'Don't you remember?' 'It was on the staircase!' exclaimed the Reverend Mother, memories suddenly flooding back. 'I remember now.' 'That's right. I don't know how you could have forgotten. Old age, I suppose,' teased Lucy and then fell silent as Sister Bernadette came in with the tea.

All the time that her cousin was thanking the lay sister, exclaiming on the succulence of the cake, the strength of the tea and the lovely heat of the fire, the Reverend Mother pondered on Shanbally House in north Cork. She and Lucy had frequently stayed there as young girls, had been to several house parties, there. Dominic and Lawrence had often been there also, she remembered. She had a memory of a dance where she had worn that green dress with all the flounces and Dominic had told her that she looked beautiful. He was, she thought, an extremely nice person, even in his adolescence.

'Two hawks,' she said suddenly when Sister Bernadette had left the room. 'I remember two hawks. There were two of them, weren't there? I remember them distinctly as a pair, two tall blue hawks. I can just see them. They were on that trian- gular shelf on the stairway, just where the steps turned a corner after the first flight. But there were two of them, weren't there? I remember them distinctly as a pair,' she repeated. 'Two tall blue hawks.'

'You're right,' said Lucy enthusiastically. 'Yes, you're right. There were two when we were young. But one of their sons smashed one, threw a tennis ball at his brother's head and it hit the hawk. I remember feeling glad that I had a little girl, not a boy, so it must have been a long time ago. A few years after you entered the convent. Those Wood boys were quite wild when they were in their teens. But you're right, Arita hawks are usually in a pair.'

'That's what Dr Scher told Father Dominic.' And then, in response to her cousin's interrogative look, she continued, 'Dr Scher met Dominic in there. He was looking at this hawk and appeared to be most distressed. He remarked on the fact there was just one and that there was a chip on its beak.'

'That happened when the second one fell against it,' said Lucy absent-mindedly. And then quite suddenly, she opened her eyes widely. 'Shanbally House, that's where those two hawks were, but it doesn't make sense that the hawk in the antiques shop came from Shanbally House. Don't you remember? The place was burned to the ground by the Republicans in revenge for the burning down of the home of one of their men. It happened some time ago. Dreadful business, wasn't it? Not that they were injured in any way, though one of the gardeners was shot, but an elderly couple like the Woods, turned out on the road at that hour of the night. They must have been almost as old as you are now, weren't they?'

The Reverend Mother didn't bother to argue. Lucy was, in fact, less than a year younger than she was. However, faithful attendance at both a hair stylist and a beautician made a difference. The use of high quality hair dye which tinted the grey hair, not to the corn-coloured hue of her youth, but to a delicate shade of ash blonde; her face enhanced with a creamy veneer of flattering foundation and powder, which skimmed over any wrinkles; both of these made her look very much the younger of the two.

'And it was definitely burned to the ground, wasn't it?' The Reverend Mother did not bother to wait for an answer. It had only been about six or seven months ago and she had read all about it on the *Cork Examiner*. 'So what would a ceramic hawk from Shanbally be doing in an antiques shop on Morrison's Island? Who owns the place, anyway?'

'It's owned by a man called Peter Doyle. You know he runs the Merrymen Light Opera group. I don't know much about him, apart from the fact that he's one of the Doyles of Fermoy. You remember that lovely old house near Fermoy, the one that was burned down about four or five years ago – this Peter Doyle, apparently, is a grandson of the elderly couple there – strange isn't it, how all those big houses of our youth have no families left in them – how all the young people have gone to England. Well, he came back from England and he's made a great success of that place in Morrison's Island; that antiques shop. I went in there once. Bought a nice old crystal glass vase, a gorgeous one, specially designed to show off those long-stemmed roses, the rim has little v-shaped slots so that each flower head is held separately. A lovely vase. Even I can arrange a bouquet in it without having to call for the housekeeper. Made by the Cork Glass Company. Their stuff is pretty rare these days. I think that the company went out of business in the 1830s.'

The Reverend Mother pondered on a crystal vase from a company that had gone out of business over ninety years ago. There was something in the back of her mind. A sudden picture from the past. A sunny June morning. A walk through a stretch of woodland, going through the iron gate into the walled garden, picking some long-stemmed roses. And the voice of her hostess. *Be careful, Dorothea. I cherish that vase in memory of my grandfather. It's lovely old Cork Glass. They've gone out of business now, of course* . . . 'The Ronaynes,' she said aloud. 'They had a vase like that. I remember the V-shaped slots'

'Their place was burned down last year,' said Lucy. 'Nobody hurt, but the house was destroyed. They went off to England. Haven't heard anything about them for a long time.'

'I'm sure that they had this beautiful crystal glass vase, a Cork Glass vase, specially made to display rose blossoms. I remember it.'

'Old Cork cut glass. Much better than that stuff from the Penroses in Waterford,' said Lucy complacently.

'So you bought a Cork Glass crystal vase like that at Peter Doyle's shop, Lucy. That's interesting!'

'Could be a coincidence, something salvaged, though I thought I heard that place was burned to the ground, too. It's just a shell now. Odd, isn't it?'

'Very,' said the Reverend Mother. She could see that Lucy was thinking hard.

'Do you know,' she said, grimacing slightly, 'it's strange, but Rupert and I, with his partner and wife, went to see *The Mikado* the other night, put on by Peter Doyle and his Merrymen, in the Father Matthew Hall, and I kept thinking that some of the Japanese stuff that they had on stage was familiar. Do you remember the Japanese bedroom at Shanbally House?'

The Reverend Mother thought about it. She did remember that bedroom. It had been the night after she had danced with

Dominic Alleyn. She remembered how she had retired to her room that night, full of romantic notions of marrying him. Aloud, she said, 'That's interesting! Could there be a possibility that he had anything to do with those burnings, what do you think, Lucy?'

'Unlikely!' Lucy's eyebrows shot up. 'Come on, Dottie. What on earth put that into your head? Peter Doyle? Why suspect him? He's one of the Doyles of Fermoy. His grandparents were thrown out of their house and the place burned to the ground. Not a thing left. He has the reputation of being a bit wild, drinks quite a bit with that young barrister, Tom Gamble and that crowd. But it's ridiculous to think that he might be part of the IRA.'

'I suppose that it does seems ridiculous. He's made a great success of his shop, according to you. But tell me this, Lucy, where does all of his stuff come from?'

'Buys at auctions, country house sales, things like that, I suppose.'

'And the Japanese screen?'

'Yes,' said Lucy slowly. 'Yes, I did think that I had seen that screen, the one that was used on stage for *The Mikado*. Very pretty blues. It had three panels, two of them were perfect, but one had a slightly faded bit at the bottom.'

'I remember it,' replied the Reverend Mother, nodding. 'And I know where it came from. Do you remember that we shared that bedroom once when we visited Shanbally House when we were quite young? Dominic and Lawrence had been in it, but they were moved upstairs to one of the smaller bedrooms when we arrived. Don't you remember Lawrence was furious about it? You remember what a temper he had when he was young? But you must recollect the Japanese bedroom, Lucy. I can picture it so clearly and I remember the third panel of that screen. Stained with water. A paler bit, shaped like a pointed mountaintop, just as though something had splashed it.'

'You had a theory, do you remember?' put in Lucy mischievously. 'We laughed so much that we fell back on the bed with our legs in the air, crinolines billowing up and we didn't hear the chambermaid when she knocked and she came in and she looked so astonished at the sight of us, with those frilly pantaloons sticking straight up in the air from out of those crinolines. What a sight we must have looked!' Lucy started to laugh at the memory. 'We laughed even more then,' she finished.

'I remember,' said the Reverend Mother, a smile twitched at her lips. Odd how such memories from the distant past lingered at the back of the mind and then suddenly came forward in full colour.

'Could have been a different one, though,' argued Lucy. 'A lot of these grand old houses had Japanese stuff.' She took a bite from her cake slice and stared meditatively at the mist-streaked window.

'And the water splash on the third panel?' queried the Reverend Mother and Lucy pursed her lips.

'Still, even if it was the same one, the very same screen, then it could have been nothing to do with these people in the antiques shop,' she said after a moment's thought. 'It could have been looters. Went in when the place cooled down and snatched what they could and then offered it for sale to an antiques dealer.'

'But Shanbally House was supposed to be destroyed, everything in it gutted,' argued the Reverend Mother. 'I remember reading all about it. The lead on the roof went on fire. It dripped into the house and it burned for days. They had the fire brigade standing by, but they could do nothing. No one would have been able to get near it. I do remember reading about it on the *Cork Examiner*. They said that they were cutting down all the timber near to the house just in case the trees caught fire, too.'

'Peter Doyle!' said Lucy. 'I can't believe that he would be involved with the IRA in such a racket. And his own grandparents burned out of their house.'

'But, Lucy, do we know for certain that this Peter Doyle was the grandson of the Doyles? Whose son was he?'

'One of the twins, I suppose. Do you remember them in their pram when we stayed there that May? Two fat boy babies in one enormous pram on the top of the steps. You said that they looked like a pair of Buddhas.'

'They were both killed at the Battle of Ladysmith,' said the Reverend Mother. 'Neither had married. I wrote to sympathize with their mother and she sent back a very sad letter to say that there were no more of the family left behind to carry on the name.'

'So they were.' Lucy was silent for a moment. 'Was there a sister?'

'I don't think so. And if she had a boy, he wouldn't have been a Doyle, would he?'

'So you think that this Peter Doyle is a fraud?'

'I think it is a possibility. And I think that Dominic recognized that hawk.' Not even to Lucy would she mention the confession that Dominic heard, a confession that sent him to his brother, the prior for advice. Lawrence had told her in a moment of anguish, a moment of despair at having failed his brother. It was not for her to talk of this to Lucy. On the other hand, Dominic's death had to be looked into. A man who would kill a harmless priest might kill again in order to ensure his own secrecy. She would have to make sure that did not happen; that no more lives should be lost.

'But at 17 and 18, one does not notice the furnishings so much,' she said aloud. 'Come on, Lucy, rack your brains. Remember that blue room. Any more Japanese stuff? They usually had a theme in those bedrooms, didn't they? I'm sure that the blue room was Japanese.'

'I remember the curtains,' said Lucy. 'We stayed there a few years ago. I remember that I thought they were just plain, just cream-coloured, but when I woke up on the first morning that we were there, the sun was shining and then you could see a Japanese pattern, faintly blue on them. You remember those hand-painted blue bamboo pictures . . .'

'Anything else you can remember from the house?' asked the Reverend Mother. The saboteurs were unlikely to want to waste time unhooking threadbare curtains while the building burned.

'There was that carved gilt wood mirror, do you remember that? It was in the hall, behind that table, a very nice table. Regency. Beautifully carved legs. They called it the sofa table, but I never remember it standing by a sofa. It was always in the hall and it used to be piled high with gloves, and whips and hats, and some old copies of *The Field* and cricket stumps when the boys were young, all that sort of thing. I used to think that it would look lovely if they cleaned the mirror and took the junk from the table, but they were very easy-going people. Sad – that burning of Shanbally House. He died of a heart attack, you know, soon after they settled in England. She is still there, over in Kent, but I heard that she's not too happy. A bit old to make new friends. And what about Jonathon Power? He's supposed to come from a place near Tipperary, on the Cork/Tipperary border.'

'So he says.'

'You nuns have such lovely trusting natures.'

'What's he like, Jonathon Power?'

'Well, they are very unalike, the two of them – in appearance and in character. Jonathon is the worker, very quiet, perhaps a bit shy. I went in there one Saturday with Rupert. Peter Doyle was busy with another customer so we watched Jonathon for a while. He had a bottle of turpentine and he was cleaning a muddy-looking old picture – generations of turf smoke on it, I would imagine – well, he was making a wonderful job of it. And someone told me that she bought a Georgian lap desk there and it had been beautifully restored. Peter, of course, is the showman and he was making a big thing of pointing out the bits of restoration and insisting that he wanted her to be happy with them, but she was delighted with the desk. Beautifully hand-polished, too. Rupert thought that Jonathon must have been trained in some London show-rooms. He's a bit older than Peter, I'd say, though I think I heard that they became friends in France during the war.'

The Reverend Mother got to her feet. 'Let's go and have a look at the place, at that antiques shop.'

'What! Out in the rain! Over to Morrison's Island!'

'You have a chauffeur, don't you? By now, he will have had his cup of tea in the kitchen. He'll enjoy a drive.'

'Perhaps it's closed.' Lucy pouted a little, holding her hands out to the fire. Not for the first time, the Reverend Mother thought that her cousin reminded her of a pampered Persian cat.

'Come on,' she said bracingly. 'Fresh air will do us good. No, they won't be closed. It's only four o'clock on a Saturday afternoon. The shop will be full and we'll be able to browse in peace.' The Reverend Mother got to her feet and took her cloak from the back of the door. 'Come on, Lucy, you can buy me a present for my feast day.'

'I thought that was in early March; I'm sure it was. I remember bringing you very expensive hothouse flowers,' said Lucy. She glanced through the window and shuddered. 'Although there isn't much difference in the weather, I have to admit.'

The Reverend Mother touched the bell. 'Mrs Murphy and I are going out,' she said when Sister Bernadette appeared. 'Could you let her chauffeur know that we are ready now.'

'Let's hope it isn't flooded,' said Lucy bitterly as they drove along the quay towards Morrison's Island. Nevertheless, her blue eyes were alert and interested and her cousin knew that the sharp brain behind them was working through memories of the big houses of the past.

An abominable business, this burning down of homes, thought the Reverend Mother. Looking back into her youth, she remembered them as places of great beauty. And then her conscience pricked her. What was it that she had heard from a pupil of hers? Every big house is burned down in retaliation for the destruction by the army of a Republican's home. A cottage, they reasoned, was of the same importance as the grand houses of the ascendancy class, who were alien to the country by race, upbringing, accent and religion.

Most of the Anglo-Irish had been given land in the time of Oliver Cromwell; the general paid his officers with huge grants of the fertile acres of the 'Golden Vale', the rich pasture-lands of Cork, Tipperary, Waterford and south Limerick. They built their houses, mostly castles in the beginning and then, in the eighteenth century replaced these with those beautiful Georgian and Regency houses that they filled with lovely furniture and the best of what Ireland could produce in silver-ware, crystal and lovely carved arbutus wood. They had periodic trips to London returning with valuable paintings and some-times furniture but, overall, they bought from the country in which they had made their home, and encouraged the native arts and crafts by their patronage.

There would have been rich pickings in these houses.

'I'll just drop you off by the front door, Mrs Murphy,' said the chauffeur over his shoulder. 'There's no room in their car park. I'll find a place by the Holy Trinity Church and come back. There seems to be a lot going on here today.'

And it seemed as though the murder of the priest in the nearby Holy Trinity Church had brought business. There were many expensive cars parked, not just in the shop car park, but also along the quay in front of the antiques shop.

The Reverend Mother got out of Lucy's car and surveyed the place with interest. Morrison's Island Antiques was painted on a board above the front door, beautifully lettered in an elaborate Gothic script, she thought, looking at it with approval. The shop, itself, seemed to be occupying a couple of floors of a former warehouse on the corner between two streets.

There had been a time when Morrison's Island had been a major trading post for the late-medieval city of Cork. Their own family, the grandparents and parents of Lucy and herself, had once owned a building there for the storage of wine from France or Spain and tea from India. That had been on the quayside. Less expensive warehouses were built on the back streets where as many warehouses as possible had been squashed into its limited area. In these two laneways, facing them, some builder had made the most of the space, building terraced warehouses, back to back, each with a frontage on to one of those narrow lanes that segmented the triangular area of the former marsh into a thriving merchandise sector in the eighteenth century. It might have been a disadvantage that there was no back entrance or exit, but the river access was the most important fact for these warehouses, and no doubt the builder had profited hugely from the rents that he was able to charge.

But now the centre of commerce had moved further down-stream, to the place where the custom house fronted the two channels of the River Lee. The warehouses of Morrison's Island, except for a few that faced the river, had been allowed to decay peacefully. Some were, thought the Reverend Mother, looking downright dangerous. Others, she guessed, might be used as places for the homeless to crawl into and to spend a night in relative shelter.

But the young men who ran the Morrison's Island Antiques Shop had made a wonderful job of converting the old building on the corner of the quay. Walls had been cemented and painted, windows had been restored to their former Georgian splendour, a new front door, Georgian in style, painted in a striking black with brass fittings, and a splendid brass knocker, gave a great welcome to the discriminating buyer. Even from a distance there was a well-lit-up interior, tasteful blinds half-concealing, half-revealing the treasure house within to attract customers. Few people, seeing those windows, would be able to resist coming in.

'Made a very good job of it, haven't they?' said Lucy. And the Reverend Mother nodded an agreement, leading the way towards the shop.

Ever since Dr Scher had told her of a single and damaged Japanese Arita hawk which had taken Dominic's attention and had caused the grief and upset of that saintly man, and ever since Lucy's identification of the possible origin of the Japanese hawk with a chipped beak, the Reverend Mother had grave suspicions about this place. And her cousin would be the one to help her draw the right conclusions.

Lucy, unlike herself, had stayed out in the world, had gone on living the sort of life that she had lived as a girl. Both had been from the family of very prosperous wine merchants, who was on easy terms with a good proportion of their best clients, people who lived in these wonderful old Georgian houses and who had inherited a taste for good wine from their ancestors. Her father had often stayed in these places and had brought with him his daughter and his orphaned niece. But that was all a very long time ago and although the memories would be useful, Lucy had gone on visiting these places. And as a solicitor's wife, she told herself, Lucy was used to being discreet about her husband's legal affairs.

Lucy made straight for the stairs. The solitary Japanese hawk was not visible now, but there was a beautiful gilt wood mirror and her cousin had stopped in front of it, gazing as though entranced with its beauty. The Reverend Mother joined her.

'Nuns have no use for mirrors,' said Lucy in her usual clear tones. 'I can't buy you that for a present.'

'Nonsense,' said the Reverend Mother. 'How on earth do you imagine that we manage to get our veil properly pinned to our wimple unless we have a mirror?' Without vanity, she contemplated her image, the pale oval face and green eyes, shrouded in white and black and she repositioned a long pin above her temple. A beautiful mirror, she thought as she stood there. Yes, it was from Shanbally House. She could remember Lucy, even at seventeen, confident and dictatorial, gazing into that same mirror, then spotted and dirty, picking up a pigskin glove from the silver tray on the table below and scrubbing at the damp dust, remarking loudly, 'How can a girl see her face in that?' And one of the Wood boys, perhaps the one who dropped dead of a heart attack after his house was burned down, had shouted from the balcony at the top of the stairs, 'Mirror, mirror on the wall, who is the ugliest of them all?' It was well polished now and showed every detail of the elderly face that looked into it.

'That's it,' came Lucy's murmur now and then she passed on up the stairs. 'I know what I'll buy you for your feast day, Reverend Mother,' she said standing on the top step and calling down to her cousin, 'I'll buy you a silver tray for your letters. You keep them in such an untidy heap. It's just what you need.'

'Do you know, I would like that,' said the Reverend Mother sedately. She continued to examine the paintings on the wall of the stairs, but listened intently as Lucy, now back downstairs, was explaining to Peter Doyle about a feast day gift for her clerical cousin and describing the sort of tray she wanted to buy. The shop, it appeared, was full of silver trays and Lucy did a good job of exclaiming and enthusing and then regret-fully finding a fault. After a few moments the Reverend Mother went down to join Lucy as the short, dark-haired man rushed around bringing back examples of all shapes and sizes of silver trays. A very good salesman, she decided. He seemed to be genuinely putting himself in the position of the customer rather than endeavouring to make a sale at all costs.

'This one might suit you,' he said eventually, producing a rectangular tray. 'Not as popular as the round ones, but somehow I feel that there is something pleasing about it. Old Cork silver, too.' He took one look at Lucy's mink coat and decided not to talk about prices. 'It wasn't in the best of condition when we got it, was it, Jonathon? You spent hours on this one, didn't you?' He had raised his voice a little and the tall man in the background who was hand-polishing a pretty Queen Anne desk came over to join them.

'Don't know what on earth it was used for, but it was as black as my boots. In a terrible state. It's a beautiful piece; but it's still got some scratches on it. I couldn't get rid of them. Let me hold it under the light here and you can see them. Myself, I don't mind these on an antique piece, but there are some don't like them. And, of course, it has got one handle missing. Personally, I don't think it a good idea to put a modern handle on it, but if it distresses you, then perhaps we could do something about that. But, I myself, I wouldn't do that.' He was confident and assured. A man talking on a subject that he knew well. Perhaps he had been trained in the trade of restoration in England. Would that have been a likely career for one of the Irish ascendency class? Not in her day, but perhaps she was out-of-date in her notions.

'How about that one, Reverend Mother?' Lucy placed a gloved finger on the edge of the tray. 'That would fit all of your letters, even foolscap size.'

'That would be lovely, thank you very much, Mrs Murphy,' said the Reverend Mother. 'That would be a very useful feast-day present.' She wondered whether Lucy would want to ask the price, and moved away to look at the desk that was being transformed. Something familiar about this, also, but perhaps they were common in houses that she visited in her youth. And then she suddenly remembered.

'Has it got a secret drawer?' she asked as Jonathon Power came to join her.

'Press that knob,' he said with a very charming smile. He was a handsome young man, she thought. Quite different in appearance to Peter Doyle. Very much the English type, tall, blond and blue-eyed. She made a show of trying to find the knob, but she could have done it in her sleep. She could picture the house that it came from, also; could see the light slanting in through the corner window of the lobby where the desk stood and making a pathway on the frail pink flowers of the old faded carpet.

'Well, do you need any further convincing?' Lucy was, thought the Reverend Mother, unusually silent when they left the shop and walked over towards the Holy Trinity Church. Her cousin had a sharp brain, though, and surely they had garnered enough evidence to satisfy her.

'I just can't imagine two such charming young men joining in with the IRA on that awful burning-down of houses. It just seems such a terrible thing to do. Perhaps they just turn a blind eye to whosoever comes offering to sell the stuff.'

'Well, you know them better than I do, but I tend to be a bit cynical about "blind eyes". Half the suffering and the abuse that goes on in this city is the result of those famous blind eyes. Myself, I like to look the truth in its face, however ugly it may be,' said the Reverend Mother trenchantly.

'You're just so strait-laced and intolerant,' complained Lucy. 'Surely, if they were criminals, they wouldn't organize a musical society and spend time giving such pleasure to everyone. Peter was saying that he thought they probably didn't make much out of it, what with the hire of the hall and paying ushers and having costumes made and that sort of thing.'

'I don't suppose that they do,' said the Reverend Mother thoughtfully. A new idea had come to her. 'Who are in this musical society, the Merrymen, is that right?'

'Well, there's that young barrister, Tom Gamble, the son of old Judge Gamble. And his sister, Marjorie – you know her, the headmistress of Rochelle School – and one of her teachers, and there's one of the Beamishes, the oarsman, that fellow that had been chosen for the Olympics, Robert Beamish. He's supposed to be engaged to the teacher from Rochelle, one of the Morgan family from Fota, I think. And there's James O'Reilly from the Savings Bank, his wife, Rose, she's a soprano, oh, and oddly enough, there's that girl, Eileen MacSweeney, works in a printers off South Terrace, you know her, don't you? The *Cork Examiner* praised her singing voice. Wasn't she something to do with the IRA at one stage?'

And then Lucy fell silent as she saw outside the Holy Trinity Church, a big picture of a blurred old photograph of Father Dominic inserted inside a glass case, draped in black, and announcing beneath it that the funeral would be on next Wednesday morning.

Eileen, thought the Reverend Mother. Well, that could be a connection. But that meant that the idea that had come to her was incorrect. In any case, she would soon find out. She looked up at the photograph of poor Dominic and thought that he might have meddled with very powerful forces.

'I wouldn't say that there is anything wrong with these two,' Lucy was saying. 'Two very nice, very straightforward young men. You know, I just can't believe that they are tied up with the IRA.'

The Reverend Mother led the way to the car, thinking hard. The carefully wrapped silver tray was under one arm and before she got into the back seat of the car, she slid it from its wrappers and gazed at it thoughtfully.

'That's it,' said Lucy in a low voice and with a hasty glance to make sure that the glass panel between them and the chauffeur had been securely closed. 'I remember it distinctly. It didn't have a handle on one end and that was where people put their whips when they came back from riding. I suppose that was why it was left on the table for gloves and things. It was useless as a tray once the handle was broken.'

'Another reminder of Shanbally House,' said the Reverend Mother as she climbed into the car. 'The picture is beginning to be filled in, isn't it, Lucy?'

SIX

St Thomas Aquinas:
Ad primum ergo dicendum quod melius est intrare
religionem animo probandi, quam penitus non intrare,
quia per hoc disponitur ad perpetuo remanendum.
(It is better to enter religion with the purpose of
making a trial than not to enter at all, because by
so doing one would afford the possibility
to remain always.)

Dr Scher arrived at the convent soon after supper that evening. The Reverend Mother heard his voice in the hallway, joking with a new recruit. It would be a few minutes before he arrived at her room, she guessed. The girl was homesick and her tear-stained face would make him take trouble with her. She would not last long in the convent, in the Reverend Mother's opinion. Probably quite unsuitable, she had thought from the time when she had first interviewed her, but the parish priest had recommended the girl so highly that she had been given a month's trial. That was before she had heard that the girl had been seeing visions, just like Saint Bernadette at Lourdes and had imagined herself as a saint in the making. So far, all of the Reverend Mother's tactful proposals that she go home for a few months and return to the convent in January, if she was still set on being a nun, had not borne fruit and so she had tried another tactic which was to ignore the tears and wait patiently for sense to dawn. Hopefully by the end of the month the girl would be back in her father's farm in north Cork. Judging by the giggles that greeted Dr Scher's feeble jokes, she was tiring of the angelic and melancholic pose adopted when first admitted to the convent.

And then there were Dr Scher's footsteps on the stairs. He was going to visit Sister Assumpta. He would spend five or

ten minutes listening to her complaints, prescribing some innoc-
uous medicine. No doubt, he would also make a point of asking
any nun that he happened to meet about how she was feeling
and would listen carefully to the answer and recommend something for a troublesome cough, or feelings of indigestion. A kind
man, she thought.

Sighing heavily, the Reverend Mother turned her attention
back to her work.

A leaflet or circular asking for funds had, she discovered
many years ago, far less impact than a personal letter, tailor-
made for the individual, alluding, if possible, to a piece of
family history, a subtle reference to a shared background, a
recollection of a grandfather who might have made the family
fortune. Most of the businessmen and the professionals, the
lawyers and doctors of Cork, had risen out of the poverty of
tenant farmers. Denied professional outlets in the past because
of their nationality and their religion, their wits had been
sharpened and they had gone in for trade, and then accumulated
shiny new possessions and newly built houses in the affluent
suburbs of Blackrock and Montenotte. Money, though, since
it had not come easily, remained of great importance to them
and, even when it was for charity, they liked to receive good
value in terms of public recognition for it. And, since it was
a closely-knit community in this small city, every begging
letter had to be quite different to the others. If possible, she
found, it was better to ask for a donation to a small individual
charity than to that vast crater of poverty that existed side by
side with conspicuous wealth in the city of Cork.

Jimmy's delight in his rubber boots had given her the idea
of setting up a rubber boot store in the convent, each pair to
be presented as a reward for good work, for regular attendance
or anything else that her fertile imagination could devise until
at least all of the infants were equipped. And surely, the hardest
heart could not refuse the price of a pair of wellingtons for a
needy child. And then she would find an obliging reporter on
the *Cork Examiner* who would be happy to write an article
about this quirky charity and would not be too proud to include
a list of those who had donated.

'I remember how generous you were when I appealed for

help to furnish the infant classroom,' wrote the Reverend Mother, 'and so I venture to make another call on your kindness. Do give my best wishes to your wife and tell her how much I enjoyed talking over old times with her at the bishop's fete. And that I still remember the lovely visit that my cousin and I paid to her parents in their beautiful house beside Blackrock Castle. I shall always remember the enormous Monkey Puzzle tree in the back garden!' Judge Gamble, the only son of a prosperous trading family, had married a rich wife from the Protestant ascendancy and he surely could spare the price of a few wellington boots from the money he accumulated from his years in the law. And this personal note ensured that her letter would be handed to him and not put into the waste-paper basket by some ignorant young clerk of the Protestant faith who did not know that Reverend Mother Aquinas was an important person in the city of Cork. Smiling slightly at her pretensions, she signed the letter, inserted it into its envelope and then carefully placed it on top of Lucy's present, her new silver tray from the antiques shop.

And, of course, it must be the tray that she remembered! Few trays could be missing that second handle, she thought suddenly, as her forefinger traced the engraved hallmark on its base. She had forgotten, but now she remembered an end-of-September day. Lawrence, standing in the hallway of Shanbally House and saying that Charles Wood had probably taken a handle off so that it did not get in the way of people's whips when they laid them in the tray. She and Lucy had giggled at that, she remembered. It was, somehow, characteristic of the Woods that no one would mind if one of their sons did something like that. The whole place was so easy-going with meals at any time that was convenient for hunting in the autumn and winter and tennis in the summer. The atmosphere had suited Dominic, but there had been times when it had annoyed Lawrence intensely. A very driven personality, Lawrence, even back then in his youth, taking holiday assignments about reading and essay writing with great seriousness. It could have been predicted that Lawrence would have been the one of the two brothers to attain high honours, though few would have guessed at the position of Prior of the Capuchin order in the city of

Cork for the eldest son of a rich Protestant landowner. Amazing how controlled Lawrence was these days. There had been a time when anything had caused his temper to erupt.

The Reverend Mother took out another envelope and wrote: The Manager; Cork Savings Bank; 97, South Mall; Cork City. And then she began her letter. This time she did not endeavour to establish a personal connection. The man was from Dublin. But she did ask for an interview to discuss the convent's account and she knew that he was unlikely to refuse. Her sharp eye had noticed a chequebook from the Cork Savings Bank when Peter Doyle opened a drawer to put away Lucy's cheque. It made sense, of course, that they banked there. A clerk from that bank, Mr James O'Reilly was, apparently, one of their operatic group. In any case, she thought, I do need to discuss the possibility of a tactful overdraft, without any crippling interest payments, of course.

When Dr Scher tapped on the door, she tucked the letter beneath many others. By the time that he came in, the pile of envelopes were neatly arranged in the new silver tray.

'Where did you get that?' Her words of greeting and remarks about the weather had passed over his head. He had noticed the silver tray. His eye went to it immediately.

'In the antiques shop on Morrison's Island; my cousin, Mrs Murphy, very kindly bought it for me as a feast-day present,' she said demurely. 'Perhaps I'd better hide it when the bishop comes to call. It has an expensive look, doesn't it?'

'Very expensive, very rare, if it is what I think it is. Surely, it is a piece of Cork Silver. Queen Anne, I would say.' He took the pile of letters, deposited them untidily on the desk and brought the tray to the window.

'Pity about the missing handle,' he said when he brought it back.

She took it from him firmly. 'On the contrary, Dr Scher, the missing handle is of vital importance,' she said, putting the tray back onto her desk and re-arranging the stamped letters with meticulous care. Now that Dr Scher was here, she was uncertain how to lead up to the matter on her mind.

'Tell me about the weapon used to kill Father Dominic,' she said.

'Not your missing handle,' he retorted. He was looking at her in a slightly puzzled fashion.

'No, of course, not,' she said placidly, tucking her hands into her sleeves and waiting patiently.

He gave one more glance at the silver tray but then turned his attention back to her.

'Patrick and I keep talking about that,' he said. 'I thought that it might be something like a very fine, thin stiletto, but Patrick wasn't keen on that idea. It could be, but I told you about that, a sharpened knitting needle, but somehow, unless it was very expertly done, I just don't think that was it. It wouldn't be fine enough. The entry wound was very small; no sign of force or anything like that. Something very smooth, not rough in any way. Whatever killed him, it just slid in and punctured the brain.'

He eyed her carefully and although she was sure that she had allowed no sign of distress to escape, he said unexpectedly, 'You may be consoled to know that I don't think he suffered. Death would have been instantaneous.'

'He knew that it was coming, though,' she said. 'I could tell that by the expression on his face. I think that he recognized his assailant – was surprised. I told you that and I am sure of it.'

Dr Scher made a half-gesture, a slight pursing of the lips, a movement of the hands, but said nothing.

'I know what you are going to say, or what you would say if I were one of your students at the university,' she said. 'You would have a lot of long Latin medical terms, but I knew Dominic, knew his expressions and I do think that he recognized the person and feared his ending.'

And then, when he still said nothing, she added, 'And, I think that may tell us something valuable, that he was astonished to see that person coming to confess and that he feared they were a danger to him.'

'Or else that he saw something in their hand.'

'That is very possible,' she admitted. 'I thought of something today. My cousin was joking with me today when she was buying me the present. I looked at a mirror, a gilt wood mirror, and she said "nuns don't need mirrors".'

'And you replied?' He looked puzzled.

'I replied that of course nuns need mirrors, or how could they pin their veil to the wimple.' The Reverend Mother got to her feet, went across the room and took something from a drawer. He was looking even more puzzled when she returned, both hands hidden in the wide sleeves of her habit.

'This is one of the pins that we use to fasten the veil to the wimple and to pin the wimple itself. The convent has a lot of these pins.'

'May I handle it?' he asked respectfully.

The Reverend Mother suppressed a smile. 'There is nothing particularly sacred about a pin, Dr Scher. Women use them to pin on their hats. We may have slightly larger ones.'

'About nine inches long,' said Dr Scher, picking up the pin and examining it.

'Yes, there are several layers of material to be caught and pinned into place so we buy the largest size.' She could see a question on his lips and decided to wait for it. Her mind was still slightly unsure as to the next step to be taken. Dr Scher, she thought would normally have joked about her murderous capabilities, but he was a sensitive man and knew that her sorrow over Dominic's death was very real.

'Well, I can tell you that this is a very possible weapon, in fact it fits my memory of the wound very well. Something like this would slide in through the ear with no tearing of the skin. A pinprick, we say, don't we? Patrick will be interested to see this.'

'He'll soon be here.' The Reverend Mother glanced at the clock. 'That sounds like him now. I've just heard the doorbell. I had not thought that he would come as late as this. He'll be in soon, once he has seen Sister Mary Immaculate.'

'I would take a bet on it that he was still working up to now. There are so many witnesses' statements to be gone through. The police take everything down in shorthand and then transcribe the whole thing. People can get very chatty out of nervousness,' said Dr Scher. Meditatively, he inserted the tip of the hat pin into his ear, but then put it down and began busily scrubbing at the damp pane of the window with his handkerchief. 'Terribly unhealthy place this city,' he added.

'No wonder that people are dying of TB and of bronchial pneumonia all over the place. Moulds form at the sides of these damp windows even in the best cared for houses. I'd have cured most of my patients if I could have prescribed a dry, cold winter and some nice sun through the summer.'

He was talking, thought the Reverend Mother, to give her a chance to recover herself and she appreciated his kindness. She, had, she guessed, gone pale when he had put her hat pin in his ear. When Sister Bernadette ushered in Inspector Cashman, they were both sitting in silence. By this stage, the Reverend Mother had made up her mind.

'Thank you, sister,' she said gravely, interrupting Sister Bernadette's hospitable offers of fresh tea and cake, 'I think that we are still quite well supplied.'

Patrick sat down, shaking his head as Dr Scher lifted the teapot in an enquiring fashion. He looked tired and discouraged, thought the Reverend Mother. She didn't suppose that Sister Mary Immaculate had enlightened him about anything much. She had been declaring to all that she had nothing to say. Like a good penitent her eyes had been shut throughout the short time that she spent in the cubicle. She glanced at the clock. Half past seven. A late hour for him to be still working on a Saturday, she thought. The city was burning with indignation at the murder of one of its favourite priests, the saintly Father Dominic. The Saturday *Evening Echo* had compensated for the lack of new progress to be reported in the Monday morning's *Cork Examiner* and had speculated freely on the possible involvement of paramilitary organizations, such as the Irish Republican Army, or the Anti-Sinn Féin Society. Everyone who had visited Father Dominic's confessional stall had been urged to contact the Civic Guards instantly if they had not already done so and there was an open invitation to the citizens to speculate on what might have happened.

'How are things going, Patrick?' she asked and he gave a weary sigh.

'We've had lots of statements, Reverend Mother, but of course, it is impossible to know how many people went to confess to Father Dominic.'

'No time limit on those outpourings?' asked Dr Scher.

Patrick gave a reluctant smile. 'That's part of the problem. If things seem to be slowing up, people go off to another stall. I've done it myself. You see it all the time. One poor soul with a lot on their mind can occupy the cubicle for anything up to half an hour. The person on the other side might get tired, go out, another one pop in, taking his place and this can go on for a long time. That's what seems to have happened.'

'Have you had many witnesses, Patrick,' she asked.

'Not too many, yesterday morning, but the *Evening Echo* came out earlier than usual yesterday afternoon. I'd say that they rushed it out. Had a big photograph of Father Dominic on the first page and an appeal for help about those who were present at the Novena, and especially from those who either went to confession to Father Dominic, or who tried to go. We've had queues at the barracks since then. And all of today. I've only just finished up. One man had something interesting to say.'

'Have some cake if you don't want tea. Sugar will give you energy,' said Dr Scher hospitably. He cut a generous slice and put the plate down beside Patrick. 'Interesting?' he queried.

'That's right.' Patrick had a bigger notebook in an inner pocket of his jacket and now took it out. It had a meticulous drawing of the confessional stall, neatly executed in ink and pencilled numbers on either side. 'Number twelve L,' he said and then, almost apologetically he continued, 'he had a tale to tell of being on the right-hand side and then he made way to allow a pregnant woman to go ahead of him and then the woman at the top of the left-hand queue insisted that he go ahead of her.'

'Cork politeness,' said Dr Scher with a grin. 'And was the good father alive when he went in.'

'Yes, and in good form. That's the only question that I ask, you understand,' said Patrick hastily and with an embarrassed look at the Reverend Mother. 'But the most interesting bit was that when he came out, he saw a woman in a huge shawl, that covered her from head to toe, going into the right-hand cubicle. This woman hasn't come forward, but someone else remembered her and another witness remarked that the woman in the shawl must have been a respectable woman because she didn't smell.'

'Didn't smell,' repeated the Reverend Mother thoughtfully.

'I like your drawing' said Dr Scher, examining the notebook. 'You're a bit of an artist on the quiet, young Patrick, aren't you?'

'It reminds me of those drawings of cranes that you used to do when you were a boy.' The Reverend Mother spoke absent-mindedly. 'And number 12 R, the person who went into the right-hand cubicle, after the woman in the large shawl?'

'Number 12 R was a small boy, eight years old. He went in, stayed only minutes, then came out, and according to his mother, he burst into tears and said . . .' Patrick flipped open another page of his notebook and read out: 'The child was still upset, but his mother related that his words at the time were: "He wouldn't speak to me,".'

'She is correct,' said the Reverend Mother gravely. 'I heard the words from the child myself. I began to worry then.'

'And after the child . . .?' Dr Scher looked from one to the other.

'The next person, number 13 R, related that the priest's head was turned away from her and she thought he had just forgotten to close that shutter and so she went out again very quickly. And she waited for some time, but there didn't seem to be any movement in the queues on either side and so she went further up the church. That happened with quite a few people. Though it appeared that no one else went into the right-hand cubicle.'

'That's odd,' said Dr Scher.

'Not really,' said Patrick. 'People wait until someone comes out and then they go in. If no one was coming out of the right-hand cubicle, then no one would go in. That's the way that it works, Dr Scher. Number 13 R said that she told the next person that the shutter was open and the priest must have forgotten to close it and that person left also and went with her friend to another confessor, further up in the church.'

'More Cork politeness,' said Dr Scher.

'We're a very religious and polite people,' said Patrick, taking the proffered slice of cake.

They were talking to cover her silence, but she felt unable

to join in the banter. She saw Patrick steal a glance at her and then, unlike his usually taciturn self, he started to talk to Dr Scher about how he used to go down the quays and count all the metal struts on the unloading crane so that he could make his drawing more accurate. And then he ran out of anecdotes and looked at her enquiringly.

'There is something else, Patrick, that I need to tell you about,' she said. 'Dr Scher may have reported to you that he saw Father Dominic in the Morrison's Island Antiques Shop and that he was looking distressed?'

'That's right, a ceramic, was that it, Dr Scher?'

'A Japanese Arita hawk,' said Dr Scher.

'Whatever that is,' said Patrick with a smile.

'A hawk made of a particular clay and then hardened; in other words, porcelain,' said the Reverend Mother with precision. 'I was intrigued by this, especially as I had a memory of a Japanese Arita hawk from a house, from Shanbally House, where I stayed in my young days.' She paused for a moment and then said quietly, 'I have a memory of Father Dominic and his brother, the present prior, staying there in Shanbally House, also.'

'It burned down last year, didn't it?' Patrick's face was full of interest. 'But I thought that everything in it was destroyed. It burned to the ground, roof, windows, everything. Just a shell left.'

'Wasn't it burned down by the IRA?' asked Dr Scher.

'Possibly,' said the Reverend Mother cautiously and then turned back to Patrick.

'I talked with my cousin, who shared my youth; we were brought up together. She wished,' said the Reverend Mother demurely, 'to buy me a feast-day present. We went to Morrison's Island Antique Shop where she bought me a silver tray.'

'Missing one handle,' put in Dr Scher.

Patrick was beginning to guess what might come next.

'Missing one handle,' she agreed. 'And that missing handle is significant. Both of us, my cousin and I, remembered a silver tray with a missing handle on the hall table at Shanbally

House. It was used, when I was young, to hold gloves and riding whips and I think that it went on being so used later on. And while we were there, we saw other familiar objects. Not the single Arita hawk, which Father Dominic had been examining. That had been removed, probably after his query. As Dr Scher will tell you, they mostly are a pair. The one in the antiques shop was a single hawk, but my cousin, who went on visiting Shanbally House after I joined the convent here, remembered that one hawk was broken when one of the Wood family boys threw a tennis ball at his brother's head and hit the hawk instead.' She suppressed a smile at the look of pain on Dr Scher's face and went on to explain about the chip from the beak and about the missing handle from the oblong silver tray. 'And there was also a gilt-edged mirror which both of us remembered from Shanbally House,' she finished.

'So there may be a connection,' mused Patrick. 'I must visit the shop again. We had a reported sighting of Peter Doyle in the church before the Novena began. I thought that it was odd, though my informant seemed trustworthy and he would have known the man well. There's no doubt about that. I was surprised, but I interviewed him because of that as well as because of what Dr Scher noticed. I thought it was strange, but Mr Doyle was adamant that he had not been inside the church. He seemed to be genuinely surprised, I thought at the time. But now I have two strange things. A Protestant in a Catholic church and a friar in an antiques shop.' He seemed to be thinking hard.

'Well, thank you, Reverend Mother,' he said after a moment. He seemed to hesitate and she was quick to respond.

'Thank you for coming, Patrick,' she said gravely.

'Shanbally House?' he said slowly. 'Surely, the IRA was supposed to be responsible for burning it down. But why then were some artefacts from the house in that antiques shop? The IRA were accused of many things, but looting was not one of their crimes. Discipline is very strictly enforced; everyone knows that.' He rose to his feet. He did not, she noticed, appear to want an answer to his question. 'Now I had better get back to the barracks, and so I will wish you both a good evening,' he said and she let him go without the formality of ringing a bell. It looked as though he were thinking hard and did not want any interruption to his thoughts.

SEVEN

St Thomas Aquinas:
'*Religionis status ordinatur ad perfectionem caritatis,
quae se extendit ad dilectionem Dei et proximi.*'
(The religious state is directed to the perfection
of charity, which extends to the love of God and of
those who are near to us.)

When Sister Bernadette, wreathed in smiles, came in to announce that Mrs Murphy was on the phone, the Reverend Mother jumped thankfully to her feet, glad of the opportunity to escape from the dismal company of Sister Mary Immaculate who had not been feeling well all day, complaining of a bad headache that she had been suffering for days. On a Sunday, in the afternoon, most of the nuns, the professed sisters and the lay sisters, had visitors or were on outings with friends and relations. Sister Mary Immaculate, however, had no visitors and with the air of a martyr, had declared her intention of bearing the Reverend Mother company. She had ensconced herself beside the empty fireplace and sat there, propping her head on her hand, and from time to time sighing heavily. The Reverend Mother, busily sorting through various bills, placing them in two piles, 'urgent' and 'can wait', did her best to control her irritation.

'May I help you in any way, sister?' she had enquired, but Sister Mary Immaculate had just continued to sigh and so the telephone call, which might have exasperated the Reverend Mother normally, was greeted with alacrity.

'And how are you on this fine day, Mrs Murphy,' she enquired and heard Lucy's chuckle on the other end of the wire.

'I'm going to take you for a drive, Reverend Mother,' she announced. 'Rupert has fallen asleep on the sofa in front of the fire, buried under the Sunday newspapers, so you and I are going for a little drive, and perhaps get away from this

awful rain. I'll call for you in twenty minutes, so get on your
best bib and tucker.'

'Where are we going?' enquired the Reverend Mother. She
should, she knew, say that she was too busy, but the temptation was too great.

'South of France,' said Lucy and rang off instantly.

Doesn't want the ladies in the telephone exchange to know,
thought the Reverend Mother. She gave a quick glance at the
monotonous drizzle that filmed the windowpanes. South of
France would be very nice. Poverty, she had decided some
time ago, was made infinitely worse by climate. Imagine the
poor of the south parish in the South of France, living in dry
houses, used mainly to shelter from the heat of the sun, always
warm, no expensive turf or coal, no urgent need for starchy
foods. No damp, no patches of mould, no problems with
washing clothes. 'They could at least keep themselves clean,'
she had heard a St Vincent de Paul worker remark and
wondered how clean that charitable lady would be if she had
no money to buy firewood or even turf to heat water for
washing clothes or bodies. And not even a garden to hang out
the wet garments for the odd hour of wind and sunshine.

'I'm afraid that I shall have to ask you to return to the recreation room as I am going out in a quarter of an hour, Sister Mary
Immaculate,' she said. It was an unbreakable rule that her room
was always locked while she was not there herself. There were
too many confidential reports and records about children and
members of the community in desk drawers and boxes for her
to run the risk of inquisitive eyes seeing them.

'I'd better go then, Reverend Mother,' she said in a martyred
fashion. 'I would not like to spoil your outing. Goodness
knows; you work very hard! If I've said it once, I've said it
a hundred times. "Don't bother the Reverend Mother; she's a
very busy woman." That's what I say to the young sisters. I
like to think that I save you quite a lot of annoyance in that
way, Reverend Mother. You're going out with Mrs Murphy, I
suppose. And I wouldn't like in any way to interfere with your
pleasures.'

She makes it sound as if I were off to the *Folies Bergère*,
thought the Reverend Mother. Aloud she said, 'You are very

good, though please bear in mind that I would always wish to be available if any sister desires to speak with me.' She stayed still and presented an inviting, she hoped, countenance towards her deputy for another few long moments. But as there was nothing said, no sound except the occasional sign, and as she had, surreptitiously, managed to finish sorting her bills, she hazarded, 'But, of course, sister, you yourself, are wise enough to know that the best possible recourse, if one is troubled, is one's confessor.' With that, she, also, rose to her feet and went towards the door where her outdoor cloak hung. It was still damp since early-morning mass when the chaplain had detained her outside the church door. His action of holding the umbrella over her head had been well meant, but it had resulted in a cascade of drops spilling down the back of her serge cloak. Still, the back seat of Lucy's car was always piled high with luxurious rugs and frequently a couple of stoneware hot water bottles were placed at the passengers' feet. She fished out her keys and stood with them in her hand.

'I suppose that you won't want to keep the chauffeur waiting,' said Sister Mary Immaculate. She slid past the Reverend Mother and went in the direction of the recreation room. Just as well, perhaps, as the elderly chaplain liked an after-dinner nap. There were peals of laughter coming from the recreation room and the sound of young children's voices, high and excited. There was a toddler there, too, judging by the sound of running footsteps. Fascinated by that large expanse of shiny floor around the central table and trotting like a little horse, like all small children who visited the convent. There was something very attractive to them about being allowed to run and run around the long table and skid on the well-polished floor. For a moment, the Reverend Mother felt a little ashamed to be releasing Sister Mary Immaculate to spoil the fun, but luckily at the last moment, the nun began to climb the stairs to the dormitories. Perhaps she had failed in the past to impose her authority on a two-year-old and didn't feel up to a tussle. In any case she had been complaining of a headache for the last few days and going to bed on Sunday afternoon would reinforce her complaints.

'Mrs Murphy's car is just coming down the street.' Sister

Bernadette came flying out of the kitchen and hastened to open the front door. 'Isn't it great the way the streets are so empty on a Sunday.'

'Thank you, sister.' The Reverend Mother tried not to rush furtively down the path. She had a feeling of escape. She was, she had to admit, looking forward immensely to an afternoon in the company of her cousin. Lucy and she had always been close and after the death of Lucy's parents, they had been brought up together. Perhaps this accounted for the fact that, though very different in every way, and leading extremely different lives, their minds were always in tune. She had to school herself to wait impassively while the chauffeur jumped out of the car, threw open the back door, and carefully handed her in.

'Oh, a hot water jar, what luxury,' she sighed. The ceramic container, shaped like half a little barrel, had a flat bottom, a rounded top and a chimney-like little spout right in the centre. She placed her cold feet on either side of the spout, curling them over the curved surface of the heater.

'You look tired, you're very pale. Let me tuck the rug around your knees. What dreadful weather for June!' With one hand, Lucy flicked closed the partition between the back seat and the chauffeur and then placed a cosy rug upon her cousin's knees. The Reverend Mother leaned back against the cushions and sighed a sigh of guilty relief.

'You'll never guess where we're going,' said Lucy as the big car slid away down the wet street.

'Not the South of France, then. Oh, what a shame!' murmured the Reverend Mother, savouring the warmth of the comforting heater at her feet.

'No, we're going to see the Abernethys, or at least, Marigold Abernethy. Her husband died last year.'

'I know. I wrote to her.' How many of those letters of condolence had she written during the last few years? The ranks of the moneyed friends of her youth who had frolicked in the big houses around the county of Cork had thinned drastically during the last five or six years. So many of those splendid houses had burned down. And then death or emigration, which was a kind of death, had accounted for most of the people that she and Lucy had known so well during their girlhood.

'And why are we going to see Marigold Abernethy?' she asked.

'We're not,' said Lucy. 'Well, we are, but in reality we are going to see her cook. It just suddenly came to me. You know how Marigold Abernethy talks, it all flows out in that strange accent of hers, that weird mixture of an English accent and a strong west Cork accent, and when you go home all sort of things that she says echo in your mind. And one of them just came back to me this morning. Rupert was reading out an advertisement for a cook at the Imperial Hotel. It was saying that they wanted a cook who was proficient in French cooking, and Rupert said, "Let's hope that he or she can cook good Irish sausages and potatoes, and that would be a change."'

'And the Abernethy's cook?' queried the Reverend Mother.

'I'm coming to that,' said Lucy. 'You see, Rupert is very fussy about his food. I couldn't get him to like visiting the Abernethys. He didn't mind "him" so much and "she" amused him, but the food was always awful, but then when she said, one day a few months ago, just as we were leaving, "Oh, my dears, I've engaged the Woods' cook . . ." well, that's what came back to me. Because when Rupert was talking about a new cook for the Imperial Hotel, well, I suddenly thought of Marigold Abernethy and her new cook. When we were coming home in the car, he said to me, "Well, I won't mind going there again if she really does engage the Woods' cook. I've had some great meals there, poor things."'

'And did she? Did Marigold Abernethy engage the Woods' cook?'

'Yes, indeed she did. And, you know, it's a strange thing, but when we next went to dinner at the Abernethy house, it was just exactly as though we had been dining in Shanbally House. Everything the same, even the gravy. She's a really good cook, perhaps a bit monotonous if you live in the house, but truly excellent if you only visit a few times a year.'

'And you thought that I would appreciate this paragon; what does she serve for afternoon tea?'

'The usual cakes,' said Lucy with a deep-throated chuckle. 'But I'm sure that you will find something to admire. It's an old-fashioned idea,' she said staring straight at a point midway on her chauffeur's back, 'yes, I suppose that it is an old-fashioned idea, but I rather like doing it, popping into a kitchen just to say how much one enjoyed the cooking.'

'How very right you are, my dear Lucy,' said the Reverend Mother. 'If I do enjoy the scone and the cakes, then I shall certainly make a point of saying so.'

'You do the cake and I'll do the scones,' said Lucy thoughtfully. 'I feel that I can do justice to the scones. "It needs a light hand", do you remember that your father's cook used to say that. It's stuck in my mind. Even your father managed to memorize that. Do you remember him going down to the kitchen? You and I used to giggle on the stairway when we heard him say, "You have a very light hand, God bless you, Mrs O'Hara!" and whenever we went out for afternoon tea, he used to say to whatever hostess we had, "Your cook has a very light hand with the scones; scones take skill." We used to laugh a lot about that,' said Lucy.

'I remember,' said the Reverend Mother. She thought about this cook, now employed by the Abernethy family, but previously in the service of the Woods. And very, very pleased to be back cooking in a nice house rather than a back-street bakery, according to Lucy. A wasted talent. No one thought much about the servants when these big houses were burned down. Pity was always poured out for the sad fate of the owners, but the servants suffered also. Their fear and shock were almost as much, they invariably lost their job and their place to live and they had no background of money, no relations in England, to cushion the shock. She wondered whether the Republicans considered this matter when their lorries roared up to these unprotected houses.

Marigold Abernethy was touchingly pleased to see the Reverend Mother. There was a glowing fire on both ends of the long drawing room and an exquisite Regency table already placed between the two sofas. A lace-trimmed linen tea cloth lay folded upon it and Marigold had nodded at a parlourmaid who had come in about ten minutes after their arrival.

'Of course, there are so few of us left now.' Marigold was talking about a ball held long ago at the Imperial Hotel. The Reverend Mother listened with seeming attention, but allowed her eyes to wander over silver candlesticks, velvet curtains, two-hundred-year-old pieces of elegantly carved furniture, an exquisite pair of glass chandeliers, an oval Adam mirror, a shelf of beautiful Belleek china. Could all of these items be spotted in the short interval of time before the house was set on fire, or was there, perhaps, a preliminary visit, a scouting operation to make sure that the pickings were worth the risk?

'She married young Gamble, you know, and a very good match it was for him, too,' Lucy was saying and then laughed at herself. 'What am I saying! Young Gamble. He's a judge these days, of course, and as grey as a badger.'

'Yes, I've seen him. He brought along his two and a friend from England, one of the Powers from South Tipperary. A very nice young man. A great admirer of my furniture. It's been here forever, I said to him. The English like things new, of course, but this young fellow wasn't like that. He told me that his grandmother had often talked about the beautiful walnut table she used to own and he thought that it must have been quite like that one over there. Queen Anne, that's what he said. But you'll never guess what he admired most of all. Excuse me, Reverend Mother, if I just reach past you.'

Marigold took from the ledge of a bookcase a couple of large silver rings, lined with cobalt glass.

'You'll never guess what they are,' she said, looking from one to another. 'My grandmother used to have a dozen of them. She gave them to my mother when she married, but you know what it's like with a big family of boys! Only those two are left.'

'Napkin rings,' hazarded Lucy. 'No, they couldn't be – too large, aren't they?'

'No, they're not for napkins. You'll never guess unless I tell you.' Marigold looked from one to the other triumphantly. 'They're potato rings. The parlourmaid used to put a linen napkin in them and then pop the potato into the ring. It stood inside the ring and the napkin kept it piping hot. I remember

them well when I was young; I remember at least six of them.
And we have some matching salt cellars to go with them.'

Made in the days when potatoes were valued as rare and
exotic, thought the Reverend Mother. She was no expert, but
thought that the silver and cobalt potato rings might well date
back to the seventeenth century. She opened her mouth to ask
a question and then closed it as there was a tap on the door
and the well-starched parlourmaid appeared pushing a laden
trolley.

'Tea!' exclaimed Lucy, with a nice note of surprise and
pleasure in her voice. 'Oh, how lovely! You shouldn't have
gone to all that trouble. Oh, scones! I just love scones.'

Dr Scher would have liked the tea set, thought the Reverend
Mother as she accepted a cup poured from the thin spout of
a pot that looked very like the one that he had described to
her from Morrison's Island Antiques Shop. There was thick
yellow cream in a matching jug and the set was finished off
by a bowl where the sugar had been carefully carved into neat
lumps, to be lifted out by a matching pair of silver tongs. A
forgotten era, she thought, as she looked at the delicate china,
the well-polished, beautifully shaped silver, the wafer-thin
cucumber sandwiches, the hot scones carefully wrapped in a
linen napkin. Someone had even gone to the trouble of shaping
the butter into elaborately patterned ball shapes and arranging
them in neat lines on a grooved wooden platter.

'You don't worry about living here on your own, Mrs
Abernethy, do you?' she asked when the parlourmaid had
withdrawn from the room.

A slight shadow passed across their hostess's face, but she
answered briskly. 'Not at all,' she said with emphasis, her voice
going up like a musical scale. 'One can't live one's life waiting
for a catastrophe. I never even think about it, Reverend Mother.
Mind you, the gardener always locks the gates before he goes
home in the evening. No point in making things easy for them.'

No need to ask what this indomitable elderly woman meant
by 'them'. This burning down of houses was an appalling
business. A crime even if it were done for political reasons;
purely to make money, well that rendered it even more despic-
able. Once again the Reverend Mother's gaze swept the room,

one among many in this house, she knew, to be stuffed with Queen Anne, Georgian or Regency treasures. She imagined a greedy glance, masked by an air of polite interest, valuing its contents. Imagined the planning. And then the raid. Not too difficult to intimidate the elderly butler; the gardener lived in the village, and probably the gardener's boys, also. There might be a boy or two living in in order to work in the scullery or to replenish the fires, and five or six elderly women servants. That would be the only opposition that tough young men, masked and carrying rifles and cans of petrol, would face.

She examined the elaborate scrolls of the silver cake server. She had never seen a cake server quite like this. The blade had been perforated to form an eight-point sun and around it was a carefully incised garland of flowers. The hallmark was on the lifter mechanism, above the handle and she thought that she could see the Cork silver hallmark with its ship and two towers. Dr Scher would be interested in that.

'I must just go and powder my nose,' said Lucy rising and seizing her handbag. 'And dear Mrs Abernethy, please do allow me to pop into the kitchen and congratulate your cook on her scones.'

'And do tell her how much I enjoyed that feather-light sponge cake,' put in the Reverend Mother as a glance and a smile was passed between mistress and parlourmaid. No doubt, by the time that her cousin descended upon the kitchen, the cook would be ready in a clean apron and with, perhaps, a box of those delicious scones sitting on the table ready to be taken home to Rupert. Lucy would make a better job of talking to the cook – she had a way of being informal and chatty. The woman would be more reserved, and perhaps even a little overawed with someone like the Reverend Mother.

In any case, she wanted to have a chat with her hostess about this visit paid by Judge Gamble to an old friend of his long-deceased wife.

'Well, the cook was full of information,' said Lucy as soon as they got back into the privacy of the Reverend Mother's room. Nothing had been said in the car and that seemed to be a good sign that valuable information had been garnered. 'And, you know, this is interesting. There were just five of them, five blackguards, according to the cook.'

'How did she describe them?'

'Well, there was only one who spoke and he was a small man, quite slim, "not a big fellow, at all", that's what she said. But, of course, you don't argue with a man holding a rifle, no matter what his size, do you?'

'And what did he sound like, did she say?'

'"Pure Cork, a city man, from the flat of the city", that's what the cook said. She said he gave her the creeps: that he had a strange sound of him, but she was probably very frightened anyway. By the way, she has a strong west Cork accent herself. Still, she worked for the Woods at Shanbally House for at least twenty years, I'd say and they'd be having lots of deliveries, city men and countrymen. I would think that she knew what she was talking about when she said he had a "flat of the city" accent. So that rather puts paid to your idea, doesn't it?'

'Why? It's possible to mimic an accent. Do you remember Lawrence? He was a terrible mimic. Could be a bit nasty with it, too. Do you remember that butler they had in Coachford House? Lawrence used to reduce him almost to tears by calling down flirtatious and some rather improper remarks over the stairs to the maids in exactly the man's Skibbereen accent. An accent can be feigned; the stronger the accent, the easier it is to mimic it.'

'Funny to think of Lawrence as a friar, isn't it?' said Lucy. 'Still, I suppose that he always got very intense about things, didn't he? Do you remember the summer when he was determined to become the best bowman in the world? He kept practising and practising, until he nearly shot the gardener and his father burned his bow and arrows. I remember how furious he was. And he was a good mimic, wasn't he?'

Not the only one, thought the Reverend Mother, but she was scrupulously careful never to repeat anything that Patrick said. She pondered his interview with the two men in the antiques shop and his report of how Peter Doyle had put on a Cork city accent. Much easier than a west Cork accent for an Englishman who lived and shopped in the city of Cork.

This did sound as if it could have been Peter Doyle. 'But tell me what the others looked like,' she said.

'One very tall man, a fine figure of a man, big chest on him, according to the cook. Another pair, nearly as tall and one just of an ordinary size. That's really all of what she could remember of them. They were given twenty minutes to grab some clothes, but when she was halfway through stuffing things into a bag, she smelled petrol. She opened her door and saw smoke drifting up the stairs, so she screamed to the other servants to hurry up. When they got downstairs, they saw that petrol had been poured on the Aubusson carpet in the hallway. Someone had thrown a match on it; that's what she thought, anyway. She said that there was just one man there, then. He was holding a gun and there was a box of matches on the table. Doesn't make sense, though, does it? If they were going to steal something, why start the fire before they even got the people out of the house? Not that the carpet was worth much, I'd say. It was the same one, that circular threadbare one, as they had in the hall when you and I were young, but still it was very dangerous with a houseful of elderly people.'

'It was meant to get them out quickly, I suppose,' said the Reverend Mother. 'Remember wool doesn't burn very fast. It smokes more than it burns. It just takes one man with gun to usher everyone out; the others were probably in the drawing room, or the library, collecting silver and small items. They would certainly have some sacks with them. Could the cook remember anything about their appearance, colour of hair or anything, when she saw them first?'

'I asked her about that,' said Lucy. 'She said that they had masks on, right over their heads and faces, just a few holes cut out for the eyes and the mouth.'

'Of course,' said the Reverend Mother. 'We've seen plenty of those over the last few years. An old sock, usually. It would conceal the hair too, unfortunately.' She thought about Jonathon Power's dark blond hair. Few Irish people had hair of that colour. The fair-haired of Ireland were mostly a pale red gold in colour. 'So nothing but the height and the stature to identify them,' she said aloud.

'That's right. One quite short and slim, one 'ordinary', two tall and one very tall.'

'So the three tall men could have been Robert Beamish, Tom Gamble and Jonathon Power. The "ordinary" one was probably the bank clerk. I haven't seen him, but I would say that the man who gave the orders sounds just like Peter Doyle.'

'Except for the flat Cork accent.'

'He was an actor, remember,' said the Reverend Mother. 'I'm no mimic, but I expect that it is easier to mimic an extreme accent, than it would be to mimic a fairly neutral one. And, of course, if you pronounce all of your "th" sounds as a flat "t", all your "e's", as "a's", then you are halfway there. Peter Doyle, by all accounts, was a talented actor so it would not be difficult for him to play the part of a masked gunman.'

Lucy said nothing. To the Reverend Mother's slight amusement, she gave a furtive glance over her shoulder as though to check that no one had entered the room. Lucy, though probably from the relative safety of a chauffeured car, had witnessed raids and street battles over the last few years, but there was something about this cold-blooded threat of violence and robbery from seemingly respectable people that seemed to frighten her. She sat very still for a moment and then seemed to come to some decision.

'And now Dominic is dead,' she remarked. 'You do realize that he is probably dead because in his clever way he worked this out. He saw the Japanese Arita hawk, remembered it. He must have remembered it, mustn't he? Or did someone drop him a clue?' Lucy gave the Reverend Mother a sudden, sharply inquisitive glance.

'Did you know that the word "clue" – it used to be spelled C L E W – meant a piece of string, rather like the thread used by Theseus to guide him out of the labyrinth. I think it was Edgar Allan Poe who used it first in our modern sense, and then Wilkie Collins popularized it,' said the Reverend Mother. Not for anything would she betray Lawrence's confidence about Dominic's penitent who was involved in crime. In her own mind, though, she thought that it would be an extraordinary coincidence if that confession did not have something to do with Dominic's surprising visit to the premises of

Morrison's Island Antiques Shop. 'That's interesting about the word "clue", isn't it?' she asked blandly.

'Not very,' said Lucy. 'And I think you are just trying to put me off. You always think that you must know best. That's the trouble with clever people. And just you remember this, Dottie; one can be too clever for one's own good. It's never safe to meddle in other people's affairs. You have a word with this young Patrick of yours. Tell him, in confidence, of course, that you suspect those people in the antiques shop are up to mischief, that they are dressing up as IRA men and burning down houses in the Republican name, having first of all taken a few sack loads of silver, some pictures and some furniture, of course. Tell him all that and even tell him your reasons for believing it, if you like. But stop there, Dottie. I'm warning you. This is not safe. It's all very well being a martyr, but I'm sure that having a hatpin stuck into your ear is not a pleasant experience.'

'No, indeed,' said the Reverend Mother, glad to have an opportunity of agreeing one point. Lucy, of course, was right. This Peter Doyle might be a very dangerous man.

EIGHT

WB Yeats:
'You, too, have come where the dim tides are hurled
Upon the wharves of sorrow and heard ring
The bell that calls us on; the sweet, far thing.'

When Eileen arrived at the convent on Sunday night, she found that the Reverend Mother was waiting patiently in the small chapel at the back of the convent. The Sunday evening show had overrun with lots of demands for encores, so she was relieved to find the door of the chapel unlocked. Eamonn had gone like the wind down quays and across bridges and then she had run at full speed down the little lane to the back gate. She was still panting when she opened the door.

The Reverend Mother was sitting on a small chair beside the altar, not fingering her rosary beads, nor reading her prayer book, just sitting, very still, looking tired and old, thought Eileen, when she rushed in. How old was the Reverend Mother? No one knew. She had been old when Eileen's mother was a child and no one seemed to remember the time before she held command on St Mary's of the Isle. Poor old thing, thought Eileen, with a rush of compassion as she went quickly up the aisle

'I'm sorry that I am late, Reverend Mother,' she said quietly as she reached the nun. She sat down on the altar steps and looked up into the face of her former headmistress. Yes, she thought, even more lined than usual, just as though the structure of the pale skin had somewhat collapsed from sheer exhaustion and lack of sleep. The green eyes had discoloured patches under them.

'What's the matter, Reverend Mother?' she asked.

The Reverend Mother seemed visibly to rouse herself. 'No, you're not late. I remembered afterwards that you would be performing tonight. Of course, you would have to change after the show, so it's kind of you to spare the time to come to see me,' she said with an audible effort at her usual briskness. 'Sit here, Eileen. I read a very nice review about you on the *Cork Examiner*. They praised your voice and I'm not surprised. I can remember you singing 'Panis Angelicus' here in this very chapel.'

And then the Reverend Mother fell silent, a brooding expression on her face. Eileen sat on a kneeling hassock at her feet and began to feel alarmed. The Reverend Mother had been like a rock to her in life, never changing, never unsure, never upset by anything. Never totally predictable, of course, suddenly tossing a question or an uncertainty back upon you, but always a fund of information and common sense. Now, for the first time, she seemed uncertain and tentative. She looked down on Eileen with a puzzled and drawn expression on her face.

'Tell me about the group, about these people, these people that you are with for the light opera performances. What is it that they call themselves, the Merrymen, that is right, isn't it?' she said.

Eileen took her cue. The Reverend Mother wanted to talk about something, to ask her something, but she didn't want to do it immediately. She was postponing, prevaricating, something that she was against in the normal way of things, but she certainly did not look well tonight. Something was troubling her very much. Eileen exerted herself to divert and to distract.

'I could write a novel about them,' she said enthusiastically. 'In fact, Jane Austen would have had fun with them. Do you remember *Mansfield Park* and the theatricals, Reverend Mother? You gave it to me to read and we discussed it afterwards. I never liked it as much as *Pride and Prejudice* or *Emma*. I loved *Emma*! But I keep thinking about it these days. They're a weird crew, that crowd, those Merrymen, as they call themselves.'

'Who's in charge?'

Eileen pulled herself up at the quietly spoken words. There was a time when both she and the Reverend Mother had shared a dream that Eileen would sit a scholarship for the university. They had practised over, and over again, for the interview that was given to the top candidates. 'Never waste a word; this is not a chat', the Reverend Mother had advised and now she remembered that recommendation and she scanned through her mind for the relevant details about each one of those people who had decided to spend their leisure hours putting on shows for the people of Cork. Reverend Mother had a reason for her question. This was not just an effort to distract herself from her troubles.

'Peter Doyle is the one who decides everything,' she said carefully. 'Jonathon Power is a sort of partner to him in the antiques shop, I think, but during rehearsals, Jonathon says very little, except about the stage sets and the costumes – they have a cupboard full of cloaks, and gowns and uniforms and suits, all that sort of thing. Jonathon is very artistic, but I'd say that Peter Doyle is definitely in overall charge. And then there is Miss Gamble. You might know her, Reverend Mother, as she is the headmistress of a girls' school, though she's a Protestant, of course. She's sort of like a headmistress with everyone, because the others are all inclined to joke and to fool around, but she's very nice, really. Quite motherly with us all, brings sandwiches, and makes us drink milk after the performance to soothe our throats. She's very nice, really,' she repeated, thinking of how kind Miss Gamble had been to her and how careful to choose a costume that would suit Eileen's black hair and grey eyes. 'And she's right to keep everyone in order,' she added and blushed a little as she remembered some of the fooling that went on with those high-spirited young men trying to amuse the two unmarried girls, and the third married one, as well. The Reverend Mother would definitely not approve of that. Hastily she went on with her character sketches. 'There's her brother, the barrister, Tom Gamble. He's very wild. Drinks a lot. I saw him knock back almost a bottle of whiskey one night. He offered me a lift home, but I refused and I was glad afterwards when I saw his car go zigzagging down Sullivan's Quay. I thought that he would end up in the river. He's a Protestant; they're all Protestants, except for James O'Reilly who works in the

Savings Bank. He's a Catholic, I think. Well, he must be. I
was surprised when I saw him go into the Holy Trinity Church
one day last week. And he was a long time in there. I know
because I was waiting for a friend and it was a good half
hour before he came out again.' She stopped. There had been
a flash of interest from the Reverend Mother's eyes. However,
she said nothing so Eileen went on with her sketches, visual-
izing each one of the singers and looking for words to bring
them to life.

'And then there's Robert Beamish. He's the oarsman, wants
to be part of the team for the Olympics. He's a bit mad, but
very good fun. Drinks a lot, too. Just like Tom Gamble. These
two are great friends. And James O'Reilly's wife, Rose. She's
one of the three little maids. She's very pretty, dark hair and
dark eyes. I got my hair cut when I saw how much short
hair suited her. And, of course, Anne Morgan, who is the
principal lady, Yum-Yum. She's fun. She's a teacher of music
in Miss Gamble's school. She has a lovely voice. She's
engaged to Robert Beamish, though I think that she's keener
on Peter Doyle. He's a real ladies' man.' Flirted with
everyone, even Eileen, herself, she thought, but then moved
on quickly.

'*The Mikado* has been a great success for them, Reverend
Mother, and that's good because they had to spend a lot of
money on costumes. They did *Trial by Jury* last season and
that was just everyone dressed in a suit, except for Anne
Morgan who was the woman, the plaintiff. And, of course,
Tom Gamble borrowed all the wigs. Wish I had been in it. It
would have been fun to dress up as a member of the jury.'
She decided not to tell the Reverend Mother that she had tried
on the suit, an old one of Peter Doyle's and rather enjoyed
strutting around in it.

The Reverend Mother nodded. Her face was brooding and
sad. Eileen began to feel slightly alarmed. The nun was
normally so brisk and so assured. Why had she summoned
her former pupil? Why was she so interested in the people
in the musical society? Whatever it was, Eileen knew that
she couldn't stay long; her mother worried about her.
Oddly, she worried more now that Eileen was back home

and under her care again, than when she had been living
with a crowd of Republicans, in a house miles from the city.
What time was it, she wondered. She had no idea. Perhaps
someday she might be able to afford a watch. All of her fellow
actors possessed one. However, she listened carefully to the
Reverend Mother's reminiscences, spoken so quietly that it
almost seemed as though the woman was speaking to herself.

'It's strange, Eileen,' she said, 'that Tom Gamble has
forsaken the religion of his father, Judge Gamble, who was a
Catholic, to join that of his mother, who was a Protestant.
Almost like, in reverse, the two Capuchin priests, Prior
Lawrence and Father Dominic, the two Alleyn brothers. I knew
them, these two priests, when they were young, you know,
Eileen. They also were children of what they call a "mixed
marriage". It was a strange arrangement in those days – that
the girls should be brought up in the religion of the mother
and the boys in the religion of the father. It was an agreement
that had been hammered out between both churches, but I
know of many cases where it has not worked.'

'The mother probably had more influence over the children,'
said Eileen wisely. She had never known her father who had
gone off to England as soon as he had made her mother pregnant. 'My mother had a great influence over me; she taught
me to be a Republican, although she denies it now,' she added
and the Reverend Mother smiled.

'You're quite right,' she said with a quick return to her usual
briskness. 'The mother's influence can be very strong. That is
very true. In the case of the Gambles, as well as the Alleyns.
Now I mustn't keep you. I know that you must be very tired
after your night's performance. I just wanted to ask you one
question and if you don't know, it may be that the young man
who is riding his motorbike up and down the lane will know
the answer to it.'

Eileen blushed a little. 'He's just going to give me a lift
back to my mother's place, Reverend Mother. He's been having
a bit of trouble with his engine. That's why he has to keep
revving it.'

The Reverend Mother ignored this. 'This is what I want to
ask you about, Eileen. You see, I used to know people who

lived in a house in north Cork,' she said. 'It was called Shanbally House and it was burned down almost a year ago. I wonder whether the name means anything to you, but I see that it does, doesn't it . . .' The Reverend Mother broke off, but in the candlelight, her eyes shone very green, very questioning.

'It wasn't our crowd that did that, that burned down that place, Reverend Mother,' said Eileen immediately. 'I remember all the fuss about it in the newspapers, saying that it was a terrible atrocity. I remember that Eamonn and some of the other boys had a good go at Tom Hurley, wanting him to deny it in the *Cork Examiner*, but he refused. He was saying, "Who cares who did it? Why should we bother if someone saves us the trouble? The whole lot of those ascendancy houses should be burned down, in any case. They burn our places. We burn theirs. That's how it will go until all thirty-two counties of Ireland are free." That's the way that Tom Hurley goes on! He has no decency about him.'

'What did your friends think? If they knew that it was not anything to do with your organization, who did they think did the deed? Who did burn down Shanbally House?'

'We thought that it was probably that Anti-Sinn Féin gang, do you remember that I told you about them, Reverend Mother?' Eileen eyed her former teacher anxiously. The elderly nun was still very pale, but to Eileen's relief, a sparkle of interest had come back into those very intelligent eyes.

She was silent for a moment, but then spoke. 'So you would be fairly sure, Eileen, that it was not the Republicans who burned down Shanbally House,' she said thoughtfully.

'Quite sure,' said Eileen decisively. 'Tom Hurley was always one to boast of something like that, and since the house was in Cork, his district, he would know all about it.'

'That's very interesting. Do you know anything else about the antiques shop, the one that Peter Doyle and Jonathon Power run?'

The question was unexpected and Eileen knitted her brows, her interest had deepened. The Reverend Mother never gossiped or chatted. Every question would have a reason behind it. Perhaps she also had heard a rumour that these people had something to do with the Anti-Sinn Féin gang.

'I think it's owned by Peter Doyle,' she said slowly, 'but I get the impression that they all have something to do with it. Rose O'Reilly helps there, nearly every day. And Miss Gamble and Robert Beamish were looking at some sheets of typed-out figures that Peter Doyle showed them. They looked like something from the bank, bank statements. I see statements like that at the printers where I work. First, I thought that it was something to do with the *Mikado* show, but it wasn't. They had the name of the shop on them. Morrison's Island Antiques. And then Tom Gamble came along and he was having a look and he was sort of chuckling with delight. They didn't hear me. I wear very soft shoes so I had a quick look . . .' Eileen stopped. The Reverend Mother might well disapprove of her sneaking up and reading papers that were nothing to do with her. 'It's for the cause, Reverend Mother,' she said earnestly. 'Eamonn asked me to join. You see this lot are suspected of being in the Anti-Sinn Féin Society'

'Sinn Féin,' said the Reverend Mother meditatively. 'Well, my Irish isn't good. It wasn't taught when I was young, you know, but it means something like "Ourselves", doesn't it?'

'That's right, but I prefer to call myself a Republican,' said Eileen earnestly. 'I want Ireland to become a republic, not just a little island on the western side of Great Britain.'

'I think you are right to prefer the term "Republican",' said the Reverend Mother. 'There is something that I don't like about a slogan that seems centred on ourselves. The world would be a better place, wouldn't it, Eileen, if people weren't just concentrating on ourselves. Perhaps your friends in the Merrymen association may be doing just that, concentrating on themselves.'

Eileen looked at her with surprise. There was something significant about the last utterance. The Reverend Mother sat up very straight, her eyes gleaming with concentration. Eileen could almost see the sharp brain behind those eyes, working away, slotting facts into their place, weighing up alternatives. There was a long silence for a few moments and then the Reverend Mother sighed. 'Now go, child,' she said, 'and I wish you all the luck in the world. Who is the young man outside?'

'That's Eamonn, Reverend Mother.'

'Ah, the medical student. I remember him from the time when I broke my arm. Bring him greetings from me and say that I am glad he is looking after you. I hope that one day he will resume his studies.' And with that, the Reverend Mother rose to her feet, vigorously blew out the candles on the altar and walked down towards the porch door, holding it open.

'God bless you, my child,' she said, and leaning over, she signed a small cross on Eileen's forehead.

'The Reverend Mother sends you her greetings and hopes that one day you will resume your medical studies,' said Eileen as she climbed onto the seat behind Eamonn and tugged down her fashionably short skirt.

'What did she want?' asked Eamonn curiously. She guessed that he didn't want to discuss the question of resuming his studies. For all of the Republicans, life was on hold until Ireland gained complete freedom from England and until the remaining six counties were signed over to them.

Eileen gave a glance around the lane. The fog had risen, and it hung in dense soft clumps around the buildings and lane. But although it would not be sunset for another hour, the gas lamp outside the convent back gate had already been lit and cast its hazy light for about twenty feet around them. Anyone lurking in the background would be visible. As long as she spoke low, she could not be overheard.

'She wanted to know whether our lot burned down Shanbally House,' she said in his ear.

'What!' He gave a long low whistle. 'So she's onto something about that. Well, that's interesting.'

'And she probed a bit about the gang in the Merrymen. Don't know why, but she was very interested that they were all looking at the bank statements for the antiques shop, and looking very pleased over them.'

'I often wondered myself who did that job at Shanbally

House.' Eamonn had ceased revving the engine of the motor-bike and was staring ahead, twisting the handle of his bike absentmindedly. When he spoke again it was in a low voice and just into her ear. 'The burning down of that place, and some others over the last few years, is a bit of a puzzle. Not our crowd, I know that. I must go and have a chat with your Reverend Mother. Clever woman. Perhaps we could recruit her to the cause.'

'Let's go. I'll be late. Mam will worry.' But Eileen, too, was intrigued. The Reverend Mother had a very sharp brain, she thought admiringly. If not the Republicans, then who would do such a thing? The Anti-Sinn Féin crowd were, when she thought about it, fairly unlikely – why burn down the houses of their friends and supporters? She knew that Eamonn was also thinking hard as he sat for a long few moments while the engine ticked over. Perhaps between the two of them they could come up with an answer to the Reverend Mother's question.

Eileen's mother, Maureen, was at the door when they roared up the steep slope of Barrack Street. There was something tense about the shawl-wrapped figure as she peered down the steep incline and Eileen was off the bike and running up to her as soon as the bike slowed to a halt by the entrance to the small lane that ran behind the block of terraced cabins.

'What's the matter?' she asked anxiously.

'There's a man in there.' Her mother jerked a thumb towards the open halves of the front door to her cabin. 'He says that he knows Eamonn. Walked in as bold as brass. Made himself at home.'

'Oh, it's probably one of the lads.' Eileen's rapid heartbeat slowed down. Probably Eamonn's friend, Bernard, she thought, but her mother shook her head.

'Not a lad,' she whispered. 'He's a man. A middle-aged man. Don't go in. Don't let him see you. We'll wait until Eamonn comes.'

Eileen's heart missed a beat. Neither she nor her mother would be in danger, but Eamonn was. She sprinted as fast as she could up the narrow lane between and behind two blocks of terraced cabins. Eamonn was still struggling with the stiff bolt to the back yard when she caught up with him.

'Don't go in, Eamonn. There's a man in there. In my mam's kitchen. A middle-aged man.'

'One man? Not army or police or anything like that.'

'That's what she said. A man, but not one of the lads. A middle-aged man,' repeated Eileen. 'Don't go in. You know you are wanted.'

'Wouldn't send one man to arrest me,' said Eamonn confidently. He wrenched open the gate, took his pistol from his pocket and walked straight through the yard, silently lifted the latch and then violently kicked the back door open.

'Well, well, that's a nice welcome for a man.' The accent was strange, softly spoken, not sing-song like the Cork accent. West of Ireland, thought Eileen. She edged her way around Eamonn's left side. Middle-aged certainly. Old, she would have said. A soft round face with a flat nose, bald, short in stature, but with a large pair of hands.

'You can put the gun away,' he said. 'Don't like those things, much. I'm a lawyer, not a fighter. Young Bernard gave me this address. He said that you could tell me some more.' He nodded in her direction. 'You must be Eileen,' he said. 'Bernard told me about you.'

'Why are you here?' she asked. She felt slightly better. Eamonn had a gun and the stranger had made no move towards a pocket.

'All the way from County Mayo,' he said. He sat back down onto the settle, leaned over the fire, moved the crane holding the kettle over the warmest spot and then smiled with a cordial display of tobacco-stained teeth. He bent down and pulled a canvas bag from under the seat. It looked like a carpenter's tool bag, though it seemed to contain mainly large heavy books, and he took out a cake box marked 'Fullers'. By the time Maureen appeared, after timidly looking over the half door from the street, he had opened the box and produced an iced sponge cake.

'My old mother used always say that it was manners to bring a cake if you invited yourself to someone's house,' he said in his soft western accent.

'And you invited yourself because . . .?' Eamonn still held
the gun, but Maureen, reassured by the appearance of the cake,
now sitting on its paper base on the table, cheerfully produced
the teapot, ladling in a generous few teaspoons. She looked
quite excited. Eileen felt a slight pang. Her mother led such
a dull, dreary life. Only fifteen years older than Eileen herself,
she had few friends and even fewer amusements. Now she
was smiling hospitably at the stranger who seemed so much
at ease and she had an air of excitement about her.

'Because of this Father Dominic business.' The Mayo man
stretched his hands to the fire and looked around. The two
halves of the door to Barrack Street were now closed. 'It's a
bit of a long story,' he said.

'Then save it for the moment while I get my bike into the
yard,' said Eamonn. His voice was still curt and he handed
over the gun to Eileen before going out through the back door,
but she felt that he believed the man's story. Maureen watched
the singing kettle, from time to time looking hungrily at the
iced cake. She sorted out the contents of the drawer and
produced her sharpest knife.

'Would you like to cut it, sir,' she said.

'I'm Maurice, call me Maurice,' he said and rose immediately, taking the knife from her. He held it poised over the
cake. Eileen steadied the pistol, her eyes on that razor-sharp
knife and he gave her a grin. 'Careful with that thing,' he said.
'You don't want it going off by mistake and breaking your
mam's cups.'

'I wonder what Maurice from Mayo has to do with Father
Dominic from Cork,' she said, refusing to return his smile.
She felt by the cold breeze behind her back that the door to
the yard had opened. Eamonn had returned, but she did not
turn around. A Republican woman was as good as any man
once she had a pistol in her hand. Countess Markowitz had
taught that lesson to her fellow countrywomen. 'Explain yourself,' she said crisply.

'My brother was part of the Macroom crowd that killed
the British spies after they threw a woman over the head of
the stairs during the civil war,' he said. 'He was captured
and condemned to death. Father Dominic visited him in the

Cork gaol and gave him the last sacraments before they
hanged him.' His voice was unchanged, still soft and western,
but his eyes were very hard, as dark grey as limestone paving
on the wet Cork quays.

'But you stayed up in Mayo?' Eamonn took over the
questioning.

'I'm by way of being a judge at the Sinn Féin courts. Only
a solicitor, really, but needs must when the devil drives. You've
heard that expression, ma'am, haven't you?' He addressed
himself to Maureen who looked hesitantly from him to the
pistol in her daughter's hand.

'I thought that the Sinn Féin courts had finished,' said
Eileen. She had begun to believe him, though. She got up,
still keeping the pistol pointed at him and kicked open
the flap of his soft canvas bag. As she had half-noticed, the
books were law texts and the title of one was *Blackstone's
Commentaries*.

'We're a bit behind the times up in Mayo,' he said in an
easy-going fashion. 'We still see the need for the Sinn Féin
courts up there. Sent a man to a deserted island off the coast
last week for being continually drunk and disorderly and
letting out what he should keep buried. He'll stay there, too.
No guards, no locked doors, but we won't see a sign of him
until his sentence is up. The people respect our judgements.
Most of us in Mayo don't think much of these people in
power who have thrown away the six counties in the north
or much of their law, either. We still want a united republic
of Ireland, as you do yourselves.' He looked from Eileen to
Eamonn. Rapidly and efficiently he sliced the cake into four
and then eight slices.

'First one for the lady of the house,' he said and offered
the plate to Maureen. And then without a change of voice he
said, 'So who did kill the good priest? Do you need help in
judging and sentencing? Have you got a likely suspect? Don't
worry. They get a fair trial. We always give a lawyer to the
accused as well as to the Free State.'

Eileen looked across at Eamonn. He gave a slight nod. She
handed his pistol back to him and made up her mind.

'You could be useful to us, I suppose,' she said, purposefully introducing a doubting note into her voice. She allowed that sentence to sink in before adding, 'There's been something funny going on here. There's been about thirty big houses, belonging to Protestants, burned down in County Cork during the last couple of years and we, the Republican movement, have had nothing to do with more than half of them. It's been a puzzle. I think it's possible that Father Dominic's murder might have had something to do with these burnings.'

'We thought it might be the Anti-Sinn Féin movement,' put in Eamonn.

'Anti-Sinn Féin! Seems unlikely. Why burn down the houses of their own people?'

'Tom Hurley thought it might be to discredit our movement.' Eamonn sounded dubious.

'What do you think, Eileen?' Maurice looked straight across at her.

Eileen thought about her conversation with the Reverend Mother.

'I was talking with someone who seemed to be thinking that some people who run a musical society and an antiques shop might have something to do with it. She seemed very interested in them and she cross-questioned me about them. Wanted to know everything about them . . .' Eileen tailed off and waited for the next question.

'Well, tell me. Go through them one by one.' From his canvas bag he took a notebook and pencil. As she went through the members of the musical society one by one he made some notes, writing in shorthand, she thought as she saw the squiggles on the page.

'So this fellow, James O'Reilly, takes drugs?' He had a sharp way of questioning that annoyed her.

'Eamonn heard a rumour about that,' she said briefly.

'Never like drug takers. Would murder their own mother to get supplies. Bank clerk, isn't he? He won't last long if this gets out. Wonder if he confessed to Father Dominic and then got the jitters. Might have murdered him to keep him quiet.'

'If he told it under the seal of confession then Father Dominic could not have told anyone,' pointed out Eileen. She wondered whether he might be a Protestant.

'Drug takers worry about flies on the wall. But go on, who's this person that you were talking to? She? So who is she?'

'She's the Reverend Mother of a convent where I went to school,' said Eileen defiantly. 'She knows everyone in Cork.'

'Got her finger on the pulse, has she?' If he was amused, then at least he concealed it. 'And who do you think that this Reverend Mother of yours might suspect of the murder of Father Dominic? Not this James O'Reilly, I gather.' His soft voice still held that undercurrent of hard steel.

Eileen thought back to the conversation. 'I think,' she said. 'I don't know, mind you, but I had a feeling that she might suspect Peter Doyle, the owner of an antiques shop just near to the church. He's an Englishman and he runs a musical society. I think that she might suspect him and his friends of having something to do with the burning down of the big houses.'

'So, Peter Doyle, owner of an antiques shop. Any evidence, so far, that he went into a confessional box and murdered Father Dominic?'

'I'm working on it.' Eileen faced him defiantly. It occurred to her that she had seen James O'Reilly go into the Holy Trinity.

'Well, keep working,' he advised and held the plate with its remaining four slices towards Maureen, before helping himself to another piece. 'Go and talk some more to the Reverend Mother of yours. She probably knows more than she's telling you at the moment. Why should Father Dominic be involved? That's what we have to find out. A good priest like that to be killed by an Englishman. Well, I don't like the sound of that. I think I'll start collecting some evidence for the prosecution. I've my eye on a couple of lawyers. Nobody has been appointed yet, but I'll persuade one of them to do judge. The man I have in mind has plenty of long years of experience. He'll make a good job of it. I would myself, of course, but when it comes to Father Dominic's murderer, I'd prefer to step down from the bench and be the prosecutor.' He tossed the remainder of his slice of cake into his mouth, chewed for a few seconds, and then said in a low voice, 'Doesn't really matter who is on the bench as long as he can sum up well. It will be for the prosecution team to find the evidence. Once we have that, there will be only one possible sentence. And that will be death.'

NINE

St Thomas Aquinas:
'*Rapina est gravius peccatum quam furtum, quia per rapinam non solum infertur alicui damnum in rebus, sed etiam vergit in quandam personae ignominiam sive iniuriam. Et hoc praeponderat fraudi vel dolo, quae pertinent ad furtum.*'
(Robbery is a more serious sin than theft, because robbery not only inflicts a loss on a person in his things, but also leads to the ignominy and injury of his person, and this is of graver import than the fraud or guile which belong to theft.)

'**M**r Murphy, the solicitor, is here to see you, Reverend Mother,' said Sister Bernadette. There was a slight note of astonishment in her voice and a look of avid curiosity in her eyes.

'Goodness, he's early!' The Reverend Mother looked at the clock. Half past eight in the morning.

'That's right. I got such a surprise, Reverend Mother. Came to the door himself, too. Not the chauffeur either and when I . . .'

The Reverend Mother missed the rest of the sentence as she swept rapidly past Sister Bernadette. Why on earth was Rupert calling at half past eight in the morning? Surely, something could not have happened to Lucy, she thought as she went through the parlour door in her usual calm fashion, turning to click the door closed, before greeting her guest. But he jumped up, came rapidly across and took her by the hands.

'Nothing's wrong with Lucy, don't worry, it's not that at all.'

She recovered her composure, freed her hands gently and indicated a chair. 'Do sit down, Mr Murphy. Would you like a cup of tea?'

'No, I won't, thank you, Reverend Mother. And I won't detain you for long. Lucy was going to telephone, but then she thought that it would be best if I dropped in on my way to work. I'm going to give my clerk a shock arriving as early as this, I'll tell you that, Reverend Mother. Never been in as early as this for a good twenty years. But you know what Lucy can be like when she is in one of her efficient moods. She was up and dressed at all hours, and had me out the door before I knew where I was, not even time for a second cup of tea.' He stopped and then said gravely, 'This will be a shock to you, but the Abernethy house went up last night.'

'Went up?'

'Up in flames.'

The Reverend Mother drew in a breath sharply. Could this have anything to do with their visit? But a moment's reflection told her that these raids, whosoever was responsible, would have to be planned well in advance. She took in another deep breath as unobtrusively as she could and waited for more information.

'Marigold Abernethy is fine,' he said reassuringly. 'She and her servants were given refuge by the local vicar. Nice fellow. Lucy rang to enquire and she spoke to his wife and then to Marigold herself. She said Marigold was in fine form. Spitting fire, apparently. Saying that the whole lot of those rascals should be hung. Oh, and there was one other thing that Lucy told me not to forget to tell you. Apparently, the cook had something to say that Marigold told Lucy. Unfortunate woman, it was second time around for her as she used to be cook to the Wood family; you remember them, don't you?'

'Yes, indeed,' said the Reverend Mother gravely. And then she waited. The news of the raid on the Abernethy household would now be all around Cork. Lucy would have been one of the many who had spoken on the phone to the charitable vicar and his wife, and, of course, to Marigold herself. The telephone exchange ladies had probably begun broadcasting the news last night. There was no ostensible reason why poor Rupert had to be bundled out of the door without his second cup of tea in order to report to the Reverend Mother. Lucy could just as well have telephoned her cousin. However, this news about the cook would be of private significance and so she turned an expectant face towards Rupert.

'Oh, yes, this will interest you, Lucy thought,' he said. He tilted back his chair and balanced on its two back legs and she resisted the temptation to reprove him as though he had been one of her scholars. 'Apparently, the cook remarked that it was the same crowd that raided the Woods' place last year, "the same useless shower of Shinners" were her exact words, if you will excuse me, Reverend Mother.'

'I see,' said the Reverend Mother. The cook, she thought, might be a fine hand with the scones, but her use of words was inaccurate. The five men who raided those two houses, and perhaps many others, were neither 'useless' nor could they be labelled as 'Shinners' or Republicans; she was fairly sure on that point. They were, however, dangerous, ruthless men, out for plunder and using a musical society as a cover for their activities.

And they may have been responsible for the death of a very nice man and a saintly priest. At the thought of Dominic, she knew that this was information that had to be passed on instantly; these men must be stopped before anything else happened. She turned to Rupert.

'It was very good of you to spare the time to come to bring me the news, Mr Murphy. Are you sure that we can't offer you anything? A cup of tea? Some toast, perhaps?'

He took her offer for the dismissal that was intended, managed to right his chair without cracking its back legs and rose to his feet with a good-humoured smile.

'Don't you trouble about me, Reverend Mother. I know that you are very busy. My clerk will have the coffee pot warming as soon as he hears me at the front door. I'll leave you in peace, now, and allow you to get on with your valuable work.' He fumbled in his pocket as they went together to the front door and counted some copper coins into the palm of his hand.

'Must get rid of some of these. They ruin the set of my suit jacket, so my tailor is always telling me,' he said gaily. There were a few lucky children around and when they saw him, they rushed to open the gate for him. To their huge delight, he presented each with a few pennies. A nice man, thought the Reverend Mother as she went back inside. Lucy had been lucky.

She was not due in the classroom for another hour and with some luck, she would get hold of Patrick before he went out. She went to the back corridor, a place of maximum inconvenience, draughty, cold and utterly lacking in privacy, which had been designated by the bishop's secretary as a suitable place to house this new-fangled telephone for the use of the convent. How would she phrase a request for Patrick's presence, she wondered? And then she was relieved to see that Sister Bernadette was lurking there, probably disappointed that she had not been requested to show out the affable solicitor. That was a piece of luck. The telephone exchange would not be interested in an underling like Sister Bernadette, who used the telephone mainly to order groceries and who might well just be reporting a minor pilfering to the barracks' telephone number.

'Oblige me by phoning the barracks, sister, and ask whether Inspector Cashman can spare a few minutes.' It was a nice, neutral message, she thought, and the telephone exchange would have news that was more exciting this morning. By now, all Cork would be looking for details about this latest atrocity and taking sides with the bitterness that was still the legacy of the Treaty negotiations. She went off to prepare for the first lesson of the day and awaited the arrival of the inspector.

The children were out in the playground for their mid-morning break by the time that Patrick arrived – on his bicycle, to the disappointment of the small boys who loved the sight of the police car.

'Sorry there's been a bit of a delay,' said Patrick, carefully wheeling his bicycle through the gate and padlocking it to the iron fence. 'We've been very busy this morning,' he added.

'I'm sure,' said the Reverend Mother. She felt a little apologetic. He looked very tired with black circles under his eyes. There would be great pressure on him to solve the murder of such a popular priest, and, of course, he would have a hundred and one other routine matters requiring his attention. And now there was another house burned down, just outside the city, this time.

'Ask Sister Mary Immaculate to take my place, please,' she said to one of the older girls. Her deputy would wear a martyred expression at losing a portion of the mid-morning break, but she could not help that. Patrick's time was of importance and so as soon as the nun appeared, she briskly ushered him through the garden and into the small chapel. They would have privacy there, would be able to avoid wasting time on hospitable offers of tea and cake from Sister Bernadette and the short walk enabled her to condense the information that she needed to pass onto him. She pushed open the heavy door and went through into the dim damp interior of the small chapel.

To her immense surprise, the centre door of the confessional stall opened and Dr Scher struggled to his feet.

'What on earth are you doing in there?' she said tartly.

He ignored that, just stood there, looking thoughtfully at the three open doors of the solitary confessional stall in the small chapel.

'Interesting, this business of casting your sins upon a priest, telling him the secrets of your soul. Have you ever read Freud, Reverend Mother?'

'Never,' she said firmly. She knew what he was thinking. Freud, or no Freud, confession, for so many people, was a good way of unburdening themselves. For the depressed and the despairing, it might well be a lifeline. Her mind went again to Dominic and the long queues that were reputed to wait patiently outside the confessional in the darkest and most obscure part of the church.

'They have ten of these confessional boxes in the Holy Trinity Church,' he remarked as though his mind had followed hers. 'Do you have only one because nuns have so few sins?'

'We have as many sins as others, different, perhaps; but only one priest,' said the Reverend Mother. She thought briefly of her own lack of charity towards Sister Mary Immaculate, but decided her sins were none of his business. She was glad to see him, though. His knowledge of antiques would be of assistance to her when she struggled to remember what she had seen during afternoon tea with Marigold Abernethy. She seated herself on one of the chairs at the back of the church and Patrick carried over two more for himself and Dr Scher.

'Not much room in that little confessional cubicle of yours, Reverend Mother,' said Dr Scher. 'Still, at least your chaplain has a cushion on his seat, not like that poor man over in the Holy Trinity Church. Why on earth did they make these places so small? Another couple of inches and the priest would be more comfortable and have more space to get away from an assassin.' And then when she did not reply, he said, 'What's the problem?'

Patrick, she noticed, was also looking at her with concern and she pulled herself together, sorting out her thoughts and slotting each fact into its relevant place. Patrick was a very busy man and she did not want to keep him long. But just as she opened her mouth, Sister Bernadette was at the door after a perfunctory knock.

'Excuse me, Reverend Mother. There's an urgent call from the barracks. Inspector Cashman is needed. There's trouble at the barracks. His sergeant is on his way with the car.'

'You must go,' said the Reverend Mother instantly rising to her feet. 'Don't worry, my story will keep.' There had been, she knew, a strike on at Andersen Docks. Desperate men will take desperate measures and she did not want to be the cause of any loss of life. Patrick's presence would have a calming effect. She accompanied him to the door and then returned and sat back onto her chair.

'Can I help in any way?' Dr Scher was looking at her keenly with that look of concern on his face.

'I need to write a letter to Patrick.' She thought about it for a moment. It was true that there was no urgency, no immediate threats. The deed had been done. Nevertheless, she felt an urge to unburden herself of what she had so carefully recalled to her memory when she had heard the message from Lucy.

She made up her mind. 'Well, if you will be so good and can spare the time, please come back to my office and help me with it.' He might, she thought, also deliver it. It would be best if he were there to interpret when Patrick read the letter. 'Would you go and ask Sister Bernadette to bring us in some tea while I collect my thoughts,' she finished.

He gave her plenty of time, probably lingering in the kitchen and joking with the lay sisters who worked there. By the time he and Sister Bernadette appeared with the tea trolley, the Reverend Mother had filled a page of writing paper with a long list. She waited impatiently while the usual ritual of praise and jokes were gone through, but once the strength of the tea and succulence of the fruitcake had been praised and Sister Bernadette had gone off back to the kitchen, closing the door behind, she read aloud. 'Dear Patrick, My cousin, Mrs Murphy and I had tea with Mrs Abernethy yesterday afternoon . . .'

'By chance, of course,' interrupted Dr Scher.

'By design, of course,' she retorted quickly. 'Now, I may finish?'

He replied by popping a large piece of fruitcake into his mouth and chewing vigorously.

'My cousin and I had tea with Mrs Abernethy yesterday,' she went on, reading from her page. 'I understand that the house was burned down last night. We went to have a word with the cook, as she, formerly, had been cook to the Wood family of Shanbally and so had been present when the house there was destroyed. She gave an interesting description of the five men, all masked and carrying rifles and cans of petrol. This is how she described them: there was one very large man with broad shoulders and a big chest, two other tall men, an ordinary-sized man and one quite small and slim – he was the one that did the talking, in a "flat of the city" Cork accent. These,' said the Reverend Mother raising her eyes from her page, 'were the cook's words. I think that I will leave it to Patrick to draw any conclusions, but here is what I need your help with. This is what I recollect of objects that might be small enough to be removed with ease and valuable as antiques.' She read aloud from her list, going through everything that she remembered. When she lifted her eyes from the page, he was nodding thoughtfully.

'Most of what you remember, Reverend Mother, is already in that shop. Neither you nor Patrick would be able to tell one piece of china from another or one piece of silver from a totally different maker. I'd re-write that letter. Just give the lad a couple of things that he can't miss. That cake server with the lift mechanism on the handle, that sounds quite unique to me and the potato servers, well, I've never seen one of those before. And the cobalt glass would make them stand out from ordinary silver napkin rings immediately. And describe cobalt, say it is a deep but bright blue, lighter than navy blue, but deeper than azure; that would be a good way to describe it, I think. Say that they are bigger than napkin rings.'

She obeyed, crumpling her first piece of paper and putting down a detailed description of those two objects, reading it back to him, before signing the letter.

'Next time you go visiting one of those big houses, Reverend Mother, tell me and I'll go along with you. I'd say that I could value and put a name to a lot of the stuff that you are trying to describe; but, as it is, you will only confuse Patrick by talking about silver sugar tongs and cream jugs,' he said bluntly. 'So you think that one of these people from the antiques shop may have killed Father Dominic, do you? It seems very likely. It's quite a lucrative business, an antiques shop, but, of course, it's much more lucrative if you don't have to pay for the goods that you have up for sale. A little expenditure on polishes and cleaners, a little time from that talented Jonathon Power and then sit back and allow the money to roll in.'

'Rent,' suggested the Reverend Mother.

'I think I heard that they bought it outright from Judge Gamble. He owns most of these derelict old warehouses. They had to spend money, of course, in doing it up.'

'What brought them here,' she wondered. 'What brought them over to Cork?'

'May have heard about these raids. Someone might have said, "What a shame that the contents of those houses were lost when the place was burned down".'

The Reverend Mother thought through the various members of the music society. 'And the forming of the Merrymen, quite soon after they arrived here, if my memory doesn't fail me . . . That would have been to get recruits.'

'Young men with expensive habits, plenty of brawn and courage. People like Tom Gamble and Robert Beamish,' said Dr Scher.

'And James O'Reilly?'

'The bank clerk? Well, I suppose that he might have been useful to them in some way. Might help with the accounts, perhaps, taxation – that's a tricky one in Cork city at the moment; the blackguards are trying to get us all to pay up for the couple of glorious years when the tax offices were burned down and nothing to replace them. Also James O'Reilly has a pretty little wife with a very sweet singing voice. I saw her in *The Mikado*. No, he would have been useful to them and they would have been useful to him. Gave him the means to buy an expensive house and car. Raised his status in the bank to be well in with some prosperous business people. *Who you know* is very important to Cork people. You wouldn't believe what I can get away with if I drop your name into a conversation.'

The Reverend Mother ignored this attempt to tease her. She was silent for a moment, thinking through the ramifications of the Merrymen Light Opera group.

'And, of course, Tom Gamble's older sister, Marjorie, would have lent respectability.'

'And a source of pretty girls with good singing voices from her school,' said Dr Scher. 'There would be no reason why she should have to know anything. A rather strait-laced lady, but I'd say that the plans to raid houses would have been carried out in those late-night drinking sessions in the Imperial Hotel.'

'And Dominic, Father Dominic . . .'

'Stumbled across something . . .'

'And was murdered in his own confessional box,' said the Reverend Mother. It had been a bleak end for a dedicated man who had done his best to bring hope and comfort to all.

'Murdered, I would say, by the woman in the shawl. Unless, it was Sister Mary Immaculate.' Dr Scher took a look at her and she could see him decide not to pursue that joke. 'A shawl could have been a disguise,' he said hurriedly. 'These old shawls are more like a blanket and from what I saw, the light is very poor in that part of the church.'

'Peter Doyle is an unobtrusive sort of man,' said the Reverend Mother looking back over her visit to the Morrison's Island Antiques Store. 'Someone like Mr Jonathon Power would stand out in a crowd, here in Cork where people are not big.'

'What about Robert Beamish or even Tom Gamble, the barrister. Both of these are Cork men and they are very tall.'

'The exceptions.' The Reverend Mother brushed this aside. 'Generations of good feeding is needed to produce these six-footers. In a church you could see fifty men look like Peter Doyle, but only one or two that might match the height of one of the Beamish, or Gamble families. And remember that only women wear shawls.' She got to her feet. 'It's very kind of you, Dr Scher, to offer to deliver this letter for me to Patrick and I'm sure that he will find you most helpful about antiques. Now I fear that I must go as I have a lesson with my senior girls.'

TEN

W.B. Yeats:
'Too long a sacrifice
Can make a stone of the heart.'

E amonn was late in arriving on Monday evening. Eileen was about to walk to Morrison's Island as quickly as she could and had set off down the South Terrace when he touched her on the shoulder.

'Only half an hour late,' she said. She had hardly known him at first. His dark good looks were obscured by a large cap that came down over his eyes, almost to nose level and he wore a sack over his shoulders, tied in front with a piece of string. Bernard was behind him, also dressed as a dock worker, his very red hair covered by a similar cap.

'Had a consignment from Dublin,' Eamonn said, with a hasty look around to make sure that no one was near to them. For a moment, she envied him, envied them both. She had enjoyed these dangerous assignments, dressing up, outwitting the police and the army. She half-wished she were back in the farmhouse again with the crowd of young Republicans. If it were not for Tom Hurley, she would think about returning. She was sick of being an ordinary office girl, sick of pretending ignorance of the Republicans and of their views and their ambitions. She wanted to come out in the open and boldly declare, 'I am a rebel.'

'Let's see if the old bike will start. I left it down the lane here,' said Eamonn. He led the way to a coal yard and once they were through the door, he removed the cap and the sack and shoved them into his saddlebag.

'I'd be quicker walking,' she said. Nevertheless, she was relieved when the engine roared and the motorbike went hurtling through St Mary's Isle, down the quays and drew up with a flourish in front of the Father Matthew Hall.

'I dropped in to see your mam,' Eamonn said over his shoulder. 'I told her that the show would be finished late tonight and she wasn't to worry. I'd get you home safe and sound. I think we should have a little snoop around that shop when they've all gone home.'

'What . . .' she began. But the bell from the Holy Trinity Church had begun to toll and she jumped from the back of the bike as soon as he had slowed down.

'See you after the show,' said Eamonn and Eileen rushed into the hall, hoping she would not be the last to get dressed. Most of the others seemed to be in the backstage area and she could see from the flash of silk robes and artificial flowers that she was probably the last to arrive. She rushed into the women's cloakroom and began to dress as quickly as she could. She combed back her hair, fastened it on top of her head, but when she had settled the wig on it, she discovered that there were no flowers left. They went through dozens of those silk flowers. Anne Morgan, in particular, had a habit of throwing her roses into the audience at the end of each performance. None were left in the women's cloakroom.

Bother, thought Eileen, I'll have to get one from the costume cupboard. Quickly she slipped down the corridor and went in. It was more of a small room than a cupboard, but they always called it a cupboard. Two hanging rails, filled with kimonos, gowns, sailors' jackets, a few old suits, elaborate cloaks and huge petticoats, spanned the depth of the small room with a large trunk at the back wall. There was no need for a light; the room was illuminated by a street gas lamp just outside the window. Eileen thrust her hand into the trunk, pulled one of the roses out, pinned it onto her wig hurriedly and went to the door. She had just opened it when she heard a voice and then another voice. There was such a note of anger, and of violence, in the tone of this second voice that she stepped back abruptly into the shelter of the deep-set doorway.

It was Peter Doyle and someone else. Peter Doyle sounded furious. The other voice was low, almost a whisper, with a pleading note, but whoever it was, Peter Doyle's voice overrode him. This was no ordinary argument, no usual impatience, not Peter's jokes or sarcasms. For some reason, the sound of

his voice made Eileen feel slightly afraid. She huddled into
the dark space of the doorway, unwilling to interrupt. There
had been a feeling of tension backstage last night, quite unlike
the usual merry jokes and banter that went on after each
performance. At the time she had wondered what was wrong
and now she thought she might be about to find out.

Peter Doyle seemed to be having a vicious quarrel with
James O'Reilly, the bank clerk. Eileen slid the door almost
closed behind her so that the dim light from the north-facing
window would be blocked off. She did not close it completely,
though and left it open an inch. The click of the door latch
would have alerted them to her presence and she was curious.
She had never heard Peter Doyle speak like that before now.
He seldom showed himself to be annoyed and relied on jokes
and occasional sarcasms to impose his will on the company.
But now there was a note of violent anger from his voice.

'Shut up,' he hissed. 'For God's sake, James, shut up and
mind your own business. I don't want to hear another word
from you, you cowardly idiot. You've been well paid – no
hesitation about taking the money, is there. Oh no, your hand
is always out. Goodness only knows you do little enough for
it. Now just you do what you're paid to do and keep your
nose out of everything else.'

Eileen moved back another step, her rubber shoes making
no noise. She was glad that her robe was a pale shade of grey.
It would not show up and she could flatten herself against the
door to the cupboard where the costumes were stored. A
moment later, Peter Doyle passed her. She could not see him
well in the semi-darkness of the passageway, but as he went
by there was a pungent smell of sweat. Peter was a very trim,
well-groomed person and she had never before smelled sweat
from him. And it was quite chilly in this damp building. So
why was he sweating so heavily?

Nervously, Eileen stayed very still in the deep alcove. She
was wishing herself elsewhere, but at the same time, the
adventurous side of her was wishing that she had come out a
little earlier and had heard what James O'Reilly had said. And
why did Peter talk about paying him? None of the actors were
paid. Any money left over from the ticket sales after the rent

was paid were usually dedicated to buying new costumes for the next performance and perhaps for a celebratory dinner for the cast and orchestra. Peter Doyle had explained this to her when she had come along to audition for the part of Pitti-Sing. Eileen felt a cramp coming to the calf of her leg and resisted stretching it. James O'Reilly would move away in a minute and she didn't want any suspicions about her eavesdropping on them.

But he didn't move away. She could hear the rustle of artificial silk. He must be yanking up the robe that he wore for his part of Pooh-Bah. She risked turning her head and moving it a little forwards. Her eyes were getting used to the dark in the passageway and now she could see him. He was pulling something out of his pocket, a small silver box. The light from the half-opened door to backstage caught the sheen of the metal. He was opening it and then she heard a loud sniff and glimpsed something white between his fingertips.

So that was it. Eamonn was right. Peter Doyle was a drug taker. She knew all about drugs. It was one of the things that she had been warned about when she joined the Republicans. Tom Hurley had lined them all up, girls and boys, and had threatened to shoot the first person that he caught with what he called 'white powder'.

And that was what James O'Reilly was doing, taking a pinch of white powder from a small silver box, like a woman's powder compact. He held it to one nostril, sniffed deeply and then did the same with the other nostril. Eileen shrunk back against the deep doorway, praying that he would not need to get anything from the wardrobe cupboard.

And then the tall figure of the Jonathon Power came from the direction of the stage. It seemed almost impossible that he would miss her, but all his attention was focussed on James O'Reilly. And she heard his voice, usually so low and pleasant, sounding, now, quite harsh.

'That's right, feeling better now, are you? Have another pinch.' He waited, his tall broad back shielding the bank clerk from Eileen's eyes. 'That's it,' he said after a moment, and then, in a menacing whisper, 'just remember, James, you won't get the money to fund that expensive little habit just from your salary in the bank. You need us more than we need you. Just you remember that.'

And, then, to Eileen's relief, he took the man by the arm and led him back down the passageway and towards the stage. As noiselessly as she could, she turned the handle of the door to the costume cupboard, closing it gently behind her and went back in. She would stay there for some time until everyone was busy. She did not want anyone to know what she had overheard. With slightly shaking hands, she busied herself tidying the trunk of wigs and headdresses, replacing hat pins in their box, taking out all of the flowers that the female members of the cast pinned to their black wigs and arranging them according to their colour on a tray with meticulous care.

'Oh, that's nice. I love those deep pinks, don't you?' Anne Morgan came in, her face as pink as one of the silk flowers and not yet properly dressed. Flirting with Peter Doyle, thought Eileen, but, good-naturedly, she helped the girl to find a wig and a few roses. Anne was friendly and effusive.

'I'm glad that you took them all out and sorted them,' she said. 'I'm always in a rush and I always get one of those droopy white ones when I scrabble around for them.' She pinned a pink rose to her wig and twirled around, singing, *'The sun, whose rays are all ablaze . . .'*

'You have a beautiful voice,' said Eileen admiringly and, to her immense surprise, the girl kissed her impulsively. 'You're in a good mood. You've been kissing the adorable Robert, is that it?' she said with a teasing smile. She half-wondered whether Anne Morgan, also, sniffed white powder from a little silver compact box.

The young teacher giggled a little. 'What! Robert! That big brute! He's the one that does the adoring, I'll tell you that.'

'Perhaps it's someone else, then,' said Eileen. She would prolong the conversation for another few minutes and when they both arrived, neither Jonathon, nor Peter Doyle would suspect that she had been listening in to that dangerous conversation.

'What about Peter Doyle?' she enquired, doing her best to sound knowing and innocent at the same time.

'Dear Nanki-Poo! Well, of course, I adore him! Don't you?

Or do you go for our strong, silent man, Jonathon? Get me another pin; will you, Eileen, like a darling? I want to fix that rose just over my ear and I don't want it to come loose.' She tucked a curl back beneath the wig, took out her powder compact and powdered her nose. Not silver, noticed Eileen, ordinary steel and that did look like ordinary face powder.

'Or do you prefer my Robert? All those muscles! Don't you admire them? Not as much as he does himself, of course!' Anne Morgan was determined to keep the conversation going along the same track. Her voice was light and teasing, but Eileen had the impression that her thoughts were elsewhere. Was the engagement over, then? Anne, she noticed, no longer wore that diamond ring.

'I'll leave him for Miss Gamble since you have been so mean as to pinch Peter from her,' said Eileen. It was a joke, of course, but not that good a joke as to warrant the torrent of giggles that came from Anne Morgan. For a few seconds, she reminded Eileen of a school friend, but Anne Morgan was no schoolgirl. She was a teacher after all, had been teaching music in Miss Gamble's school for the last year. She must be about four years older than Eileen was, but she seemed determined to keep the conversation going along the same rather juvenile track.

'Can you just see them? Miss Gamble and the sexy Peter Doyle! No, I can't! She'll live and die a headmistress of Rochelle School. I don't suppose that she'll ever get married. In any case, the trustees of the school don't like married women. She dropped me a hint about that when I was interviewed for the job of music teacher. She said that it was a job for life if I was dedicated and hard-working, but that of course it would not fit in with other responsibilities like . . .'

'Like?' queried Eileen. It was just as well to prolong this conversation. And if the two of them arrived together back-stage, busily gossiping, then she would not be suspected of eavesdropping.

'Like looking after a husband, and having children, of course. But go on, what about Robert Beamish for you? To tell you the truth, it's all over between the two of us. I can't stand a jealous boyfriend.'

'I've got a boyfriend, already,' said Eileen. It was not strictly true, but it would prolong the conversation. 'My boyfriend is just as handsome as Robert Beamish is. He's one of the strong, silent, intellectual types. Oh, and by the way, he will be in the audience tonight,' she said. 'I'm going to have to fly straight after the show. Will you put my robe away for me? And if I don't see Peter, will you tell him why I had to go?'

'What does he do? Your boyfriend, I mean.'

'Oh, he's just a student,' said Eileen hastily, Anne Morgan was hardly listening, just too occupied with pinning the silk rose in the most flattering position over her left ear and gazing at her face in the mirror. She'd remember afterwards though if anyone wondered where Eileen had gone. As it was, she seized Eileen by the arm and began singing the first verse of 'Three Little Maids from School' as they did a polka step down the corridor, only stopping hastily as Miss Gamble peered out from the kitchen.

'Stop making such a noise, you should be saving your voices,' she said, as though they were schoolchildren, thought Eileen feeling rather amused, but Anne Morgan immediately stopped and muttered an excuse. Eileen thought of the banter that went on in the printer's shop and decided that she was glad not to be a teacher and have to behave in a prim way.

'How old is she, anyway?' Eileen whispered in Anne's ear as they went to take their places in the line-up backstage.

'Well, Tom, Mr Mikado, he is thirty, he told me that one day,' Anne whispered back. 'He said that it was his birthday and he was thirty years old and when he went through the records of his law cases, he found that he had pleaded thirty cases in court as a barrister. And so he was going to have a double celebration. And he's Miss Gamble's younger brother. So she's more than thirty.'

'God, I wouldn't like to be over thirty, would you?' Eileen felt appalled at the thought. What would she be doing when she was over thirty, she wondered. Not still working in a printer's shop, even though it was fun. No, she hoped for something better. I think I would like to be a doctor, or perhaps a lawyer, someone who could defend her fellow party members if they were arrested, she thought. She might have a word with Bernard about the law courses in the university. And then her mind went to Tom Gamble sitting placidly in a corner, dressed in the robes of *The Mikado*. How long had he been a barrister? Thirty cases didn't seem a lot in about eight or nine years. What did he do with his time? And, more importantly, how did he manage to afford to drive a Bentley? They were a rich crowd, all in all, these members of the Merrymen group. The cars that were parked in the yard next to Peter's antique shop showed that. Peter himself had an Aston Martin.

'Sounds great, doesn't he?' whispered Anne in her ear as Peter's tenor voice singing, 'A Wandering Minstrel I,' sounded out, clear and strong, from the front of the stage.

Eileen nodded. It was interesting, she thought, that Peter was always so much better on stage than he was at rehearsals. Something in him always rose to the occasion. A daredevil, by nature, she thought. Her eyes went over to James O'Reilly. He would be a very different type. Even his choice of occupation showed that. After all, the life of a bank clerk wasn't very exciting, was it? It was amazing, though, that someone from such a dull, safe occupation as a bank clerk, should chose such friends, amazing that he had joined this group of rather wild young men, big spenders, big talkers, Tom Gamble, Robert Beamish, Peter Doyle. Even Jonathon Power was very confident and always willing to take a risk, perhaps that was why a person like James O'Reilly was led into taking drugs. He couldn't keep up otherwise. But what did Jonathon mean when he'd said, 'You won't get the money to fund that expensive little habit just from your salary in the bank.' It sounded as though the man had the habit previously. And how did being a member of the Merrymen make him able to afford drugs? None of them was paid. So who paid James O'Reilly and why? Eileen turned the matter over in her mind, listening with half an ear to Robert Beamish's pleasant baritone voice singing to the accompaniment of roars of laughter:

> So he decreed, in words succinct,
> That all who flirted, leered or winked
> (Unless connubially linked),
> Should forthwith be beheaded, beheaded, beheaded
> Should forthwith be beheaded.

'Who did you think was the best, now that you've seen the show twice?' she asked Eamonn when she met with him after the show. The two of them stood for a moment and then moved away and walked towards the river. The rain had stopped and gas lamps shining on the water made the place look quite festive.

'The girl who sang the main part, Anne Morgan, was that her name?' he said promptly and she was half-sorry that she had asked. If he had said that she was the best, she would have immediately pointed out that Anne Morgan possessed a far more outstanding voice, but now she felt slightly annoyed. That was the worst of the Republicans. They were so high-minded that they would not even tell a polite lie. And then she felt ashamed of herself. She would not swap someone like Eamonn with his high ideals for a man like Peter Doyle, no matter how good a flirt he was, nor for any other of the Merrymen.

'How much would a bank clerk be paid, Eamonn?' she asked into his ear as they stood gripping the chain and swinging it idly to and fro.

'Four hundred and fifty pounds a year,' he said promptly, without turning his head towards her. His face was turned down-river and his eyes were fixed on the burned-out remains of the city hall. 'Or, at least that is what my mother tells me. When I said that I couldn't go back to university yet, she wanted me to try to be a bank clerk. As if they'd have me!' Eamonn gave a shout of laughter and turned his face back towards her. It was difficult for him, she knew. His well-to-do family was appalled at his decision to throw up his studies at the university and join the Republicans. At least my mother prays for the whole island of Ireland to be free, thought Eileen. She worries about me, but she has some understanding of what I am trying to achieve.

'About nine pounds a week,' repeated Eamonn. 'My mother makes money a god.'

Nine pounds a week! Eileen thought about that sum. Very good money if your needs were not extravagant. A man could get married upon nine pounds a week, just as James O'Reilly had got married to Rose. But what if a man had expensive habits? Then in his ear, Eileen whispered, 'How much does it cost to buy cocaine, Eamonn?'

'Jesus, Eileen, don't ask me things like that. I haven't a clue,' said Eamonn impatiently. 'And don't go talking about cocaine to me in front of your mother. She'll have a fit.'

Eileen ignored this. She was thinking hard. Thinking about those expensive cars; the gorgeous clothes that Anne Morgan wore; the magnificent pearl choker necklace around Marjorie Gamble's neck. And the words spoken by Jonathon Power to the bank clerk, James O'Reilly.

'Perhaps they sell drugs,' she said suddenly. 'I always thought that it was weird that they opened the shop after the play was over. They talked about selling antiques to the playgoers, but it's a funny time of the night to be selling that sort of stuff. Would it be easy to get hold of drugs in Cork, Eamonn?'

'Pretty easy,' he said guardedly.

'How do you know?'

'The lads at college used to talk about it; used to talk about buying them down the quays from sailors – probably all talk,' he said impatiently. He seemed to be thinking hard. He released the chain and stared into the murky waters of the River Lee. 'I was reading a book about the Hell Fire Club in Dublin,' he said slowly after a minute of silence. 'Perhaps these people have some sort of club like that, drink and drugs and devilish acts. They might even, and perhaps the Reverend Mother suspects that, they might even have killed a priest as a sort of demonic act.'

'Let's go and have a cup of tea and a sandwich and then we'll come back and have a sneak around,' suggested Eileen. 'In any case, they might be keeping an eye on me. We'll go on your bike. We can leave it somewhere on the South Mall when we come back and then walk across Morrison's Island. No one would notice us. We could just peep in the back window of the shop to make sure that no one is around, then.'

They lingered over their tea and sandwich and by the time that they walked into Morrison's Island there was no one around, no cars on the road and no people on the pavements. The church had been closed and the windows of the antique shop with their beige-coloured blinds were just pale outlines reflecting the watery moonlight. But the windows were open and there was a sound of voices, laughter and then the clink of a bottle against a glass. Within the car park beside the shop there were six cars still parked there: Peter's Aston Martin, Tom Gamble's Bentley, Marjorie Gamble's Morris Austin, the O'Reillys' Fiat, Jonathon's Wolseley and Robert Beamish's handsome Alfa Romeo.

Eileen touched Eamonn's arm. 'Be careful,' she whispered. 'They're all still around. Let's get into this doorway. They'll go home soon.'

There was an old, derelict warehouse fronting on the car park used by the antiques shop and they huddled into the empty space where once there had been a door. From time to time, Eileen found herself glancing over her shoulder, almost as though she felt that someone's eyes were upon her, but every time she turned around, there was nothing to be seen. She gazed up at the sky. The fog was lifting and the hazy rings around the moon were beginning to melt. There was something eerie about this place as it began to light up. The old rotten floorboards and the dangling pieces of plaster from the high walls were taking on a strange ghostly beauty. Eileen looked once more over her shoulder, saw something and then moved a little closer to Eamonn.

'Let's get out of here,' she whispered.

'What's the matter?' He took her by the arm and then turned to stare over his shoulder. She almost said, 'Don't!' But it was too late. She heard him suck in his breath. He dropped her arm and turned back, stepping over a large splintered hole in the floorboards. Reluctantly she turned, noticing that she was shivering. She had not been mistaken. Something was stretched on the floor at the back of the warehouse.

There was a body there. The body of a man, small, slight with one arm outstretched, the palm turned over, open to the sky, his eyes wide and staring, the moonlight making his face very white in contrast to the small black moustache.

'It's Peter Doyle from the antiques shop,' she said in a whisper. 'Is he dead, Eamonn?'

Eamonn bent down, touched the pulse in the man's neck and nodded.

'No pulse. But the body is warm, very warm.' He did not immediately stand up, though. His head was bent over the man's chest.

'Look at this,' he said after a moment. He stood up and she joined him reluctantly.

Pinned with a long, black hatpin to the dead man's chest was a small card. On it was neatly printed: 'Found guilty of the murder of Father Dominic and executed by order of the Irish Republican Army.'

'Let's get out of here,' said Eileen urgently.

'What! And leave him lying there! We can't do that.' Eamonn was a very upright person; this was only what she might have expected from him. But Eileen found herself shaking with nerves.

'We'll be blamed for it!'

'Why should anyone blame us? But they might if we walk away from this place and leave a dead man lying on the ground. If we do the right thing now, no one will suspect us.'

'They know my face at the barracks. I was identified. They have a photograph of me now. I told you. Jonathon Power took it. And what about that lawyer, Maurice? And him visiting my mother's house. Do you think that he did it? Just because of something that I said.'

Eileen, to her disgust, found her teeth began to chatter. Now, all that she could hear was that clashing of tooth enamel against enamel. But a second previously, she had thought that she heard a sound, a rustling sound, somewhere to the left of them. She turned and scanned the heaps of rubbish, the broken floorboards and the long shards of dangling plaster, eerie in the moonlight. There was a huge wooden container in a dark corner and she wished that she had the courage to go boldly over to it. As she stared, she thought that she saw a movement within it. A rat? Perhaps? A person, possibly?

'Have you got a revolver?' she whispered and he shook his head silently. 'I left it behind,' he whispered in her ear. 'Didn't want to bring it into the play.'

'I think there is someone hiding over there behind that container,' she said in his ear. She tried to sound nonchalant but still she could hear that annoying click of her teeth.

She saw him looking towards the container, but then he

shrugged and she knew that he had not seen what she had seen. And now, there was, oddly, a feeling within her that the two of them were quite alone. Whatever presence there had been, that had now disappeared.

'A rat,' he said and she wished that she could believe him.

'Who killed him?' she asked in a whisper.

He looked down at the body. There was a dark stain on the floorboard beside the man's head. She saw him bend his head to examine it.

'Has he been shot?' she whispered, and then, with alarm, 'don't touch him, Eamonn. Don't get blood on your hands.'

'Let's go.' As always, Eamonn made the decision quickly. He grabbed her arm and walked at a steady pace towards the open doorway. 'Don't look back, and don't try to run,' he whispered and she understood the reason for that. Someone had shot Peter Doyle, but that did not mean that he would shoot two young people who just strayed into the warehouse. The murderer might not be even sure that they had even seen something. She tried to walk steadily. It was very hard not to look back. In a second, someone could spring on them and knock them to the ground. She admired Eamonn intensely at that moment. He was so calm, so relaxed.

When they got to the junction with the South Mall, he pushed her around the corner. They stood there in a doorway, entwined, almost as though they were lovers, thought Eileen, but there was a deadly feeing of apprehension in her mind.

'Go across to the Imperial Hotel,' he said in an urgent whisper. 'Ask to use their telephone. Phone the guards.'

'What'll I say?'

'Just tell them that you and I found a body. Don't say anything about the card on it.'

'What are you doing?'

'I'm going to keep an eye on that lot in the antiques shop. One of them could have murdered him. We've been suspecting that they are something to do with the Anti-Sinn Féin Organisation. They could have had a falling out. Someone murdered that man not long ago, five or ten minutes ago. The hand was still warm. The chances are that it was one of them. There's nobody else around, is there?'

Eileen felt shudders pass down her body. She glanced over her shoulder.

'Don't go back there, Eamonn.'

'I'll be all right. I'm not letting them away with that. Did you see that notice on him? "Found guilty of the murder of Father Dominic and executed by order of the Irish Republican Army". They are trying to blame it on our crowd. And it's not true. There's been another ceasefire agreed. Tom Hurley told us last night. He said no more guns to be used for the moment. I'm going back there to that shop. I'm going to see if they are all there. I should know them by now after seeing that show three times.'

'Don't let them see you.' Eileen knew that she couldn't argue him out of it. The quicker she got a Garda, the safer Eamonn would be. She ran across the broad empty road and burst into the Imperial Hotel.

'There's been a murder,' she said to the uniformed porter in the hallway. 'There's a man lying dead over there on Morrison's Island.'

'I'll get the police.' He was very quick, she thought as she collapsed onto one of the padded chairs in the hallway. But, why not? Goodness knows; there had been enough murders on the streets of Cork during the last few years. A ceasefire. So that was why Eamonn didn't have a gun on him, tonight. Had the Republicans given up, then? A few big jobs for people like Tom Hurley and for the rest, for people like Eamonn, who had given up a promising university career in medicine, Bernard who had been studying law, for these and for those like them, was it nothing but a few wasted years. She sat, staring at the glowing anthracite stove in the hallway, her mind distracted from the body, lying there on the ground of that deserted warehouse.

'They're on their way.' The porter was by her side before she realized it. Those thick carpets deadened the sound of footsteps. She scuffed the pile with her rubber-soled shoe and wondered what to do.

'They asked me to tell you to wait.' He was looking at her keenly, in a fatherly way. 'So you just sit there while I bring a pint of porter to a gentleman in number 22,' he said with deliberate emphasis. He was giving her a chance to escape; she knew that and she thought that it was kind of him.

'I'll wait,' she said. Eamonn, she knew, would not run away. He would see this out. He had strong principles. She would not desert him.

There was no way that this murder was going to be wrongly blamed on the Republicans if either of them could help it.

She was at the door of the Imperial Hotel when a young policeman came cycling down the South Mall. She went through the door and down the steps, rapidly.

'Is there just you?' she asked incredulously.

'That's right, miss.'

'There might be a murderer hanging around, you know.'

He produced a truncheon and swung it with bravado. 'Don't you worry, miss. You stay here if you like.'

'It's not a joke, you know. We did find a body. My friend is over there, keeping . . . staying with the body,' she finished lamely. She didn't want to say that Eamonn was doing a spot of detection on his own account.

'Is that a fact,' he said and swung the truncheon once more.

'Come on, then. Come and see for yourself.'

'Just a moment,' he said and dug a notebook out of his pocket. 'I'll just take down a few details about you, miss, if you don't mind. Name, address, that sort of thing.'

'My name is Eileen MacSweeney and I live at 103 Barrack Street,' she said steadily. No point in giving a false name. Chances were that he might recognize her. His face was vaguely familiar. She had little faith in him, though, and was relieved when, by the time that he had finished writing, there was the sound of an engine and a police van came down the South Mall.

'That was quick! They had to get the inspector out of his bed,' said the young policeman. 'Inspectors don't do night duty like the rest of us.'

'Inspector Cashman?'

'That's right. Know him, do you?'

'He was leaving the convent school when I started,' said Eileen. She wondered what the Reverend Mother would say when she heard of this latest killing. The Reverend Mother, she suddenly remembered, had asked lots of questions about the Merrymen group and about the antiques shop. And then she had gone on to talk about the burning down of some big house, Shanbally House, she remembered the name. What would she say when she heard of the latest death? Or would she have expected it?

ELEVEN

History of Civic Guards in Ireland
*'Throughout the winter of 1922/23 irregulars destroyed
485 police stations. Some 400 guards were physically
beaten, stripped of their uniforms and had their
personal possessions stolen. One was killed. Police
morale deteriorated, but the Minister for Home Affairs,
Kevin O'Higgins, and General Eoin O'Duffy, refused
to arm the guards'.*

Patrick recognized Eileen as soon as he arrived. Turned into a very pretty girl, he thought. It was a shame that she had become so wild. There were stories about her in the barracks. Still, at present, there was nothing against her, so he greeted her formally, thanked her for the information.

'Will you show us where the body is, Miss MacSweeney?' He began to walk rapidly across the South Mall as he spoke and then slowed down a little to stay beside her.

'He's in a warehouse, one of these derelict ones, just across the road from the antiques shop.' He saw her look at him closely as she said the last two words and he wondered what she knew.

'And your friend, who was with you?' There was a solitary motorbike parked down outside the back of the church. There had been a story, he remembered, about Eileen MacSweeney on the back of a motorcycle during a jailbreak.

'He's keeping an eye on the people in the shop.'

'Why?'

'Someone murdered him. He was dead when we went into the warehouse, but he's only just dead. Eamonn, my friend, used to be a medical student. He said that the corpse's hands were still warm, so he was only just after being killed. There's no one else around except them. So it must be one of them.'

Or you or your young man, thought Patrick, but he said

nothing. He crossed the road over towards the church and put
his hand on the motorcycle engine. Still warm. They could
not have been there too long. It had taken about ten minutes
for the police to arrive. Luckily, he had been still up when he
was summoned from his room in the barracks.

'The dead man is over there,' pointed out Eileen and he
allowed her to lead him back across the road. He beckoned
to the duty sergeant and the man joined him, shining a very
powerful torch onto the dead man's face.

'Looks as though he's just asleep, doesn't he, but my friend
said that he was dead. Felt his pulse. He used to be a medical
student,' said Eileen. 'I thought that he was asleep for a minute.
"Death-counterfeiting sleep." That's from Shakespeare, *A
Midsummer Night's Dream*. Did you study that at the Brothers?'

He could hear the defiant note in her voice. Probably scared,
he thought.

'Hmm,' said Patrick. He bent down, touched the man's neck,
and then the hands. Cooling, but not yet cold. Eileen did not
call his attention to the card on the man's chest, but he saw
her look at him as if to check whether he had noticed it.
She had gone very silent. Perhaps she thought that he would
be friendlier as they had been neighbours once.

'Not been long dead.' A young man had joined him.

'No,' said Patrick. Strange, that their arrival had not caused
any interest in the crowd inside the antiques shop. There were
snatches of melodies, laughs, and then a very English voice
calling out, 'Mind that vase, Anne!'

'I've been keeping an eye on them. They all seem to be
there. My name is Eamonn. Eileen and I found the body. Not
long dead, when we found him. The hands were still hot.
That's why I thought that it must be someone nearby who
killed him. There was no one else around, except the rest of
the crowd in his shop.'

'You know him, then.'

'Eileen does. It's Peter Doyle, the owner of the shop.'

'How many doors to the shop?'

'Just the one. There's no back door. These old warehouses
were all built back to back, I think.' From a good family, that
'th' was very carefully pronounced. A fellow about my own

age, thought Patrick. One of the ones who had everything, even a university education being paid for by parents, no doubt. One of the poor fools sucked in by the Republican movement. The sooner all that was finished, the better for the country. Aloud, he said, 'Perhaps you would give me a statement and then you and Miss MacSweeney can be off home.'

Very clear, very concise, that statement. A clever fellow, no doubt. Somehow, thought Patrick as he scanned what he had written, I don't see him coming over here to Morrison's Island, with a girlfriend on the back of his bike and assassinating a man, sticking around, sending for the police and waiting for them to arrive. It didn't make sense. He took a quick glance downwards at the body and the white card, very visible by the light of the sergeant's lamp.

'Perhaps you could sign this and then print under it the words: "Found the body just after midnight".'

'I didn't write that card, you know,' said Eamonn, showing that he had seen through Patrick's trick, but he signed his name with a flourish and then printed the words. He did not appear to take much trouble over the word 'found' or indeed over any of the other words.

'And an address, please.'

'I'm staying with Mrs MacSweeney, Eileen's mother, on Barrack Street, not sure of the number,' said Eamonn defiantly.

More likely out in some IRA safe house in west Cork, thought Patrick, but he had other things of more importance to see to, so he allowed the address.

'Thank you, both of you, you may leave now,' he said formally. A quick glance had been enough to see that Eamonn's handwriting was quite different. He had scrawled the words at top speed and had not even glanced at the card while doing so. Patrick dismissed the pair from his mind. The sergeant would see that they went off.

Now he had to tackle the jolly crowd inside the antiques shop. He waited until the motorbike revved up and went off in the direction of the quays before he walked over to the door to the antiques shop. It was unlocked and the decorative brass knob yielded to his hand.

And then his way was blocked by a large man.

'Who the hell are you?'

'Inspector Patrick Cashman, sir. It's Mr Robert Beamish, isn't it?' It was easy to recognize this man. His photograph was in the newspaper often enough. There were high hopes of him putting Cork on the map by winning a gold medal for rowing at the Olympics.

'That's right. Want something?' The voice was offensive, but the man was probably drunk. There were a lot of empty bottles on a tray on the counter next to the cash machine.

Patrick ignored him. He walked forward. 'Could everybody sit down, if you don't mind? I think it would be best. Sergeant, bring some chairs. Yes, Miss Gamble, will you and the other two ladies sit on that couch, please.' He waited calmly until they were all sitting down. They seemed to be completely at ease, amused, perhaps. There had been a certain amount of talk about people, who had too much to drink, driving noisily through the streets of the city. Letters had been written to the *Cork Examiner*, saying that the police should be doing something about it. Perhaps they thought that was why he arrived after midnight. He looked around. Perhaps if I could take everyone's name and address,' he said briskly. 'Miss Gamble, could I start with you?' He caught the eye of James O'Reilly. The man looked quite happy, sharing a low-voiced joke with Robert Beamish. The bank manager's words came back to him. *I'm worried about that young man.*

They were all there and seemed quite content, if a little puzzled, to give their names and addresses. The three women. Marjorie Gamble, the headmistress, Anne Morgan, the teacher and Rose O'Reilly, James's pretty young wife. And then there were the men. Robert Beamish and James O'Reilly, Jonathon Power, the Englishman and Tom Gamble, the barrister. Tom was the first to notice that someone was missing.

'Hello! Where's Peter?' he asked.

'Went to the back to get some wine,' said Robert Beamish. 'I'll go and get him and tell him that the Bull is here.' He was on his feet in a moment, and made his way to the back of the shop, shouting, 'Where are you, Peter, old fellow? The Bull is here. What have you been up to? Come on, out you come and keep your hands above your head!'

Very funny, thought Patrick and kept his eye on the faces in front of him. None of them showed even a flicker of anxiety. Patrick nodded at the sergeant to join the search and waited in silence while the heavy footsteps sounded. These buildings did not go back too far, about forty to fifty feet wide, he reckoned. Robert Beamish was taking a long time over the search.

'No sign of him. Had a bit of trouble with the gas. Dark as hell back there.'

'Perhaps he's upstairs.' Jonathon now showed a trace of anxiety, but surely, that was natural. Patrick allowed him to run up the stairs, and the sergeant followed like a well-trained dog. Still no sign of anything other than puzzlement on the faces and not even much of that.

'Perhaps he went out,' suggested Patrick quietly when Jonathon returned. He watched their faces keenly. They seemed puzzled, but not concerned.

'That's impossible, inspector,' said Marjorie Gamble. 'We've all been here, standing around, having a glass of wine after the show, just as you found us. Peter went off to get another bottle of wine – it was probably about ten minutes ago. It's impossible that he came back without anyone noticing and even more impossible that he left the building. There's only one door, only one way out of this building. It's only the other day that I told Peter that he should really get an outside stair-case built from one of the windows upstairs. The place would be a terrible deathtrap if there were a fire on the ground floor. He must be somewhere,' she finished. She sounded impatient, but not particularly worried.

'He is,' said Patrick bluntly. He looked around at all of the faces. The light was good here. An old chandelier converted to gas hung right overhead and the clear, white beam illuminated the group. Each of the seven faces turned towards him was showing a mixture of concern, exasperation and incredulity.

'I'm sorry to have to tell you that Mr Peter Doyle has been found dead in a warehouse across the road from here.'

'What!' Miss Gamble was on her feet. 'There must be some

mistake, inspector. Peter is here, somewhere in this building.'
She looked with some exasperation down at the young teacher,
Anne Morgan, who had suddenly begun to sob. 'Don't be
ridiculous, Anne,' she said harshly. 'This is nonsense. We all
know that Peter is still in the building. Let me look.'

Patrick allowed her to go. His eyes were on James O'Reilly.
The man was very white. He looked even more upset than
Jonathon Power did. And yet Jonathon and the dead man had
been friends before they ever came to Cork. He remembered a
piece in the *Cork Examiner* about them when the shop had first
opened. Had been in school together, he seemed to remember.
Both of Irish origin, they said, and were curious to see the land
of their ancestors. Some sort of story like that. Now Jonathon
seemed to be thinking hard.

'Are you certain that it is Peter, inspector,' he said.

'Certain,' said Patrick. 'The people who found the body
identified him and I knew him instantly. You may remember
that I was in your shop a few days ago. It would be good,
though, if you would kindly pop along to the barracks tomorrow
morning and make a formal identification. Not tonight, I think.'
He purposely nodded in the directions of the empty wine bottles
and Jonathon gave a wry smile.

'Well, perhaps not, inspector. Don't worry. We have hard
heads. I was just saying to Robert that we would go for a walk
by the river before driving home.'

'There's no sign of him.' Miss Gamble was back, her face
quite pale now.

'He's been identified by those who found the body,' said
Jonathon. 'And the inspector met him here a few days ago.'

'I don't want to delay you in getting home,' said Patrick. 'I
think that if we have a joint statement from you all. Perhaps . . .'
he looked from Jonathon to Miss Gamble.

'You do it, Marjorie,' said Jonathon. 'You will be better at
that sort of thing.'

Marjorie Gamble's statement was very clear. They had
come to the shop, as they usually did after a show, they would
have a glass or two of wine, discuss the evening and then go
home. As far as she could remember Peter had left them about
a quarter of an hour ago, he had gone to the storage rooms at

the back of the shop to choose another bottle of wine – and there were nodding heads when she said that. Jonathon had asked Robert to help him to carry down a table that he had been working on upstairs. Miss Morgan had gone to the bathroom – Anne Morgan nodded at that – and Rose O'Reilly had gone to look at one of the newly cleaned pictures. James O'Reilly went with Tom – my brother, inspector – to check on some bank statements that Peter couldn't understand – and Marjorie Gamble, herself, had taken off the glasses to be washed, as Peter didn't like putting red wine into glasses that had held white wine previously.

'So it is possible that Mr Doyle might have slipped through while you were all busy.' Patrick held his indelible pencil poised for a second and watched the faces.

'I suppose it might be possible now that you say it,' admitted Marjorie Gamble reluctantly. 'He might have wanted some fresh air.'

'Anybody else anything to add to Miss Gamble's statement?' Patrick allowed his eyes to rest for a few moments on each face. All were shaking their heads. They wanted to finish with the matter and to talk it over with each other. He wondered whether to demand the key and lock up the warehouse, but he didn't think that he could do that. After all, the murder had not occurred there, but in the derelict place across the road. He read his statement aloud and then laid the notebook on the counter. There was a pen there and a bottle of ink, black and indelible, he noticed with interest. He opened the bottle, dipped the pen in it and said, 'Now could everyone print their name and address beneath the statement.' Surely, there would be enough letters in every name and address to compare with the printing on the card. He had a strong intuition that this was not an IRA killing.

'I'll leave you to the sergeant,' he said. This would give him a good excuse to wander over the premises. He would have to check that there was no possible exit from the warehouse.

The whole affair was very puzzling, he thought as he made his way towards the back rooms. A glance was enough to show him that there was no chance of anyone leaving the premises from the small windowless room where the wine bottles were stored in racks. There was a small cloakroom with lavatory bowl and hand basin next door. That had a tiny window cut in the wall, not much bigger than a hand span in size. Must be the end-of-terrace wall. He came back out and looked around, getting his bearings. There was another small window, not quite so small, in that same end-of-terrace wall. It still didn't look big enough to get out of and it had a diamond patterned metal screen over it and a silver candlestick, complete with a cream-coloured candle standing in front of the screen. Patrick reached up and touched the screen. Carefully screwed to the wall, he noticed, before he ran upstairs, noting the open-tread staircase that was fastened to the blank wall. When he got to the top of the stairs, he looked around. Just one enormous room with a high ceiling. Large windows here, but nobody could get out of them. They were a good twenty feet above the roadway. Everything was wide open and could be seen from downstairs. There was no doubt now in his mind that Peter Doyle must have slipped out of the front door while nobody was looking.

But it did seem impossible that two people might have left, unseen, through that front door and that only one came back.

Unless, he thought, that they are all in it. Unless they made a pact to lie.

He came back down. By now, all the names and addresses had been printed onto his notebook. He was right about the ink. Thick, jet black ink. He had left the card on the body, but tomorrow he could compare the two. Something occurred to him then and he went back up the stairs and stopped in front of a picture. It had a card under it giving the name of the artist and the date when it was painted. He reached out and touched it. Not too dissimilar, he thought and came back down.

'Who does the lettering on the cards?'

'I do.' Jonathon Power had a puzzled look on his face.

'And where do you keep the cards?'

'Here.' Jonathon produced a bundle from under the counter.

'I may keep one?'

'Yes, certainly, inspector.' The man was even more uneasy.

'Just one more question, sir. Who would own this business after the death of Peter Doyle?'

There was a very long pause this time. The man had gone pale. After a few more moments, Miss Marjorie Gamble intervened. 'Don't look so worried, Jonathon. The inspector is not accusing you of murder. He just wants to get the facts so it is quite all right to tell him. You are a partner, aren't you?'

'Yes, I s . . . s . . . suppose so.' He stammered a little over the words.

'Well, I'll let you all go home now. You must be tired. And you'll pop into the barracks tomorrow morning, Mr Power, will you, and make a formal identification of the body. As early as you please. The barracks will be open. Just tell the man on duty that I sent you, if I'm not in when you come.' Something more should be said, thought Patrick. Wishing them a good night or a pleasant end to their evening seemed a little strange after telling them that a close friend had been killed. He contented himself with a brief nod to the sergeant to open the door.

'You have a quick look around,' he said the sergeant. 'I'm going across the road to have another check and then young Conor can get off home.'

It was only when he was standing in the derelict warehouse, across the road from the antiques shop, that he suddenly thought of what Miss Gamble had said. Her brother Tom and James O'Reilly had been checking through bank statements. Why? What had Tom Gamble to do with bank statements? James O'Reilly might be of help with technical problems, but surely, a bank statement was a bank statement, a simple account of sums deposited and sums withdrawn.

I'm worried about that young man. Those words kept recurring in his mind.

A young man who lived in a style well beyond his income, who looked ill, who had a strange glitter in his eyes.

And then there was that Tom Gamble. Another man who spent heavily, perhaps. He seemed almost to live in the Imperial Hotel. Patrick reflected that he had seldom passed the place or had gone in there without seeing Tom Gamble, at all hours of the day as well as at night. And Robert Beamish. The family had money, probably were happy to spend on tuition, trainers, on expensive boats, but he, too, lived a very high life. There were lots of young Beamishes. Would the family generosity maintain all of them in that style, or did Robert Beamish have some other source of income?

All in all, he thought wearily, he had his suspicions about that crowd. In all probability the Reverend Mother was correct: they were behind many of the burnings down of the big houses. But he could not see why on earth any one of them would have murdered Peter Doyle, who was probably the man who masterminded the operation.

Except perhaps the quietly spoken Jonathon Power. If he were a partner, then he would now inherit the business. And that seemed to be doing very well.

TWELVE

Civic Guard Handbook:
*'The Civic Guards are directly controlled by, and
accountable to, central government.'*

'So, it was the Shinners that killed the fellow,' said the
superintendent when Patrick put his head around his
superior's door on Tuesday morning. 'You've had a
night of it, haven't you? Pity you didn't think to detain the
two who found the body; I know that name, Eileen
MacSweeney. She's been in trouble before and the fellow that
she was with, he was one of them, as well, I'd guess. I'd have
thrown them in a cell for a few hours and got something out
of them. You've seen this, of course, pinned to the man's
chest, I understand. What do you think? The Shinners without
doubt, is what I'd say. To give them their due, they try to
make life easy for us. Love to lay claim to their crimes.' He
took a piece of card from the top of his letter tray and handed
it over to Patrick.

'Yes' I've seen it. "Found guilty of the murder of Father
Dominic and executed by order of the Irish Republican Army."
Could be the Republicans, I suppose,' said Patrick. He held
no brief for the rebellious Sinn Féin, but the nickname,
'Shinners', grated on him. 'Seems a bit odd, though, doesn't
it, superintendent?' he went on. 'How did they know that Peter
Doyle killed Father Dominic? We don't know that ourselves.
It seems unlikely. Why should he?'

'Well, I put that very question to Dr Scher when he brought
the card in before he started on the autopsy. He had some
story about seeing Father Dominic looking upset about a
ceramic bird of some sort when he was in Peter Doyle's shop.
Perhaps Doyle stole something belonging to the priest and
when he was challenged, he killed the good man. Let me
have your report on last night when you have the time.' The

superintendent returned to his work on the wages sheet and
Patrick retreated. The superintendent was a Protestant, a left-
over from the former police force, the Royal Irish Constabulary,
and as such did not perhaps know that Capuchin priests were
not allowed to possess any goods.

'Let me know when Dr Scher has finished the autopsy,
Tommy,' Patrick said as he passed the sergeant on the desk.
'Tell him I'd like to have a word when he's free. Trouble you
for five minutes, Joe,' Patrick continued as he leaned into the
open door of the office where his sergeant was sitting. Sergeant
Joe Duggan was on his feet in an instant, notebook in hand.
He followed Patrick into the inspector's office and took a seat
on the other side of the desk.

'Well, another body,' said Patrick with exasperation, 'and,
for the life of me, I can't see any possible connection between
a Capuchin friar and an Englishman who owned an antiques
shop, though, apparently Dr Scher saw Father Dominic in the
shop on the day before he was murdered.'

'The superintendent thinks . . .' Joe gave a hasty glance at
Patrick's face and then stopped.

'Let's go through the notes again,' said Patrick wearily.
'Could it possibly be true that Peter Doyle murdered Father
Dominic?' he said. 'The Republicans usually get their facts
right – that is if that card isn't just put there to mislead us.'

'It's like them, though, isn't it? They usually like to claim
responsibility. The whole city is up in arms about the murder
of Father Dominic. And, of course, newspapers have been
speculating about whether it's a Sinn Féin atrocity. They
would want that wiped off people's minds. In any case, if
the IRA execute the man who murdered a popular priest
like Father Dominic, then it will boost their recruitment at
a time when lots are falling away from them.' Joe looked
again at the card that Patrick had placed on the desk between
them.

'Well, we'll see. I suppose we must take into account that
there may be some connection between the two murders;
that one resulted from the other. We should be able to solve
Father Dominic's murder. After all, that church was full of
people. Surely, we can get some good evidence. Now, let's

see—' he leafed through his notes – 'yes,' he said, 'after the woman in the shawl, there was that little boy who said to his mother that the priest wasn't talking. That wasn't like Father Dominic. He was very kind to children. I remember going to confession to him myself when I was about that age and he was asking me to say a prayer for him and joking that he was a terrible sinner. This means that the last person to see him alive might well be the woman in a shawl,' he finished.

'Who has not come forward,' said Joe.

'A very big shawl, apparently,' said Patrick, looking back at his notes. 'Two or three witnesses described it as one of those old-fashioned shawls, not the newer kind of black or brown, but one of those big, plaid shawls, floor length. That was mentioned by everyone that I've interviewed.'

'What about the evidence from the garage man about seeing Peter Doyle, small man with a moustache standing at the back of the church?' asked Joe.

'You're thinking along the same lines as I am,' said Patrick. 'You're thinking that Peter Doyle might have disguised himself as a woman in a shawl and killed Father Dominic.' He brooded on this for a minute while Joe waited respectfully. The IRA were usually very accurate at assigning crimes and had a good knowledge of what went on in the troubled city, so it was certainly worth considering Peter Doyle as a possible killer of the priest. Joe, he thought, was sharpening up immensely and was becoming a very useful assistant. He resolved to make as much time as possible to discuss matters with him. 'And you know,' he continued, 'nobody looks too closely at someone going into confession and if the shawl was pulled forward, right over the face, and perhaps across the mouth, no one would notice the moustache. The church is pretty dark, anyway, and that particular confessional is in the darkest part of the church. People said that Father Dominic chose it for that reason. He had lots of the Republicans coming to confess to him and he knew that some of them were shy of being spotted, espe-cially if their faces were on posters around the city. Now let's have another look through all of those statements. I don't think there were any more mentions of the woman, if she was a woman, in the shawl, but I just want to check.'

'Easy enough to fade out of sight,' said Joe. 'And if it was Peter Doyle who dressed up, well, remember he was an actor. I saw him in *The Mikado*. He was very good. Really looked as though he was enjoying himself, too. He'd have the confidence to do something like dressing up and joining the queue for confession. Did anyone give a good description of the woman in a shawl? Is that what you're looking for?'

'I've found it,' announced Patrick. 'Nothing like taking notes of everything said, Joe. Never be tempted to skip someone who seems to be going on and on. You never know what might be important. It was the woman, with the little boy, who said this. "A woman in a shawl came out. She seemed a very respectable woman. She didn't smell like they usually do." Do you see, Joe? They do smell, these poor things, don't they? So if this woman didn't smell, it seems likely that she wasn't really what they call a "shawlie", but someone dressed up, disguised. Could have been Peter Doyle, couldn't it? He was quite a small man.'

'Wonder what he did with the shawl.'

'Dropped it somewhere. There's always someone poor enough to pick up something like that. Or else it's in the river. Wouldn't tell you much, I'd say.'

'I can guess where he got it, if it was Peter Doyle, or someone else who wanted to murder Father Dominic,' said Joe. 'The Holy Trinity have a charity for old clothes for poor people. And they send everything they get to the laundry, first. That shawl probably came from there. They leave a big box at the back of the church, near to the bell rope, out in the open there so that they can keep an eye out that someone doesn't pinch the lot. But otherwise, I'd say that it would be fairly easy, if you had a bag, to just grab something and no one would notice.'

'A respectable, well-dressed man like Peter Doyle?'

'Well he could just hang around a bit and then snatch. Or, more likely, he could bring along something like a pair of old trousers, or a pair of shoes or a few things like that and make a show of unloading them and then just take a shawl when no one was looking.'

'Of course. I've suddenly remembered. Someone actually saw him. It was that fellow from the garage on Morrison's Island. Let's see. Here it is: ". . . English fellow that runs the antique shop, Mr Doyle; I thought it was a bit odd to see him. Him being a Protestant. He was standing at the back of the church, just beside the bell rope. It was before the Novena began." And he knew Doyle well as he filled his lorry with petrol.'

'Well, that proves it,' said Joe. 'I was right! What an earth would a Protestant be doing hanging around just before the Novena started. He grabbed a shawl, most of these shawls are floor length – and he wasn't a big man, was he? Then he went into the little room by the bell rope, the place where they keep the brooms, the buckets, and the polishes and put it around him. Took a bit of nerve, but I'd say that he had it.'

'You're probably right,' said Patrick absent-mindedly. He was leafing through the rest of his notes. The woman with a shawl had been noticed by a lot of people, but no one else had anything of interest to say about her. 'Nobody remarked on how long she was in the confessional,' he said aloud.

'Doesn't take too long to kill someone with a sharp knife through the ear,' said Joe.

'Not a knife, I think. A hat pin, I'd say,' said Patrick. 'The Reverend Mother showed me a hatpin that nuns use. It looked able to do the job, according to Dr Scher. Look at it.' He took the pin from the drawer and laid it on the table. It exactly matched the pin that had fastened the card to the dead man's jacket.

'A reporter from the *Cork Examiner* to see you, inspector. Will I bring him in?' Tommy put his head around the door after a perfunctory knock.

'No, I'll come out,' said Patrick. These reporters had no idea of time. And if he were once ensconced in the office, he would expect a whiskey. The superintendent had got a lot of reporters into bad habits by producing a bottle automatically. Patrick had no intention of following in his footsteps.

'They've got hold of the IRA involvement,' warned Tommy, as Patrick rose to his feet, 'and it wasn't me that told them.'

It probably was, thought Patrick. Tommy was a terrible old gossip and loved to drop heavy hints that would immediately be picked up by a sharp reporter. Five minutes and any young man worth his salt would get everything he wanted to know out of Tommy.

'No harm,' he said and was amused to see the look of relief on Tommy's face. He stopped at the door. 'Hand me that card found pinned on the man's chest, Joe, will you and I'll bring it out to show to him. We might as well get all the information we can.' Virtually the whole of Cork city read the *Cork Examiner*, either a copy that they bought, or one that they picked up from a rubbish bin on the street, or found left lying on a seat of the tram. It was a good way for the police to appeal for information.

'Morning, Bob,' he said when he came out to the desk.

'Busy day, inspector.' Bob would be slightly annoyed not to be taken into his office, but he couldn't help that. 'Start as you mean to go on', had been his motto, when he had first been appointed as inspector, and he had kept to it. 'Time is of the essence', he had read in a law book and that applied to the solving of crimes and all other police business.

'Tommy's probably filled you in on the basic details,' he said briskly, 'but you might be interested to see this. Give me a piece of paper and a pencil, Tommy, and I'll make a copy of it so that you can take it away with you, Bob. Any questions?'

This part of the job was getting second nature to him, now. Best to tell rather than to allow them to guess; that had been his policy from his first days as an inspector.

'The Civic Guards are very grateful for all the assistance that they have had about the tragic death of Father Dominic Alleyn,' he said as he traced an outline of the card onto the piece of paper. 'Now they are appealing for help with this second murder.' And then, with a quick eye at the lettering, he began to print the words on the note found on Peter Doyle's body. 'We'd be grateful,' he continued, speaking slowly so that Bob could keep up with him, 'we'd be very grateful if anyone who was in the streets around Charlotte Quay, Morrison's Quay or anywhere on Morrison's Island yesterday night – between eleven o'clock and midnight, especially, could contact us,' he said. The writing on the card was quite difficult to reproduce, he thought, with a glance back at the card. Whoever wrote it made their letters strangely. The letter 'o' in the word 'found' was a thin oval, whereas the 'o' in 'order' and the 'o' in 'of' were both fat and round. A disguised hand, he thought, but was careful to keep a blank face as he painstakingly copied the message, letter by letter.

'You'd have a good camera at the *Examiner* offices, wouldn't you, Bob?' he said. 'What about taking a picture of this and printing it on the front of the *Evening Echo*.'

'Who knows, someone might recognize the handwriting,' said Tommy wisely.

'Ab-so-lute-ly,' said the reporter enthusiastically. 'Really appreciate this, inspector. Will give you a bit of a write-up, too, don't you fear – "in the competent hands of Inspector Patrick Cashman" – that sort of thing.'

'Send me a few competent witnesses and I'll be happy,' said Patrick sedately. The *Examiner* man, he thought, had done him a favour. The act of copying, letter by letter, had alerted him to something he had not noticed before. 'I'll leave you now, Bob,' he said. 'I'm a bit snowed-under this morning. Tommy will take care of you; will let you know if there is anything else.'

'Dr Scher's just arriving, inspector,' said Tommy. 'I know the sound of that old Humber of his.' He beckoned to a young Garda. 'Just mind the desk for me for a moment, sonny, while I show the reporter out.'

He would be off to the nearest pub where the reporter would buy him a few drinks and put it down to the *Cork Examiner*'s account, thought Patrick, but it was no business of his.

'Ask Dr Scher to pop in and see me if he has a moment,' was all that he said as Tommy took down his coat and fished an umbrella from under the reception desk. Patrick did not enquire why a man going to the door needed an umbrella and an overcoat. The superintendent was in charge of the barracks and Tommy, like his superior, was a Protestant – left over from the R.I.C. Everyone knew that Tommy was privileged.

Dr Scher, he thought, looked slightly worried as he ushered him into his room.

'Can't stay long. I've had a call from my housekeeper. She had a call from Reverend Mother Aquinas.'

'I'll go with you.' Patrick made up his mind instantly. 'We can talk on the way.' He took the card from the desk and, putting it carefully into an envelope, he placed it into his jacket pocket, put on his coat and popped his head into Joe's room. 'Be back in an hour, Joe,' he said briefly and then followed Dr Scher.

'Anything interesting about the autopsy?' he enquired as he eased himself thankfully out of the rain and into the shabby front seat of the Humber.

'Well, body of a man aged early twenties, well-nourished, fit, healthy, identified by friend and employee, Jonathon Power, as one Peter Doyle, aged approximately twenty-two, owner of antiques shop . . . Cause of death . . .' Dr Scher delved in his pocket, made a pretext of studying his notes, but Patrick knew that the words were on the tip of his tongue.

'The cause of death, Patrick, you will be interested to know, was, once again, a hatpin, this time left within the ear, a very long hatpin, just like the one that the Reverend Mother showed you, a hatpin with a black top, made from Bakelite, and a steel pin exactly nine inches long. Well, what do you think of that, Patrick?'

'Strange weapon for the IRA,' said Patrick. He looked out through the windscreen, the rain was still pouring down, but the sooner they got to the convent, the sooner they would find out what the Reverend Mother wanted with Dr Scher. 'I'd have thought that it would be much easier to shoot him.'

'I'll get your old bus going,' he said and plunged out into the rain again. It seemed almost a relief to put all his energies into swinging the starting handle and a source of great satisfaction to hear the engine roar in response. At least something was going right this morning. He got back into the front seat and waited while Dr Scher eased his bulk to an easier position behind the wheel.

'I suppose that we'll get a summer some time,' he said, conscious that Dr Scher turned and looked at him closely before pressing the start button. He had sounded bad-tempered and irritable. He could hear the exasperated tone in his own voice.

'I'm a bit puzzled about that card left on the dead man's chest,' he said in explanation as they swung out onto Barrack Street.

'I've seen that,' said Dr Scher. 'I unpinned it from the chest of the cadaver, very neatly attached to the lapel of his expensive suit. Our murderer seems to have lots of hairpins. One on the jacket and another one in the man's ear; pierced the ear and went through to the brain. A very good quality of hairpin, both of them,' he added.

'Anything else of interest?' asked Patrick. He wished that someone had taught Dr Scher to drive properly. It was an unnerving experience to be in a car with him as he swerved from side to side of the narrow street. 'Tell me later,' he added hastily as Dr Scher turned to face him, shooting out from Barrack Street right into the path of the traffic on Sullivan's Quay. Several horns blew angrily and Dr Scher laughed. Patrick braced himself and thought about the handwriting on the card.

The Reverend Mother looked even paler than usual, he thought, when they arrived at the convent. She had been standing at the window of her room, looking out into the rain. When she turned around to face them, he could see, even in the bad light, that she had deep shadows under her eyes.

'I'm sorry to have troubled you, Patrick,' she said gravely. I was going to write to you, but somehow I thought it might be easier to explain to you face to face. I have grave suspicions about this Peter Doyle who runs the antique shop and of those associated with him in the Merrymen Light Opera group.

'You won't have heard the news yet,' he said, 'but we had another murder last night. Peter Doyle was found dead some time after midnight. His body was lying just inside the doorway of a derelict warehouse. He had been pierced though the ear, into the brain, with a blacktopped hatpin. The body was still

warm when the police arrived. The body was discovered by
Eileen MacSweeney and her young man.'

'After midnight,' she said thoughtfully. 'That's strange. And
Eileen . . .?'

'Show her the card, Patrick,' said Dr Scher.

Patrick took it from his pocket and held it out.

'"Found guilty of the murder of Father Dominic and
executed by order of the Irish Republican Army".' She read
aloud. There was a puzzled look on her face. 'The Republicans,'
she said thoughtfully. 'Odd method to choose, wasn't it? I
would have thought that if one possessed a gun . . .'

'True,' said Patrick. 'Unless, they thought that by giving
him the same death as Father Dominic . . .'

'Possibly,' she said thoughtfully. 'A difficult way to murder
someone out in the open, I would have thought. Quite different
in one of those terribly narrow cubicles in the confessional.
There's barely room for the priest's shoulders. Father Dominic
could not have got away. But a young, active man like Peter
Doyle, and out in the open . . .'

'Body was not moved, I'd say,' said Dr Scher. 'As far as I
could tell, he was stabbed in the ear and fell to the ground
and was not moved after that.'

'Was Peter Doyle unconscious at the time of death, Dr
Scher?' She was focussing on the anomalies of this strange
murder.

'Ah, Reverend Mother, you have a sharp brain,' said Dr
Scher admiringly. 'I think it is possible that he might have
been unconscious, but I examined the body carefully and there
were no bruise marks so it's not possible to be sure.'

'And there was no one else around on Morrison's Island at
that time of night, was there?' she asked.

'On the contrary, there were lots, just across the road. All
the performers of the show, of *The Mikado*, except Eileen,
who had gone off with her young man, but all the rest of
them, they were all still there. All of their expensive cars
were parked by the antiques shop and every one of them
there, drinking wine and eating sandwiches. Eileen
MacSweeney went across to the Imperial Hotel and got the
porter there to call the guards. And her young man, Eamonn,

stayed, according to himself,' Patrick opened his notebook, '"to keep an eye on them".'

'Why?' asked the Reverend Mother and Patrick nodded.

'That's what I asked myself. After all, if it were a Republican murder, why did the pair of them hang around? Why run a risk? Though my superintendent is wondering why I didn't throw the two of them in a cell. Anyway, I sent the pair of them home and then went across the road to the antiques shop, told them of the death and interviewed them all. Not too much to show for it. Peter, apparently, had gone down to the back room for a bottle of red wine as he didn't care for white wine. They thought that he was only gone for a minute or two, but . . .'

'But when you're drinking, time passes quickly.' Dr Scher gave a wise nod.

'Why did Eamonn feel that he had to keep an eye on them?' asked the Reverend Mother.

'He was very honest about it. He said that he knew it was not a Republican killing and therefore it had to be one of the man's friends.'

'And could it be?'

Patrick thought that he saw a glint of interest in the Reverend Mother's eyes. She was worried about Eileen, he thought.

'Not, if everyone was telling me the truth,' he said briefly. 'And if someone was lying then everyone was lying. There's absolutely no way out of that place except for the front door, or the front window. You know how they are built, terraced and back to back, just one tiny window at the Charlotte Quay end. They were all in the front of the shop, the bottles and the glasses were on the counter. Jonathon had asked Robert to help him to carry down a table that he had been working on upstairs. Miss Morgan had gone to the bathroom and Rose O'Reilly had gone to look at one of the newly cleaned pictures, and then, it seems they all started drinking again and didn't notice the time passing until I arrived. Took me ten minutes to arrive, I'd say, add another three or four for Eileen MacSweeney to get across to the Imperial Hotel and get the porter to phone the duty sergeant. He came straight upstairs to me. I hadn't gone to bed and I went immediately.' He thought back on the evidence that he had taken the night before. And why should anyone of them murder Peter Doyle? And if someone did, why should everyone else lie to protect the guilty person? Once again, he wondered whether they were all in it. That was the only possibility that seemed to make sense. The Reverend Mother wore a very pensive look and he waited for her to respond.

She seemed to think for a moment, and then to make up her mind. 'Patrick, on Saturday afternoon, my cousin took me to the antiques shop to buy me a present.' She got to her feet and took the silver tray from her desk. 'I chose this.'

'Good piece of Cork silver,' interjected Dr Scher.

'Yes, but that wasn't my reason for choosing it. Both my cousin and I remembered a silver tray, with one missing handle, just like this one, lying on the hall table of a house, Shanbally House, which you may remember was supposedly burned down by the Republicans some time last year.'

'Supposedly . . .' put in Dr Scher, and Patrick nodded quietly. Things were beginning to come together. Suspicions that had been in his mind during that midnight interview seemed to crystalize.

'The ceramic hawk, Dr Scher,' he said. 'The superintendent said that you reported Father Dominic was upset about a ceramic hawk. Did you and your cousin notice the ceramic hawk, Reverend Mother?'

'Yes, indeed, we both remembered the hawk, a Japanese Arita hawk. It stood on a shelf in the corner of the stairs in Shanbally House. I remembered two hawks. And when I remarked on it, my cousin recollected how one was broken and the other damaged. The hawk in the antiques shop was damaged on the beak. There were other things in the shop, also, that we were sure came from that house.'

'So you think that Peter Doyle was connected with the Republican movement,' said Patrick.

The Reverend Mother shook her head. 'I am fairly satisfied that he was not,' she said. 'Forgive me if I don't mention my source of information.'

Eileen MacSweeney, thought Patrick, but he nodded. Bother,

he thought, just when things were beginning to get sewn up, they began to unravel again.

'There were other pieces, other antiques, vases, furniture, as well as silver, from houses that my cousin and I remembered, but that had been burned down, supposedly by the Republicans.'

'That's very interesting,' said Patrick.

'When I was young, my cousin and I often visited the houses of the Anglo-Irish. My family were wine merchants and they supplied most of those families,' she said quietly. 'Father Dominic is an old friend of mine. He and his brother, the present prior of the Capuchins in the city, Prior Lawrence, they also knew all of these houses. I have a very clear recollection of us all as visitors, spending time in houses that have been burned down during the last few years. Many of the houses were quite shabby, even then – the Great Famine had reduced the rents. Nevertheless, these families had been in the past very rich with huge estates and the houses were treasuries of Georgian furniture, silver, glass and paintings. How easy and how lucrative to stock an antiques shop from articles from these burned-down houses.' She sat back and tucked her hands into her sleeves.

'You're suggesting that the antiques shop stocked their shelves by simply raiding these old houses of the Protestant ascendancy.'

'Very lucrative,' said Dr Scher.

'Very,' agreed the Reverend Mother. 'Think of the price of your coffee pot, Dr Scher.'

'A spectacular fire in the front of the building and a lorry around the back,' said Patrick.

'Precisely,' said the Reverend Mother. Patrick was glad to see her smile. He was beginning to feel a certain excitement rising within him. He hadn't noticed a lorry when he had called to the shop, but that man, who had given evidence about seeing Peter Doyle, had talked about filling their lorry with petrol. Why a lorry when anything bought in the shop could be delivered more easily in a van? He had not thought of that at the time, but now it seemed to him significant. And the man had mentioned cans. Why should people working in an antiques shop need cans of petrol? But the IRA had lorries; many of them captured from the British army. And the accounts of the burning down of those houses were all the same. *A lorry drove up, masked men jumped out, carrying cans of petrol. Went into the house and gave the inhabitants twenty minutes to get out.* Yes, it all began to make sense.

'And if Father Dominic had come to the same conclusion as you and your cousin . . .?' he asked.

'He would have tackled the man instantly,' said the Reverend Mother. 'Dominic was a very straightforward person. He would have thought of it as a matter of saving a man's soul.'

'So, Father Dominic visits the antique shop, sees the ceramic hawk, recognizes that it comes from a house supposedly burned down by the IRA, perhaps, like you and your cousin, Reverend Mother, he recognizes other things. Then he goes and has a word with Peter Doyle and Peter Doyle tells him some lie or other, perhaps, but realizes that the game is up. He has to get rid of the priest, but he doesn't want any suspicion to come to his door. And where is the last place that you would expect to find an Englishman and a Protestant,' he said to Dr Scher.

'I don't know, Patrick, you tell me.' Dr Scher glanced over at the Reverend Mother. She had a very reserved look on her face. She knows something else, thought Patrick, but she may not want to tell me.

'In a Catholic church, of course,' he said triumphantly. 'Well done, Dr Scher. Without your account of seeing Father Dominic in the shop and noticing his distress at the sight of this Japanese hawk – well, Peter Doyle would have been the last person in the world to be suspected. But, of course, Father Dominic was called the IRA priest by some people. He visited them in jail; I know that.'

'So you've solved both murders, you think,' said Dr Scher. 'Peter Doyle murdered Father Dominic. And the Republicans murdered Peter Doyle.'

'For a moment I thought that was a good solution, but now I'm not sure. The Reverend Mother doesn't think so. Her informant denied that the Republicans had anything to do with it, and I'd say that her informant was well-informed,' said Patrick. 'That young man with Eileen had the look of a Republican. A lot of those college boys joined up. He had been a medical student, apparently.' Patrick delved in his pocket, held the card out towards them both. 'And then there is this. It puzzles me a little. Do you see anything odd about this, Reverend Mother, Dr Scher?' he asked, looking from one face to the other.

'I may touch?' asked the Reverend Mother.

'Yes, certainly,' said Patrick.

She took the card, went over to the window and put it down on the small table that stood there. Dr Scher followed her.

'I had to copy this out for the *Examiner* reporter. I tried to do it like a picture image, to copy it exactly as it was written and I found . . .'

'That the lettering was odd,' said the Reverend Mother quietly, 'inconsistent,' she added.

'That's right,' said Patrick.

'I didn't notice that,' said Dr Scher and then he nodded, 'but, yes, I can see now.'

'The "o" is what I noticed first,' said Patrick. 'It's quite different in "found" to the way that it is written in "of" and again slightly different in the word "order". I think someone tried to disguise the handwriting. And yet it seems unlikely that anyone in the IRA would want to do that. We've seen some of their stuff before, just straightforward printing. Still, one never knows.' The Reverend Mother, he thought, was staring very intently at the card. It was hard to read anything from a nun's face. The white linen wimple that smoothly covered the forehead right down to the eyebrows gave them an untroubled look. He produced his notebook.

'No one knows who wrote that card,' he said, 'but I thought that I might collect samples of handwriting from everyone possible that night and so I wrote out a statement here, mainly based on what Miss Gamble told me, and then I asked everyone to print their name and address beneath it.'

'Printing so that you could compare with the card. But

you don't really suspect any of that crowd, do you? Why should they kill Peter Doyle, even if he killed Father Dominic? Father Dominic was nothing to them.' Dr Scher sounded impatient.

Patrick's eyes were on the Reverend Mother. After a moment, she placed a forefinger under the 'o's of Jonathon.'

'I noticed that, too,' said Patrick.

'I remember admiring the sign outside the shop. The style is Gothic, very well done. He is a most artistic young man,' said the Reverend Mother. 'This is a modified style, of course, but the letter "o" has that angular shape.'

'And, apparently, he is the partner. That's what he said, anyway. Miss Gamble was talking about him selling up and going back to England. It would be interesting to look at the bank statements. If we are right and they are getting all of their goods free of charge, then the profits, once they had paid for the renovation of the shop, must be enormous.'

'Doesn't strike me as the type who would kill a harmless old priest, though, does he?' said Dr Scher. 'I'd have thought that the other fellow, Peter Doyle, would have been the more likely of the two. What do you think, Patrick? And you, Reverend Mother? You met them both, didn't you?'

'"There is no art to find the mind's construction in the face",' said the Reverend Mother.

Probably Shakespeare, thought Patrick. A fleeting thought crossed his mind. Would he have been a more educated person if he had stayed on at the convent, rather than going to the hard labour and monotonous rote learning which brought the Christian Brothers such good examination results from slum children like himself. Eileen, he remembered, had quoted Shakespeare last night.

'I think that it makes sense that it is a revenge killing,' said Dr Scher decisively. 'There must be a connection and that makes sense. Don't you agree, Reverend Mother?'

'And the only people who would want to avenge Father Dominic would be the Republicans, is that what you are thinking, Dr Scher?'

'No family, had he, Reverend Mother?' asked Dr Scher. 'Except for that elderly prior, his brother, poor man.'

'None, except for the prior,' said the Reverend Mother. And then there was a silence. She seemed, thought Patrick, to be thinking hard and when she spoke, it was with her usual decisiveness.

'I would say, Patrick, that both murders were committed by the same hand. A murder breeds fear, and fear, in its turn, breeds more murders.'

THIRTEEN

St Thomas Aquinas:
'Scimus quod aedificati parietes non prius
tignorum pondus accipiunt, nisi a novitatis
suae humore siccentur; ne si ante pondera quam
solidentur, accipian.'
(We know that, while walls are still new and damp,
they cannot bear weight; and if a weight be placed
upon them before they be dry, the whole building will
fall to the ground.)

From four to five in the afternoon, when the children had gone home, was always a quiet time at the convent. The Reverend Mother was conscious that she was very tired. Dominic's funeral had been sad. A pointless death, she had thought. She found anger welling up in her and tried to suppress it. Recently she had found that anxiety or emotion seemed to cause breathlessness. I must take care of myself, she thought, but knew that she would have no rest until she worked out why the gentle priest had been slaughtered. For once, the midsummer weather was kind and the Reverend Mother took herself out into the garden and admired the rows of vegetables, which, by her orders, were gradually replacing the sterile ornamental clumps of Pampas grass and the odd, starkly-solitary rhododendron.

'Vegetables takes lots of work,' warned her gardener.

'Well, you will have saved all that time that used to be spent mowing grass and pruning bushes,' said the Reverend Mother crisply. She wasn't going to have any criticism of her lovely vegetables. Rows and rows of dark green potato leaves, runner beans shooting up higher every day, feathery carrot foliage; whenever the Reverend Mother felt depressed, she came out and looked at them and diverted her mind by planning. By the autumn, they might be able to offer a midday meal to the children. She gave herself a little treat by imagining their delight at the sight of a heaped plate.

There was a snail-infested summerhouse at the bottom of the garden, near to the river and she eyed it with sudden interest. It had been donated about two years ago by the heart-broken father of a new recruit. He imagined, no doubt, his pious daughter sitting there with her rosary beads. The reality of teaching ABC to slum children, however, proved too much for the carefully nurtured girl and she had left the convent after the first six months. The Reverend Mother had thought of mentioning the summerhouse at the time, but then refrained. It might be useful one day.

'Hens!' she said aloud and then turned away as she saw a few heads of nuns who were enjoying the sunshine turn towards her. She walked briskly towards the summerhouse. Yes, it was ideal. And a sawmill not far away! She was sure that she could get them to donate a cartload of sawdust from time to time to cover the concrete base and with a bit of luck they might even donate a few planks to make perches. She was a little vague about the needs of hens, but very sure of their benefits. They surely would not cost much to keep. Hens could eat the slugs and snails that infested this damp land around the river. They would also consume waste from the kitchen and in return, they would produce eggs that could be made into nourishing dishes for the children.

Feeling cheered up by this idea, the Reverend Mother went indoors to find Sister Mary Immaculate.

'Oblige me by chaperoning me on a walk,' she said briskly. The woman had been complaining of a headache and would be the better for a little fresh air and exercise, but only sighed heavily at any suggestion that she should go out-of-doors. However, there was a rule somewhere or other among the tons of paper that she had inherited, that stated sisters should always be accompanied by another when walking through the town. In order to avoid giving scandal, she seemed to remember. She, personally, never took much notice of that rule, but Sister Mary Immaculate would find it important. It worked, anyway, as the nun rose obediently at the words. She didn't look well, despite Dr Scher's tonic, thought the Reverend Mother. But

then she had looked like that since the day when Father
Dominic was found dead in the confessional stall. And the
news of the murder of Peter Doyle had brought on another fit
of hysteria, causing her to sob in the middle of the evening
meal and to declare that no one was safe these days.

What was the connection between the murders? The Reverend
Mother thought about the matter while making routine enquiries
about her deputy's state of health. After all, it may have been
a coincidence. Peter Doyle, a business man from England, a
man with a certain mystery about him; his murder was more
understandable than the killing of a saintly priest inside a
confessional stall. And the copycat nature of the murder, the
use of a hairpin, the note supposedly from the Republicans,
these could have just been an effort to establish a connection,
where, in fact, there was none. Someone may have wanted to
get rid of Peter Doyle; may have seized upon the murder of
Father Dominic as an ideal smokescreen. Somehow, she didn't
think so. And then, with a qualm of conscience, she turned her
full attention to Sister Mary Immaculate.

'Just look at the size of that runner bean. It's a good six
inches higher than it was yesterday,' she said enthusiastically
to her unresponsive companion.

Sister Mary Immaculate stared dully at the base of the runner
bean and sighed heavily. The Reverend Mother controlled the
exasperated words that rose to her mind and persevered. The
woman did not look well, she told herself firmly.

'I must bring Jimmy out here and tell him the story of *Jack
and the Beanstalk*,' she said. 'I wonder whether if I wrote out
the story a sentence at a time and got him to repeat the sentence
back to me that he might get the notion that reading is fun.'
She was talking for the sake of talking, but to her surprise,
Sister Mary Immaculate turned an animated, if annoyed face
towards her.

'That child is a liar, Reverend Mother,' she said vehemently.
'I don't think that you should encourage him to believe in
fairy stories. He makes up enough of them himself. I had to
be very cross with him when I overheard him the other day
in the playground. He was telling a very tall story about his
cousins to some of the little children. He had them all sitting

on the ground, pretending to be a teacher, if you please, and he was telling them some ridiculous tale.'

'Jimmy telling stories to the infant class, well, I would never have thought of that. Are you sure it was Jimmy?' queried the Reverend Mother. Sister Mary Immaculate sounded more like her old self. It was good to see her emerging from the terrible apathy. She would try to keep the conversation going. Nothing better elicited a flow of words from her second-in-command than a hint of disbelief.

'I assure you, Reverend Mother. He was telling the little ones that his cousins owned an underground palace on Morrison's Island and that it was full of furniture and of gold and silver.'

'Really!' The Reverend Mother was impressed. Perhaps she was doing the wrong thing trying to teach the poor child this wretched alphabet where so many letters had so many difficult possibilities and where combinations of letters laid enormous traps for novice readers. Perhaps he might learn to read from a storybook, as she believed she herself had done. As they walked out onto the street, she began to plan enthusiastically. Perhaps Eileen might help her to get a few simple sentences printed so that Jimmy could feel that he was reading a real book. Surely, she could find some money to pay for this. An underground palace sounded a wonderful idea. Could Jimmy draw pictures, she wondered. She would have to see.

'Let's walk over to Morrison's Island,' she suggested when they had got as far as the quays. The tide was in and the river full, sparkling in the unusual sunshine and not smelling as badly as usual. Nevertheless, it was a nice day for a walk by the river with a blue sky and white seagulls swooping and diving. She had planned to call into the friary to enquire after Prior Lawrence, but she thought that she would wait and see how Sister Mary Immaculate reacted to this suggestion. Perhaps she could park the woman in the antiques shop and slip away for a quarter of an hour. In any case, it would make a nice walk and she would plan ideas for Jimmy's storybook. To her relief there was just a weary sigh from her companion at her suggestion so she walked a little more quickly and set a good pace along the quays. Cork was looking its best, today, she thought.

'It seems amazing, doesn't it, that about a hundred and fifty years ago, most of our city was a marsh,' she said chattily. 'Can you imagine Patrick Street, the Grand Parade and the South Mall were river channels and between them was nothing but Dunscombe's Marsh and the Reap Marsh. And, of course, Morrison's Island, where we are going now, that was a marsh, too, used to be called Dunbar's Marsh, I remember my father telling me that and how they had to rebuild the Holy Trinity Church because of the unstable ground.'

There was no reply from her companion. Had heard it all before, thought the Reverend Mother. She knew, rather guiltily, that she tended to mention these facts rather frequently. The thought of Cork as a sort of Venice in a northern climate had always fascinated her, but that was not to say that people always enjoyed hearing her talk about it. In any case, Sister Mary Immaculate was not from Cork city, but from somewhere near to Limerick. She was patently not interested. Still, it had got them down to the 'flat of the city', as Cork people said, and now they could cross over Parliament Bridge and then just wander down along Charlotte Quay. And, after all, if she kept talking, Sister Mary Immaculate could not in all politeness keep sighing heavily. She searched through her memory for more reminiscences about the building of the modern city of Cork, of the enterprising merchants who had financed the draining of marshes, the building of quays and the roofing over of river channels. Perhaps it would be tactful to leave out the history of the Holy Trinity Church, in view of the memory that might be evoked in the woman at her side.

And then to her relief she spotted the barrister, Tom Gamble, on a ladder propped up against a lamppost. 'What is Mr Gamble doing on that ladder?' she asked chattily. 'Your eyes are better than mine are, sister. Can you see what he's doing?'

'He's putting up a poster,' said Sister Mary Immaculate. Her voice sounded a little better, a shade of animation had crept into it. 'I suppose, yes, that's right, they're cancelling the performances of *The Mikado*. I suppose they would have to, as that man is dead; he was the principal character, wasn't he?' She was beginning to sound like her old self, and the Reverend Mother felt relieved. 'Hysteria; that's the cause of all those headaches,' Dr Scher had said. 'She'll get over it. Don't encourage her to talk about it. Just ignore her. Give her plenty to do. Don't let her think that she is important. That will only encourage her.' Now the good sister was looking very disapproving, staring crossly at Tom Gamble in shirt-sleeves and an old pair of paint-stained trousers. 'You would think that a barrister wouldn't show himself up like that. Why didn't he get a man to do it for him?' she said crossly.

'Let's go and ask him.' The Reverend Mother did not wait for a reply but went rapidly across the road and stood beside the ladder.

'You should always have someone to hold a ladder for you, Mr Gamble,' she said severely. 'That's very dangerous. What if it slipped?'

A handsome young man, she thought, as he came rapidly down and shook hands. 'You're quite right, Reverend Mother,' he said. 'I had Jonathon Power, but he went back for some more posters. And how are you on this lovely day? And sister, too? You're having a walk, are you?'

His manners were very good, and so they should be. His father had sent him to one of the most expensive schools in Ireland. It was interesting, she thought, that he had been sent to Clongowes Wood College, a Roman Catholic school run by the Jesuits, but that he had taken his mother's religion and turned Protestant when he reached the age of twenty-one. She wondered whether the judge minded. Probably not, she thought. The Gambles were one of the commercial families of Cork, one of the merchant princes, as they liked to call themselves. Money would matter more than anything else would. Judge Gamble, she thought, was not a particularly religious man.

Aloud, she said, 'I'm very sorry to hear of the death of your friend Mr Doyle.'

'Terrible. Dreadful, the things that happen. Poor Peter. As if he had anything to do with the death of Father Dominic.'

'I was telling Sister Mary Immaculate about the history of Cork,' said the Reverend Mother, anxious lest the mention of the deaths might occasion an outburst of tears from her companion.

'Your family reclaimed the marsh here, didn't they, Mr Gamble?' she went on hurriedly.

And while he was telling Sister Mary Immaculate the old story about Henry Gamble who had owned the marsh, reclaimed it, built warehouses, and who supplied preserved provisions to the Peary Polar Expedition in 1824, she pondered on him. It was a familiar pattern. One generation made the money, educated the second generation – in the Gambles' case, Henry Gamble's son had risen through the ranks of clerk to become a solicitor, and his well-educated son had qualified first as a solicitor and then a barrister to become a judge – and the third generation spent it. Tom, by all accounts, was certainly doing his best to spend as fast as he could. *Rags to riches and back to rags in three generations,* her father used to say, she remembered, as Tom Gamble was giving a lively account of the shipwreck and the finding of the provisions in quite a miraculous state of preservation, eight years later. At that time, the Gambles had owned the whole of Morrison's Island, but now only the judge's house was left to the family.

'It was your family who sold the land to the Capuchins to build the Holy Trinity Church, wasn't it, Mr Gamble?' she enquired. By some miracle, Sister Mary Immaculate was looking quite interested, probably thinking of making a lesson of it for the girls, she thought.

'That's right,' he confirmed with a quick look at the beautiful Gothic limestone building across the road from where they stood.

'I seem to remember,' said the Reverend Mother, 'that my father told me that the building had to be abandoned at an early stage. Wasn't there some story that the foundations slipped?'

He stared at her. There was a certain frozen look on his face. It interested her immensely. 'No, I never heard that,' he said shortly. 'Now, if you'll excuse me, Reverend Mother, and sister, I really must go and see what has happened to Jonathon.' He wore no hat that he could doff, but he waved a hand airily and was off, walking across the road and down Queen Street. The long strides took him from their sight very rapidly.

'Well,' said Sister Mary Immaculate, in affronted tones, 'I don't think much of that young man's manners. He could have listened to you. You have so many interesting memories of the past, Reverend Mother. He could have learned from you.'

'He's probably busy,' said the Reverend Mother in abstracted tones. It was very odd, almost impossible, she thought, that Tom Gamble would not know how the marshy ground had caused the first foundations of the Holy Trinity Church to slip in 1832, and how the church was abandoned for almost twenty years and then rebuilt, adding new foundations on top of the old. Surely, Judge Gamble would have known the story from his own father and would have passed it on to his son. And if Tom had not known it, she would have thought that he would have been interested. He knew all the history of the polar expedition and of the wonderfully preserved provisions, so he was interested in family history. And yet the young man had looked at her almost with dislike, no, more like a mixture of fear and dislike, when she had talked about the rebuilding of the church.

'Let's go for a walk around,' she suggested and Sister Mary Immaculate trailed behind her as she walked briskly down the street past the friary. An odd place, Morrison's Island, she thought. A mixture of poverty-stricken lanes, derelict buildings, and expensive three and four-storey houses near to the South Mall, most of them owned by members of the legal profession, or by doctors. And then, near to the river, warehouse after warehouse. Many of those warehouses did not look in good condition. Of course, it would have been a tempting situation for warehouses as the Lee was very deep at that point and quite big ships were able to moor on Charlotte Quay. But the marsh had been the victor in many cases; the water had crept back oozing up and around foundations. Some of the warehouses still stood, a few were still used. Quite close to the river were some that had been repaired, but most were abandoned. The majority looked downright dangerous, with sagging walls and broken roofs. Some were slanted and leaning sideways. The foundations had slid, just as had happened to the original Trinity Church, she thought, looking thoughtfully at one where a front door still stood in its original framework, but at a very odd angle. The wall above it had crumbled and the sky was visible through the large gap. She would have to have a word with Jimmy about not going into those buildings. Like most of the children in her school, he was street-wise, but children could not be expected to understand that buildings, so very high above their heads, might be dangerous. Their vision tended to be at the level of their eyes.

Sister Mary Immaculate was now talking in an animated way about the dangers of keeping preserved food too long, so she listened with half her mind, while the other half thought about the first building of the Trinity Church. She wished that Dr Scher were her companion. He was a man who seemed to have garnered lots of odd pieces of information during his lifetime and she would have liked to discuss what had possibly gone wrong with the church foundations and perhaps more importantly to her now, how the matter had been remedied.

'Let's go and have a look at the antiques shop,' she interrupted the flow and headed Sister Mary Immaculate in the opposite direction. The antiques shop was not too far from Judge Gamble's house. Perhaps it had been owned by that family and when Tom became friendly with Peter Doyle and with Jonathon Power, he might have suggested that the two Englishmen could set up shop in one of their empty warehouses. Odd, though, she thought. Why did they come to Cork, of all places, from England?

To her pleasure, the antiques shop was open despite the death of its owner. Jonathon was now at the counter, but both Robert Beamish, the Olympic oarsman, and Miss Marjorie Gamble were helping. And their presence was needed. There seemed to be a large amount of people, attracted by the article in the *Cork Examiner* about the most recent death on Morrison's Island, probably, but busily looking at the various wares. Tom Gamble was there, also, pouring out glasses of sherry and handing them around. He came across to her immediately.

'Terrible, isn't it, to be open today, after the death of poor old Peter,' he said with an attractive smile. 'Jonathon shut the place for the morning, but then so many turned up to pay their respects, knocking on the door, popping in cards and envelopes. So he thought it was easier just to open the shop and allow people in today. So many seemed to want to do something, seemed to want to talk about poor old Peter, and it's one in the eye for those wretched Shinners, isn't it?'

'We couldn't tempt you to a glass of sherry, Reverend Mother, could we?' Marjorie Gamble had come to join him. Marjorie was, of course, an acquaintance. They had sat together at an educational conference and the Reverend Mother had found her intelligent and full of ideas. She smiled and shook her head, but was glad to see the woman. It would seem quite natural to gossip a little with her. Something about this set-up puzzled her.

'Your school is on holidays, of course, isn't it?' she asked. These private schools, she knew, had long holidays.

'That's right,' said Marjorie. 'We broke up a few weeks ago. I live with my father during the school holidays. Tom and I came around to see how Jonathon was managing on his own.'

'So they were partners, Mr Power and Mr Doyle,' she said. 'I had thought that Peter Doyle was the owner.'

'Yes, they were partners,' said Marjorie. 'They came over from England, together. We all became friendly with them because of the singing. Tom and I used to sing at concerts to raise money for the victims of this dreadful burning down of houses, raise money to send them off to England with a few comforts, that sort of thing. Peter came up to us after one concert and he had this idea about putting on shows of the Gilbert and Sullivan operas to raise money for worthy causes. We got Robert Beamish, the oarsman, you know, we got him to join, too. He was a friend of Tom's and he has a great voice. And I got the music teacher from my school, Anne Morgan, and the older girls became the chorus. It was much more fun for them than just singing. We had a great time. I suppose all that will be finished now. It's a shame. We've had such fun. I still can't believe that poor Peter is dead. He was always the life and soul of everything. He put so much into these Gilbert and Sullivan operas. We all loved doing them and they were a great success.'

'So I understand,' said the Reverend Mother. 'Does it have to finish?'

'Well, Jonathon is thinking of going back to England.

This might be in the nature of a closing down sale,' explained Marjorie.

So, since Jonathon was a partner, he presumably would inherit all the profit; that was interesting! What he did not sell to customers, he would probably dispose of easily to other shops and dealers. There might not be too much left, though. The amount realized by the sale today could be huge. The Reverend Mother eyed the eager crowds. There was now quite a queue in front of Jonathon and everyone was clutching some antiques. A man and his son had even carried over a small Queen Anne desk and were standing holding it, as if loathe even to put it down for a minute.

'I was telling Sister Mary Immaculate that most of Morrison's Island belonged to your family at one stage.' The Reverend Mother wished that her assistant would look a little more interested. Perhaps a sherry might cheer her up, she thought fleetingly before regretfully rejecting the idea. 'Tell me, Miss Gamble, did this building belong to your father?'

'Well, yes, I think it did at one stage. It was quite a small warehouse, I think.' She cast a glance around at the joking young men and there was an understandable look of regret in her eyes. She would miss the companionship and the fun, thought the Reverend Mother. She was not too old, would be about thirty, she thought, delving into the past. Her father, the judge was a baby when she entered the convent. She remembered hearing of his wedding with a shock of surprise. Marjorie was his elder child. Probably too old now to think of getting married, but not old enough to give up readily some amusements out of school.

'You couldn't keep the Merrymen going, could you?' she asked.

Marjorie Gamble looked regretful. 'I wouldn't think so,' she said. 'Now that Jonathon is talking of going back to England and that would be the two best voices in the company gone, and, in any case, the whole thing seemed to depend on Peter. He is, was, a great organizer . . .' She stopped, and shook her head sadly.

There was a lot to be said for the Catholic habit of breathing a prayer for the repose of the departed soul, thought the

Reverend Mother. It got the relations and friends of the deceased person through one of those awkward silences.

'He was the one that began the society, was he?' she said and Mary's face brightened.

'That's right. He and Jonathon came over from England, looking around them to see what they could do and they saw this old warehouse. I think Tom was involved somehow in the legal formalities and he got friendly with them and one night, in a bar, Peter started singing "Hark the hour of ten is sounding," from that Gilbert and Sullivan operetta, *Trial by Jury* and the other two joined in. Peter had a lovely tenor voice and Jonathon a baritone, and Tom, my brother, is a bass. And so the barman said to them, "You gentlemen should put on a show!" and that night they discussed forming a society, a society to put on the Gilbert and Sullivan operas – that's where they got the name, Merrymen from *The Yeomen of the Guard*, you know.'

'And you joined in, did you?' The Reverend Mother was puzzled about Tom Gamble being involved in legal formalities for the transfer of property. After all, the man was a barrister, not a solicitor. And she thought that Marjorie had skipped the intriguing part of the story. Cork, poverty-stricken and almost without industry or employment, haemorrhaged its own citizens to the cities of England. What had brought those two personable young men to journey in the opposite direction? Still, perhaps Marjorie Gamble, born into a wealthy family and used to a prosperous way of life, would not find anything strange in that whim or decision.

'That's right. They persuaded me into it. Tom and I used sing at parties and at a few concerts, as I was telling you. And Robert Beamish, too. He's one of our set. But, of course, it's very different singing at parties to getting up on the stage in front of God knows who and in the beginning I was quite worried about the parents in the school. Well, you know what it is like with parents, always ready to criticize, Reverend Mother?' said Marjorie Gamble as one headmistress to another.

'Indeed,' said the Reverend Mother and tucked her hands into her sleeves. There were, she thought, compensations and drawbacks in every job. The parents of the children in her

school had many shortcomings. They might neglect their
children; allow them to wander the streets at night, exposing
them to unspeakable dangers. They might arrive in the middle
of the school morning, drunk and maudlin, and insist on seeing
the Reverend Mother. They might keep her awake at night
with unsolvable problems to do with missing or brutal
husbands, unwanted pregnancies, lack of money to pay the
rent or to buy food for their children. And, of course, the
perennial problem: how to get rid of the rats. They mostly had
a touching belief in the Reverend Mother's ability to solve the
rat question.

But, she reflected, to give them their due, she had never
known any who thought it was any business of theirs to enquire
into what she did in her spare time. She turned an interested
face towards Marjorie Gamble, child of a wealthy father and
an even wealthier mother, endowed, apparently, at the age of
twenty-five, with a large fortune from her maternal grandmother, money that covered the purchase of a girls' boarding
school, and reputedly left her a wealthy woman in her own
right. The Gambles had the reputation of being great business
people. There was a saying in Cork that if a Gamble put a
sovereign under the sod in a potato row one day, there would
be a hundred pounds of sterling ready to be dug up in a few
weeks' time.

'So, you see I got the girls involved . . .' Marjorie was still
telling the story of the establishment of the Gilbert and Sullivan
group. 'We had always entered them for singing competitions,
elocution, that sort of thing, so good for their poise and the
parents were delighted to see them on the stage, just in a
group, of course, just the chorus, and their music teacher, Miss
Morgan, who has a nice soprano, she was keen to join in also.'

'And Mr O'Reilly from the Savings Bank, and his wife,
also.' James O'Reilly, she thought, was the odd one out. The
others were all Protestants. Why had he been invited?

'That's right. The two of them. Rose has a lovely soprano.'
Marjorie smiled across at the pretty dark-haired girl who had
emerged from behind a set of glass shelves with a silver coffee
pot in her hand. 'I've been singing your praises to the Reverend
Mother, Rose,' she said and Rose came across immediately.

She had, thought the Reverend Mother, a slightly anxious expression. Undoubtedly she had overheard the question about her husband. A pretty girl with a gentle, sweet expression. Very different from the sensible sharp intelligence of Miss Gamble.

'I'm looking for a matching sugar bowl for Dr Scher, Marjorie,' she said and the Reverend Mother craned her head to see the familiar rotund figure bending over a tableful of silver tastefully arranged on a green baize cloth.

'Good to see you, Dr Scher,' she said as he approached in answer to her wave. 'I've taken your patient for a little walk. Sister Mary Immaculate has been overworking and she has been suffering from bad headaches,' she explained to Marjorie Gamble. 'I shouldn't have taken her out, but I needed an escort. Our rule, you know . . .' she tailed off. She had been talking fast so that Sister Mary Immaculate would refrain from mentioning Eileen and her visits to the convent.

'I do feel rather weak and giddy,' said Sister Mary Immaculate, groping behind her for a chair and then feebly sinking into it. 'I must say that I will be glad to be back in the convent again. There's a glare from that sun and it has given me a headache. Perhaps Dr Scher . . .'

'I can go and fetch my car, if you wish, Reverend Mother,' said Dr Scher rising nobly to the occasion. He put down the coffee pot that he had been examining. There was an air of mild regret on his chubby face and the Reverend Mother felt rather sorry for him. And annoyed with herself. She should have guessed that Sister Mary Immaculate would have made a great fuss. At least the danger moment about Eileen visiting the convent regularly had passed. Sister Mary Immaculate now was completely focussed upon herself, dropping her head onto her hand and sighing gently.

'Why don't I make you a nice cup of tea, sister; you do look very pale. She would be better off sitting quietly in the back office for five minutes, Reverend Mother, wouldn't she? What do you think?' Rose came to the rescue and Marjorie Gamble beamed approval at her. No doubt she felt that it would be a shame for Jonathon if Dr Scher didn't buy the coffee pot that he was handling so lovingly.

'Great idea,' said Robert Beamish heartily. 'Take my arm, sister. Lean on me as much as you like. I'm a strong fellow, you know.'

'He swims down to the outside of Cork harbour every morning before breakfast,' said Marjorie 'Don't you, Bobby? And then climbs a few mountains before he has his dinner.' She got on well with all of those young men, thought the Reverend Mother, noting the affectionate use of a nickname, unusual between young men and women unless there was a close relationship. Perhaps she treated her younger brother's friends like that, took on a motherly role with them. Eileen had said something about that. The Reverend Mother found herself feeling rather sorry for Marjorie Gamble. She wondered whether her money brought much satisfaction. Still, the fees of Rochelle School were high and its reputation had grown. Someone, probably her cousin Lucy, had told her that girls came there from all over the country. Its headmistress would be a well-to-do woman if the school continued to prosper. Nevertheless, it may not have been the life that Marjorie Gamble had envisaged for herself when she was twenty-one years old. Not pretty, of course, that goitre had left its traces, and she was thin, with no figure to speak of, a wide mouth and heavy chin, but very intelligent, if slightly protruding eyes. And the Gamble family's dark hair, cut fashionably short, suited her face. The brother was more regularly featured; far better looking than his sister. He took after his mother; she thought, remembering Lucy's account of the society wedding of the present Judge Gamble and his rich and beautiful Protestant bride.

'That's it, sister, you lean on me.' Robert Beamish was holding out an arm. He was in his shirtsleeves and his musculature was impressive. Sister Mary Immaculate started back, staring in horror at the very idea of touching a man's bare arm.

'She'll be all right with me, Robert,' said Rose quietly, taking the nun's forearm in a firm, professional grip. 'Don't worry, Sister, you'll feel much better once you are sitting down. Just mind the step there, that's right. We have a lovely comfortable armchair over here and you can have a good rest. I'll make you a nice cup of tea and then you'll feel better.'

'You're very good,' whispered Sister Mary Immaculate. She leaned heavily on the slight figure supporting her and tottered off towards the back of the shop.

'Good, good,' said Dr Scher. 'Nothing like a nice cup of tea. Better than all the medicine in the world.' He had a relieved look on his face as he wandered back to a well-furnished table displaying the silver pots.

'I'll tell you what, Reverend Mother,' said Marjorie Gamble with a look at Dr Scher. 'I have to go out on an errand in about five minutes. I'll take the sister in my car and drop her off at the convent. Would that be a help? Or would you like to come with us also?'

'That's very good of you,' said the Reverend Mother. 'I must confess that I was looking forward to a walk. I get very few opportunities. So, if you don't mind, I'll entrust Sister Mary Immaculate to your care and walk back with Dr Scher.' And then she said impulsively, 'How wonderful to have a car!'

'My father was a little shocked, but I was determined. When Tom and I were on a holiday in London we saw lots of women driving and that did it! I gave myself a birthday present of a new car.' There was a certain bleakness about her smile and the Reverend Mother felt rather sorry for her. It would have been her thirtieth birthday and perhaps on that landmark she had given up all hope of being married.

'Well, I do envy you, Miss Gamble,' she said. 'I've often thought how wonderful it would be to have a car. Did your brother teach you to drive?' She looked across to where Tom Gamble was busy showing a woman the secret drawer on the desk that Jonathon Power had been polishing on the last occasion when she had visited the shop. So virtually all of the musical society were here. What very faithful friends, she thought. The Merrymen group must have very strong links. Everyone had rallied around to help Jonathon.

'Certainly not,' said Marjorie Gamble crisply. 'Have you ever seen my brother drive, Reverend Mother? I wouldn't advise you to accept a lift in his car. No, I hired a professional chauffeur for a week in order to teach me to drive properly. I had promised one of my aunts a little holiday so we drove along the west coast, staying at hotels and by the end of the holiday I knew everything about driving, double-declutching, what to do to the engine when it won't start. I've even taught Rose O'Reilly. I'm an expert, now.'

'What a wonderful thing for you,' said the Reverend Mother sedately. 'But now I must leave you to get on. I can see that you are very busy. I'll go and join Dr Scher and allow him to tell me all about Cork silver.'

'I can't make up my mind between the coffee pot and the tea pot,' said Dr Scher when she arrived at his side. Jonathon Power, she noticed, appeared to be busy, polishing a butter dish on an adjoining shelf, but he had an eye on this potential customer. 'Look at them, Reverend Mother. Both a gorgeous shape. Which should I have, what do you think?'

'The teapot,' she said promptly. 'You don't drink coffee.'

'As if I would pollute either of them! They're not for common use. They are to be admired. You're being no help, Reverend Mother.'

'I'd be inclined to take the one that you feel you cannot live without,' suggested Jonathon Power with a pleasant smile. He was a nicer man than his late partner was, thought the Reverend Mother. Peter Doyle would have tried to push the doctor toward the more expensive purchase. Or was Jonathon a partner? There seemed to be varying views on that. She had heard from Lucy that Peter Doyle had been the sole owner.

'The coffee pot.' Dr Scher had closed his eyes and now suddenly he opened them very widely. He had a smile on his face. 'I can just see the spot on the shelf of my little roomful of silver,' he said. 'You're right. I tried them both in my mind's eye. And the coffee pot is the one that I can't live without.'

'You'll have to give him a good discount on that, Jonathon. He's a fellow enthusiast.' Marjorie was smiling with amusement as Dr Scher fondly scrutinized the hallmark with a medical eyeglass.

'I'll give you two pounds off it, Dr Scher,' said Jonathon. 'How about that?'

'Great,' said Dr Scher absent-mindedly. He seemed hesitant to allow the coffee pot from his hands, but once Jonathon had begun to wrap it, he went briskly back to the table.

'Two pounds,' he said. 'I have two pounds to spend. Let's have a look at those spoons, Reverend Mother. What would you advise?'

'Perhaps get the coffee pot on its place on your shelf and then see what else you require,' she suggested. Dr Scher would end up buying the whole shop if someone did not drag him out. In any case, she wanted time to talk to him. 'I'll walk back with you and admire it on your shelf, if you like.'

'No sign of your intriguing potato rings, or of the cake server with the lift mechanism, either,' he said as they walked across Parliament Bridge. 'Nor, as far as I could tell, any of the other things you mentioned. I looked carefully for the Beleek china, but they have none of that. Oddly enough, and I only just noticed this – they have no china. And that bears out your suspicions. Much easier to shove silver in a bag than to take delicate china without breaking or cracking it, don't you think. But I'm absolutely certain that they don't have that silver you saw.'

'Perhaps they have a hidden storeroom,' she said. 'It would, after all, be dangerous to display items that had been recently stolen. Memories could be jogged. It seems very likely to me that there is a store room. And that would solve the problem of how Peter Doyle left the premises on the night when he was killed.'

'Pity not to have found it,' he said. 'I'd like to have seen those potato rings. Anyway, I've got a great bargain!'

'Was it cheap, your coffee pot?' she asked then. It had looked to be an immense sum when he had written out the cheque. Imagine spending so much money on a coffee pot that you would not even use. Still that was Dr Scher's affair. She was interested, though, to think upon the enormous profit from the selling of antiques.

'Very!' Dr Scher had a small smile of triumph on his face. 'I'd never get it for that price anywhere else. Did you see how I bargained with him? And then he handed me back two pounds. Unbelievable! Of course, you have to know how to barter with these fellows. I've got that ability in my bones.'

'Yes, indeed,' she said indulgently. She did not like to say that her observation of the excited faces on the crowd of people there led her to believe that everything was going very cheaply indeed. Why? If Jonathon Power was the owner now, why was he leaving Cork? Why not stay and carry on with such a profitable business? Had it perhaps become too dangerous? Was there a fear that outsiders had cracked the secret of Morrison's Island Antiques?

'Should I go and have a word with Patrick about the price of antique silver?' he asked and she shook her head.

'No, you go home and admire your new coffee pot,' she said. Patrick, she thought, had more important matters on his plate just now.

FOURTEEN

W.B. Yeats:
'But who can talk of give and take,
What should be and what not,
While those dead men are loitering there,
To stir the boiling pot?'

'The hands on the body were quite warm, almost hot, when we found it, Reverend Mother,' said Eileen. She tossed her wet hair out of her eyes. The day that had promised so well had now ended in yet another downpour. 'And that means that the man was only just dead. Eamonn told me that. He remembers learning that at university. The hands and the feet are the first parts of a dead body to cool.'

'I hope that he keeps up his studies. I'm sure that he will make a fine doctor,' said the Reverend Mother absent-mindedly. She was staring straight ahead of her, staring at the confessional stall at the back of the little convent chapel.

'But, you see, that means that that it wasn't any one of the Merrymen, Reverend Mother,' said Eileen earnestly. 'We don't think that it could be. We looked through the window and they were all there: Jonathon, James and his wife, Rose, Robert Beamish, Anne Morgan, Tom Gamble and Miss Gamble. None of them could have passed us on the street.'

'Dressed in their costumes?' asked the Reverend Mother.

'No, we leave those in the Father Matthew Hall. No, they were all in dinner jackets and black tie, the men, anyway. Miss Gamble had her usual black dress with the choker of pearls around her neck that she always wears, and Rose had a low-cut pink dress with straps over the shoulders. And Anne Morgan was wearing her blue dress with a string of white beads, knotted in the middle of the chest and hanging down to her waist, you know that's the style these days, Reverend Mother. I saw each of them quite distinctly. I counted them one by one. I did notice that Peter Doyle wasn't there, but I thought that he had probably gone for more wine or something. And after we found the body, Eamonn checked again. We could hear them, anyway, all the time that we were there, we could hear them laughing and shouting remarks and they started singing, "My brain teams with endless schemes". I could definitely hear Jonathon's voice. He's got a lovely baritone.'

'How far away was the body from the shop?' asked the Reverend Mother.

Eileen thought about that carefully. Estimating distances was an important part of Republican work and Tom Hurley had made them practise this again and again in the fields of Ballinhassig when they had first set up the safe house there.

'About hundred and fifty yards,' she said eventually. 'And we passed the shop before we found the body. They were all there then, and I'm pretty sure that they were all there when we went back towards the South Mall. I just glanced in as we passed. I was a bit shaken, but Eamonn went back instantly after I had crossed over to the Imperial Hotel, and he counted them. Three women and four men, he said. And that means they were all there: Jonathon, Tom Gamble, James O'Reilly, Robert Beamish, and then there was Anne and Rose O'Reilly and Miss Gamble.'

'And there was nobody around in the streets or the lanes when you were going towards the South Mall?' The Reverend Mother, thought Eileen, looked as though she were thinking of something else. Some idea had occurred to her. Still, she dare not ask so she continued to give the requested information.

'No one,' she said. 'We even looked down that little laneway; you know the one that runs along the backs of those posh houses that front onto the South Mall. There was no one around. I don't think that we could be mistaken, not the two of us.'

'No, I'm sure that you are both very alert,' said the Reverend Mother. 'And I do appreciate, Eileen, that you came to tell me this.'

'Eamonn is very upset about the card saying that it was the Republicans. He thinks that the police will just sit back now and blame it all on us.'

'So you still think of yourself as a Republican, in spite of your quarrel with Tom Hurley.' The Reverend Mother didn't sound surprised. She had a half smile on her face for a few seconds before she continued, saying very seriously, 'But, Eileen, I don't think that Inspector Cashman will take any easy route, will be content to lay blame without finding evidence. He has the reputation of being a hardworking and scrupulous policeman. And I am sure that all you could tell him about this second murder will be of help to him in solving both cases.'

'Do you think that they are connected, then, Reverend Mother?'

'What do you think, Eileen, you and Eamonn?'

'We're not sure,' said Eileen. 'We've been talking about it. But I wanted to tell you about that lot, well, some of them anyway, there is something funny about them. I saw James O'Reilly, the fellow in the bank, taking drugs. He took some white powder from something that looked like a woman's compact. And Jonathon Power knew all about it. And I think from something he said that they are paying James O'Reilly to do something for them.'

'Can you remember what he said?' asked the Reverend Mother. 'I'm sure that you can. I remember how very excellent you were at learning poetry off by heart.'

Eileen felt a little rush of pleasure. The Reverend Mother was always encouraging, but she was sparing of too much praise.

'Yes, I do. It really made an impression on me because up to then I thought that Jonathon was a very nice fellow. I liked him much better than any of the other four men.' She thought for a moment, trying to remember exactly how that English accent shaped the sound of the words. '"Just remember, James, you won't get the money to fund that expensive little habit just from your salary in the bank. You need us more than we need you. Just you remember that." He did sound very menacing when he said those words, Reverend Mother. I think that it scared James O'Reilly. Jonathon took his arm and led him back and I got the feeling that he was holding him up.'

'That's very interesting,' said the Reverend Mother and

Eileen got the impression that this was no news to the Reverend
Mother. People told her things, told her secrets, she just sat
there, with her hands tucked into her sleeves and it was a bit
like going to confession. No matter what you had to say, there
was no response, no gasps of horror, no disbelief. And then
Eileen thought about the priest. Of course, that was why the
Reverend Mother was so interested in this affair.

'I saw James O'Reilly going into the Holy Trinity Church
the day before Father Dominic was killed,' she said. 'I
remember wondering why he was going to confession on a
Wednesday. It seemed a funny thing for a bank clerk to be
going to confession on a Wednesday. It's mostly just women
on weekdays. Most people wait until Saturday so that they
have their soul clean for Sunday morning communion.'

'They have a half day from the bank on Wednesday,
don't they?' The Reverend Mother sounded rather absent-
minded, thought Eileen.

'And Tom Gamble, has a . . . well, he has a girlfriend,
although he's a married man. Eamonn has seen her. They're a
funny lot, all of them. And they seem to have money to burn.'

The Reverend Mother sat for a moment, deep in thought
and then she roused herself.

'"For the love of money is the root of all evil." That is from
the Bible, Eileen, and like a lot of things from the Bible,
though not everything, there is considerable wisdom in the
saying.'

'Yes, Reverend Mother,' said Eileen. The Reverend Mother,
she thought, looked very old and quite sad. She had got to
her feet and Eileen rose, also. She was beginning to follow
the Reverend Mother's thoughts. Perhaps between them they
would clear the Republicans of a false suspicion. And find out
who murdered these two very different men.

FIFTEEN

St Thomas Aquinas:
Ex nihil, nihil fit
(From nothing, nothing will be made.)

The Reverend Mother listened carefully to Jimmy's disjointed story and tried to sort the truth from the fantasy.

'So you and your cousins lit a fire in one of the old empty places,' she said, going back to his words of earlier.

'On a flagstone,' said Jimmy virtuously. 'I was the one to think of that. I told them not to light it near to the floor. All soft and crumbly some of that wood, you know, Reverend Mother.'

'But it spread.' Inevitable, of course with a crowd of excited small boys and all that lovely rotten wood, blazing like tinder. 'That was a bit dangerous, wasn't it?'

'I told them. They didn't take no notice of me. That's because I'm the youngest.' Jimmy's face wore a disapproving look, the look of a boy who knows fires should not be lit in derelict buildings. But, after a minute, a smile began to pucker the corners of his cheeks. 'You should have seen the flames, Reverend Mother. Jumping up. Size of giants, they were. You should have felt the heat from them!'

The Reverend Mother allowed him to talk. Experience had taught her that it would be of little use to express horror or to scold. The event was over until next year and by next year, any words of hers, uttered now, would be completely forgotten. Perhaps next year a bonfire could be organized on St Mary's Isle, close to the river. Not so much fun, of course, as the excitement of almost burning down a derelict building and experiencing the heat and colours of your very own fire. Nevertheless, she made a mental note to try to organize something less dangerous, but fun for next midsummer's night. If only there were more fathers around who were willing to pay some attention to the children they had generated. Perhaps Eileen could organize a few young men and Patrick a couple of bored policemen who could be assigned to look after public safety.

'What happened next, Jimmy?' she enquired, hoping that her face showed none of the horror that she was feeling at the thought of those small boys and a fire within a rotten building.

'Well, that's what I was telling you, Reverend Mother,' said Jimmy. 'The fire spread a bit and some of the floor slipped and the big piece of timber fell through the giant hole and there was a road down there and my cousin's dog got himself free and he just jumped. We was all screaming. We thought he'd be burned to death, but then we heard him barking so Bob, my biggest cousin, he's fourteen, he jumped up and down on one of the other floorboard and when he'd broke it, he smashed a giant big hole and he slipped down and then he shouted out that there were a million rats down there!'

'A million,' echoed the Reverend Mother in awestruck tones. Her mind was very busy.

'That's right and then Frank and Thady and Benjy went down and I followed them to keep an eye on them,' said Jimmy, righteously determined to prove his superior virtue and law-abiding principles. Originally he stayed with his older cousins every Saturday night when his mother worked in a public house on South Main Street but she had the impression that he seemed to be there most of the time, now. She suspected that he was rather in awe of these cousins of his, and that he was bolstering his ego by imagining that he was in charge.

'How far down was it? You jumped, didn't you? How far a jump was it?'

'About a million . . .' Jimmy's imagination began to falter.

'Like from that chair to the ground?' The scorn on his face was enough so she proceeded carefully. 'Like from the top of that table to the ground, bigger than that, are you sure, Jimmy?' Through long practice, she knew that her face bore a look of incredulous shock.

'About from the top of the curtain to the ground,' said Jimmy triumphantly.

'Goodness, gracious me. Oh, Jimmy!'

Knock off a few feet, and that would be about eight to ten feet, she thought. Far too much for an ordinary foundation.

'Tell me what happened next,' she said.

'We was all running after the dog and we was shouting, "Patch! Patch!" and . . .'

'What was under your feet?' asked the Reverend Mother.

'A road,' said Jimmy. 'I was telling you, Reverend Mother, it was a road.'

'Hard, like a road, are you sure, Jimmy, really sure?'

'Really and truly, Reverend Mother, cross my heart and hope to die! It was a real road.'

'And you were running, or were you crawling?'

'Running,' said Jimmy slightly impatiently. 'Running real fast.'

'Even the big boy, Bob?'

'He was in front. I was catching up with him. And the rats were all running up the walls and scrabbling around over our heads.'

If a fourteen-year-old could run, and if the rats were over all of their heads, then this underground road must have been at least six feet high.

'The fire was big,' she printed carefully. But then she crumpled up the piece of paper impatiently and flung it impatiently into the bin. No point in reducing the child's dramatic story to the level of a primer, she thought.

'It was a dark, dark night,' she wrote, reading aloud as she went. She would do justice to his story. As good as Mr Wilkie Collins, she thought, as she strove for a clear and dramatic retelling. 'And did you find the little dog, Patch, in the end?' she asked. She had read it through twice, had asked for his opinion, had meekly changed certain words at his suggestion, but had made no effort to get him to read it. Let him enjoy his story without any of the accompanying feelings of shame or inadequacy. 'And Patch,' she wrote and then looked at him enquiringly.

'You'll never guess, Reverend Mother!' He paused dramatically and then breathed. 'Patch got right as far as the river and we found him inside a boat eating a giant rat.'

'Inside a boat! A giant rat with a boat!' Memories of one
of Lucy's grandchildren clutching *The Wind in the Willows*
came to her mind. The little girl had been enchanted by the
story, but the Reverend Mother had regretfully rejected
the possibility of the children of her schools being equally
enthralled by the whimsical adventures of Mole and Rat in
their riverside boat.

Jimmy eyed her sternly. 'It wasn't the rat's boat, Reverend
Mother. It's that boat that belongs to Mr Beamish. The fellow
that goes rowing on the river. He's made hiself a little shed
for his boat, there under the quay. Got an iron ladder so that
he can climb down to it. And ropes that tie it up, ropes tied
to big iron handles into the side of the quay.'

'Mr Robert Beamish.' But she hardly waited for the reply.
So Robert Beamish housed his boat on Jimmy's underground
road. That was very interesting. Her mind went back to her
father's tales about the building of the Holy Trinity Church.
The foundations slipped and the building fell down, her father
had related the story dramatically, but she strove to remember
details of the rebuilding. Slab after slab of stone, she seemed
to recollect. They had built pillars with the slabs. After all,
the Cork builders had learned how to roof in rivers and streams
and lay roads above the water. She seemed to remember that
the Holy Trinity had been rebuilt using that same technique,
erecting a platform and building the church on top of it.

Churches were very important in Cork and the collective
memory was strong when it came to their history. Individual
buildings, such as warehouses, though; that might be a different
matter. It was hard now to picture how rapidly and excitingly
the landscape of Cork city changed during the 1700s. And,
of course, there must have been trial and error when marshes
were being drained, quays constructed, streams and water-
ways roofed over. That triangular piece of land, named
Morrison's Island, less than twenty acres in its entirety, she
thought, was valuable for the storage of goods, brought right
to the centre of Cork in the small ships of the day. Perhaps,
copying the second and successful attempt at building the Holy
Trinity Church, these later warehouses, also, were built above
the ground.

'And we found Patch, safe and well, eating a giant rat inside a boat,' she finished. So Robert Beamish must be aware of the subterranean remains of Morrison's Island's past. He lived, she remembered, close by, had lodgings above a solicitor's office on the southern side of the South Mall, in a house that fronted on the South Mall, but whose rear overlooked Morrison's Island. She took another piece of paper and she wrote rapidly, 'Patrick, you might be interested in Jimmy's story. Get him to tell you all about Mr Robert Beamish and his boat.' Quickly she summarized the child's words, added her memories about the building of Morrison's Island and then she put the page into an envelope, sealed it and printed 'Inspector Cashman' on the outside.

'I think that Inspector Cashman will be very interested in your story, Jimmy,' she said, crossing the room to stand beneath the map. 'I'd like you to tell him about everything if you agree? What do you think?'

'I know him. He came to school with my mam, but he lives in Barrack Street, with all the other peelers, now,' said Jimmy. He wore a wide smile. He was quite happy helping with the little children in Sister Philomena's class, but delivering the Reverend Mother's letters was his big excitement in life.

'Now let's see if we can find Barrack Street on the map,' she said. 'I'll give you a clue. It begins with the same letter as "boat". But,' she paused dramatically, 'I have another letter for you and it's for Miss MacSweeney. Now let's see, Jimmy, can you remember the first letter of her name?'

'"M" for Mam,' shouted Jimmy, his eyes swivelling towards the drawer where the sweets were kept.

'The bank manager is here, Reverend Mother. I told him that I didn't think that you were busy.' Sister Bernadette gave a perfunctory knock on the door and then popped her head in, looking pointedly at Jimmy. According to Sister Mary Immaculate, the sisters in general, both the lay sisters and the professed nuns, felt that a busy woman like the Reverend Mother spent far too long with Jimmy and paid him far too much attention. The boy would be better off sent back to the Brothers, Sister Mary Immaculate had said and then, having received a cold stare, had fallen back feebly on her usual 'I thought that you would like to know what was being said.'

'Thank you, sister,' said the Reverend Mother to Sister Bernadette. 'I'll ring when I'm ready for you to show him in. Now Jimmy, show me the way you will go to deliver the letter to Miss MacSweeney. Go there first. Yes, that's right, just near to Dr Scher.' She had little idea of how long it might take to print Jimmy's little story, but the sooner it was begun, the better. 'I'll find the money, whatever it takes,' she had promised Eileen recklessly, but hoped that this Republican printing press would be merciful towards her over-stretched purse.

'It's so very kind of you to call upon me, Mr Broadford. You'll have a cup of tea; I'm sure. Sister . . .' But Sister Bernadette had immediately fled to the kitchen to gather up a tasty snack. A bank manager was an important visitor. Even the most unworldly of the sisters knew that. The state of the weather, thought the Reverend Mother, would fill the gap nicely until tea arrived and so they discussed the terrible June, the torrents of rain that had fallen in the last twelve hours and the hot and sunny Junes of the past. He was new to his position, quite a young man for a responsible post, not too hidebound yet, she hoped as the tea trolley came in and he was cut the regulation chunk of cake by Sister Bernadette.

'I won't waste the time of a busy man like yourself,' she said briskly, once he had swallowed his cup of tea and praised the cake. 'The fact is, Mr Broadford, I find it hard to make ends meet, as you may have noticed from our account. The new furniture for our infants' class was expensive and our fundraising for it a little disappointing.' As a charity, it had not appealed to the merchants of Cork – they had found extravagant the idea of buying child-sized tables and chairs to replace the old-fashioned metal-bound desks where tiny children balanced on ledge-like seats with no support for legs or backs. She had stubbornly gone ahead, but now finances were restricted.

'Perhaps an overdraft,' suggested Mr Broadford. 'Would that suit your needs? We wouldn't want to keep you short with all the good work you do here in this convent.'

She felt her face relax into a smile. 'Would it be possible? I wondered whether His Lordship, the bishop would need to be . . .'

She allowed the words to trail away and looked at him enquiringly.

'No, no,' he said soothingly. 'Just a little arrangement between ourselves. Let me see, the bishop's secretary audits your accounts at the end of the financial year in April – so about another nine months. We'll have everything straight for him, by then, don't you worry, Reverend Mother. The thing is to have the account looking healthy at the end of each month. Try to pay your bills in the beginning of the month. Leave it in my hands. Bless you, Reverend Mother; big businesses do this all the time.'

'You are very kind,' said the Reverend Mother. She said this so often that it had become almost a meaningless phrase for her, but this time she meant it. It would be so wonderful to leave all financial matters in someone's safekeeping. She would be delighted to leave her accounts in his hands. She had often wished that some truly mathematical girl would decide to become a nun and she could hand over the money affairs to her. It didn't seem to happen, though. The mathematical girls seemed not to be endowed with vocations for life in a convent. She tended to get the dreamers, the lovers of sentimental poetry and the idealistic girls coming to her, full of enthusiasm for a life of prayer and of self-sacrifice. 'I am most grateful to you,' she added.

'I am very glad to be able to be of service to you,' he said and then hesitated a little. 'You were very good to my mother and she has never forgotten you. When she heard that I was to be promoted to Cork, the first thing she said was, "You must go and see Reverend Mother Aquinas. I owe everything to her teaching. Her name was Agatha Colfer, but I don't suppose that you remember her,' he added, though he looked at her hopefully.

'Of course I remember Agatha,' said the Reverend Mother after a hasty trawl through memory. Colfer was a Waterford name – quite unusual in Cork. 'Yes,' she said, 'I remember her well. A bright girl, a pleasure to teach.'

And an extremely stubborn one, she thought, looking back into the past. She almost smiled to think of the battles that she had with Agatha who was determined to leave school and to get a job in a public house, instead of staying on and attaining her Intermediate Certificate. But the Reverend Mother had won. Agatha had done very well at that examination and by some marvellous piece of luck had got a job as a junior clerk in a bank somewhere in west Waterford. It must be more than forty years ago, she thought, as she sent her love to Agatha.

'Are you enjoying your new job?' she asked politely. 'It must be a very rewarding position. You have the financial affairs of the city in your hands, and, of course, just as important, the welfare and progress of your staff.' It was a tiny hint, a tiny sprat to catch a mackerel, but he swallowed the bait.

'Yes, indeed, you've put your finger on it, Reverend Mother.' He gave a heavy sigh. 'That's the part of the job that worries me the most. I've got a great problem in my mind now and I don't quite know what to do about it. It's not anything that I can discuss with others in the bank and I don't want to go higher up, not if I can sort things out myself.'

'Perhaps you'd like to tell me; I can assure you that anything you say to me will be in strict confidence.' She was slightly amused, inwardly, on how things were turning out; but outwardly, she knew that her face would show nothing but polite interest.

'It's one of my young clerks. He's up to something. Moving money around from one account to others. I don't know what's going on with one of the accounts. A shop . . .' He hesitated for a moment, but she did not press him for the name of the shop. Let him tell his story in his own way.

'I've sent out statements, asking them to check, even telephoned the manager of the shop a couple of weeks ago, but he assured me that everything is fine. He'd hardly allow me to explain myself, just wanted to get rid of me.'

'He may be someone that doesn't like checking statements,' said the Reverend Mother soothingly. 'You good business people don't realize how intimidating all of those columns of figures can be. Perhaps if you suggest that he come to see you in your office and you can chat to him and explain everything.'

'I did that. Did it on Monday morning. Went in to his own place, had a word with him. Very plausible chap. Said that he needed to return to England. Needed ready money. Well, I couldn't say anything about that, could I? A man has a right to his money. But that's not the end of the story. The chap is dead, now.'

'We're talking about Peter Doyle, are we, Mr Broadford,' she put in. She tucked her hands into her sleeves and turned towards him with what she knew would be a blank face, ready to receive any confidence. It usually worked, that face. Suddenly she found herself thinking of the confessional. Thinking of poor Dominic turning a listening ear towards his murderer and her heart hardened. The killer had to be caught; had to be prevented from committing any further crimes.

After a moment, he nodded. 'And the account is closed. Everything drawn out of it. And it was this clerk of mine, who handled everything! When I cross-questioned him, he showed me the cheque that the man had filled out. Took the whole lot out in cash. Cleared the account completely and closed it – all in one transaction.'

'And the date on the cheque?'

'Thursday the twentieth of June.'

'The day before Father Dominic was killed.'

'I don't believe it.' He said the words bluntly. 'I just don't believe it. The trouble is that I can't prove it. If my clerk holds a cheque dated to the twentieth of June and swears blind that he received that cheque on Thursday morning, when, by chance, I was in Dublin, well, there is no way that I can challenge this. A man has a right to take out his own money.'

'But you are worried.'

'I am. I'm very worried. This young fellow looks terrible. I have a suspicion that he may be taking drugs, but he denied it when I asked him. He's spending high, too. Car, house, expensive wife. I've seen some of the jewellery that girl wears. And the company he keeps. I've seen him late at night coming out of the Imperial Hotel with Robert Beamish and Tom Gamble; well the Gambles and the Beamishes, everyone knows there is money there, but how can this fellow, on a clerk's salary, keep up with them?'

'Where did the money go?' asked the Reverend Mother.

'Well, I called at the shop to offer my condolences, and incidentally, try to find out why the account was closed. This chap Jonathon Power, he says now that he is the partner, but there was no talk of partners when the account was opened. It was just opened by Peter Doyle. He signed all the cheques, made the deposits, authorized withdrawals.'

'Everything done through the one clerk.'

'That's right. Not too unusual, that. People here in Cork seem to like to deal with the one person. Dublin is different, bigger place, bigger staff.'

'Did you ask Mr Power why he thought his partner closed the account?'

'He told me without my asking. Said that money was owed to people for goods and services. Said that he was going to close down the shop. Said they both had decided to close the shop and return to England. That's what he said and, of course, I couldn't prove him wrong, could I?'

'But no cheques were paid out to other people or businesses?'

'No, he explained that people wanted to be paid in cash. And there's another thing, too. I was worried about that account. I had a memory of noticing payments to some people and I wanted to check on them, but the papers about the account are missing. And they shouldn't be, Reverend Mother. Not in a well-run bank. They should be part of the end-of-year accounting.'

'But you remembered some of the payments from past statements, Mr Broadford.'

'Well, they seemed to be all to the same crowd of people – the crowd that this young clerk of mine hangs out with, not to this Jonathon Power. He didn't seem to have a bank account. I checked.'

'Perhaps another bank,' suggested the Reverend Mother.

'Checked that, too,' he said briefly. 'Pulled in a few favours. Mr Jonathon Power did not seem to have a bank account in Cork. On the other hand, there were so many of those cheques drawn to cash. Perhaps that was the way that he was paid; he might have wanted to escape tax. Though tax collection has been very lax in this country, but, after all, they did come from England, the pair of them, so tax might be a bit more of a worry over there. We were having a chat about that, myself and some of the other bank managers; talking confidentially, you understand, trusting each other to keep secrets.'

Interesting the financial network. The Reverend Mother hoped that the bishop's secretary, annoying man that he was, could not feed off these secrets exchanged between bank managers.

'And there is another thing, too, Reverend Mother.' Once started Mr Broadford had become quite garrulous. Perhaps his mother Agatha had given him a high opinion of the Reverend Mother on St Mary's Isle. 'I know I can trust you,' he went on, 'but this clerk, this James O'Reilly, had opened some strange bank accounts, supposedly some furniture shops or second-hand furniture shops in the county of Cork. But, you see, Reverend Mother, when I was a boy I heard a lot about Cork. My mother had told me so many stories about it. Even before I went out there to check, I didn't think that a place like Douglas would have a store selling furniture and antiques. And yet, there was the account, Douglas Furniture, small, but healthy. Lots of money going into it and regular money coming out of it, all out-going cheques paid to cash. And, you'll never guess, but every one of those accounts have now been shut down.' He stopped and looked at her and she looked back at him. This was Agatha's son, she thought. A decent man, well brought up, a man trying to do his best, scrupulous about looking after other people's money, and, at the same time, careful about his staff. Bearing the responsibility for their deeds on his shoulders. There was, she thought, only one thing that she could say.

'I think, Mr Broadford, that my advice would be that you place this affair in the hands of the police. Any loyalty that you owe to your staff, any paternal duty that you may feel towards a young clerk, has to take second place when one recollects that already two people have been killed, have been murdered, and that the strange tale that you have been telling me, has concerned, perhaps, the running of Morrison's Island

Antiques Shop. The murder of Peter Doyle, possibly, probably, has connections to the business that he owned, but also, there is a connection to the murder of Father Dominic. Forgive me if I don't tell you what it is. The matter is in police hands, and so, I would think, should be the very interesting account that you have so lucidly spelled out of the strange goings-on in your bank. Your feelings of responsibility for your staff do you great credit, Mr Broadford, but no one wants to see a third murder occur. I would unburden yourself to Inspector Cashman.'

It was a long speech and when she had delivered it, she sat back feeling drained. Perhaps a young man's career might be ruined by her advice. Nevertheless, she did not regret it. There was something very odd going on in Morrison's Island and the sooner Patrick knew about it, the better.

SIXTEEN

History of Irish Civic Guards
'*The Government enacted temporary security
legislation during the civil war which provided for trial
by military tribunal and death sentences. On the expiry
of these laws, crime and violence increased, witnesses
and judges were intimidated, and the Government
introduced new measures to improve security.*'

'**D**o you mean to tell me that letter has been sitting there for the whole of yesterday afternoon and you didn't give it to me?' Patrick could hear the note of anger in his own voice and Tommy took a step backwards.

'Well, it was just a little street boy, inspector. He came in here, bold as brass, and said that the letter was for you. But you were with the superintendent. I wasn't going to interrupt you. Not for a little fellow like that, not for one of those boyos from the slums. And then, there was a lot doing yesterday, so I just forgot to give it to you when you went back into your office.'

Patrick felt rage rise up within him and made a strong effort to control his temper. He held out the envelope, angling it to the light so that the Reverend Mother's elegant copperplate script was clearly visible. 'Look at that, Tommy. Is that hand-writing the handwriting of a little boy from the slums?' *And none of your damn business, in any case.* He suppressed the second sentence. No point in quarrelling with Tommy. The harm was done. Hopefully it was something that he could remedy.

'Yes, I noticed that afterwards,' admitted Tommy. 'I just didn't want him hanging around the office. Goodness knows what he would bring in, what he would leave behind him. Once you get fleas into a place, it's hard to get them out no matter how much Jeyes Fluid that you splash around the place.

I'll tell you that for a fact, inspector. I just told him to leave the letter on the counter and to get out.'

Patrick replaced back into its envelope the Reverend Mother's letter and Jimmy's story and abruptly left Tommy at his counter. 'Joe,' he said as he passed his sergeant's office, 'come and listen to this. Very important information which, unfortunately, was not given to me yesterday when it arrived.' He said the words as loudly as he could and was sure, by the bad-tempered banging on a typewriter, that Tommy on the desk had heard him.

'Didn't know anything about that,' said Joe, looking somewhat alarmed.

'No, of course, you didn't. It was that blockhead, Tommy,' said Patrick as soon as he had closed the door. *Didn't like to disturb you as you were in with the superintendent.* He took a firm grip on his temper. No sense in complaining.

'What do you think of the child's story?' Joe, he noticed, had finished the page and had gone back to the beginning again.

'Well, the Reverend Mother must know the boy and she wouldn't send this to you unless she was fairly sure that he wasn't telling lies,' pointed out Joe. He had been to the Model School, himself, but like most of Cork, he knew of the Reverend Mother. 'Yes, I see. That underground passage might solve a problem about the death of Peter Doyle, give a way for someone to get from the antiques shop and into the warehouse across the road, but I'm not sure that it gets us further along in the Father Dominic investigation.'

'Find the answer to one and you're well on the road to finding the answer to the other.' That's what he was telling himself, anyway. He walked restlessly up and down the room, thinking hard. 'I'll be off, then, Joe, to St Mary's Isle.' He had reached the door when he turned back. The child had been humiliated and disappointed yesterday. A memory of the past came to him and he heard the words, clearly, as though they were spoken in his ear. *Get out of this shop or you'll feel the toe of my boot.*

'Joe,' he said. 'Where's that very small cap? You know the one that fitted no one. Do you remember the lads laughing about it when the new uniforms were sent down, making jokes about the size of heads in those Jackeens up in Dublin?'

'I'll get it. It's at the back of the cupboard in the back hallway.' Joe, wearing a grin, was off without a question and Patrick nodded. Yes, there was no doubt that he had got himself a quick-witted assistant there.

'And I brought you a badge, too,' said Joe when he returned. 'No one will know. We've loads of those things. Though you'd better take it away from him when you've finished. Tell him that they have to stay at the barracks unless he's on duty.'

Patrick put the badge and the cap into his attaché case and he slipped past the superintendent's door. His news would keep until after he verified the child's story.

'Going out, inspector?' Tommy raised his eyes from the *Cork Examiner* and then when Patrick reached the door, he called after him, 'What shall I tell the superintendent?'

'Tell him that I've gone out,' said Patrick unhelpfully and allowed the door to slam behind him. The police car was standing in the yard, but he decided against it. For a moment, he had been tempted, thinking what fun it would be for a small boy, but then he reflected that a leisurely walk down Sullivan's Quay and George's Quay would elicit scraps of information that might be lost in the excitement of a drive in a motor car. In any case, the downpour had ceased. It wasn't exactly raining, just a little damp.

He had timed his arrival well. All of the children were in the wet playground, tearing around with an energy that made him feel envious. He stood for a moment at the railings, looking in, picturing himself fifteen years ago, barelegged and barefooted. He had not been amongst the poorest, either. He was an only child with a devoted mother. At least his father had not burdened her with a large family before silently disappearing to England. Nevertheless, he had always been conscious of a gnawing feeling of hunger and of the lovely, satisfying feeling when he won a sweet from the Reverend Mother for a particularly good piece of work. As she approached to open the gate for him, he resolved to stop at a shop in Parliament Street to buy some sweets before going on to Morrison's Island.

'Good morning, Reverend Mother,' he said loudly and clearly. 'The Civic Guards need a bit of help. I'd like to borrow one of your boys, a boy called Jimmy.'

'Jimmy. Yes, of course, inspector,' said the Reverend Mother as calmly as though she were well accustomed to such demands.

'Jimmy, Jimmy,' screamed a small girl, abandoning the game of hopscotch, which she was playing with a small empty tin of shoe polish. 'Jimmy, you're wanted!'

'The peelers want Jimmy!'

'What were you doing last night, Jimmy?'

'Jimmy's been on the lang!'

Jimmy came forward slowly. He had an uneasy look on his face and Patrick wondered if his announcement had been too public. Still, he could make amends.

'I need a bit of help, Jimmy, and I hear that you're the boy to help me,' he said loudly. He rested the edge of his attaché case on top of the low wall below the iron bars and snapped the latch open. The cap lay on top. He took it out and put it on Jimmy's head. The Reverend Mother, with a serious face, straightened it so that the brim was exactly centred over Jimmy's nose. Patrick shut his attaché case, took the badge from his pocket and apologetically handed it to the Reverend Mother. Gravely she pinned it to the ragged jersey and then stood back.

'I'll need my boots,' said Jimmy with a quick glance at Patrick's well-polished pair of leather boots.

'Yes, of course,' said the Reverend Mother. 'Run and get them quickly, Jimmy. Don't keep the inspector waiting.'

'I was keeping them for the winter, they're a bit too big for him, but I saw him look at your boots . . .' she said in an undertone.

'We'll keep your dinner warm for you, Jimmy,' she said when he returned and then firmly rang the bell for the end of playtime. The children came to order immediately, standing in straight lines as their teachers appeared at the door and led their classes back into the building. Jimmy watched them with a smile of satisfaction puckering at the corners of his mouth.

'Where are we going, mister?' he asked as they went down towards the quays. It was the first words that he had spoken and Patrick was abruptly jerked from his endless thoughts about the two murders. He took the small, cold hand into his own as they crossed Green Street. There was a shop there, what his mother would call a huckster shop, and he sent Jimmy in for a pennyworth of sweets. They seemed to have a fine selection of humbugs and liquorice allsorts.

'You keep them,' he said when the boy came out. 'I'm not allowed to put sweets in this jacket pocket. That's police regulations for you!'

Jimmy nodded. He did not smile nor did he volunteer any information. He looked rather nervous but once a sweet was in his mouth he relaxed.

'The woman liked my cap,' she said.

'That's good,' said Patrick awkwardly. The sharp, short questions that he normally used when cross-examining a witness, didn't seem to fit in this case. He wished now that he had asked the Reverend Mother to talk to the boy while he sat silently in the background and took notes. But no, that would not be enough. He needed to see the place for himself. He couldn't ask the Reverend Mother to scramble around in a derelict building or to jump down into underground passageways. The silence made him uneasy, though, so he began to talk to Joe about his own days at school and how the Reverend Mother saved him once from being slapped because he would not return to the classroom from the playground. 'I was counting ants,' he explained, 'and I just didn't want to stop.' And then when there was no response, he said, a little desperately, 'After that I went to the library and I read everything that I could about ants.'

'I can't read,' said Jimmy. 'Not at all, not even a word.' His face frowned as he looked down into the murky depths of the River Lee. A smell rose up from it. It always did, but Patrick noticed it even more strongly today as he fumbled for words. What did one say to a child? Commiserate? Reassure?

'Not – a – single – word,' said Jimmy with emphasis. He opened the bag of sweets, again, popped a second humbug into his mouth and sucked noisily.

'You're just the man for me, then,' said Patrick with a sudden inspiration. 'You'll be a man with good eyesight.' He hoped sincerely that he was not undermining some teacher's hard work, but the assertion had popped into his head.

'Reading ruins your eyes,' said Jimmy, moving the sweets to his cheek and getting words out with difficulty. And then, after a minute of sucking, 'Wot you after?'

Patrick thought about this for a moment. The whole matter seemed far too complex for explanation. Then a memory of a film that he had seen recently came to his rescue.

'Spies,' he said and Jimmy nodded an agreement.

'I'd be good at finding spies. I do a lot of work for the Shinners.'

'No more talking,' said Patrick, unsure of his ability to elaborate on that terse utterance and Jimmy nodded again. Once they had crossed Parliament Bridge and had turned down into Morrison's Island, he led the way, walking quickly and confidently along the rain-smeared pavements until he stopped in front of a derelict building.

'Don't make a noise,' he said with a severe glance at Patrick's heavy boots. And then, stepping across broken floorboards, he led the way towards the back of the warehouse. The smell of burned wood still hung around in the damp air.

Downright dangerous, this place, thought Patrick, making an inward note to have it roped off with a 'Danger' notice placed at the entrance. It wouldn't stop children going in there, of course. Mentally he drafted a letter to the town council. Waste of time, even if he managed to get the superintendent to sign it. There would be no money available; that would be the answer.

'This is the place,' said Jimmy in a low gruff voice.

Patrick opened his attaché case and took from it a torch. It was a gloomy day and there was very little light. The powerful beam of the torch made a golden pathway and lit up the underground passageway. Without hesitation, Jimmy jumped down. Patrick, hampered by the case and half-wishing that he was not wearing his new uniform, lowered himself carefully to the level.

'Want to see the treasure?' asked Jimmy and without waiting for an answer, he led the way confidently, going in the Parliament Street direction, Patrick reckoned. He tried to keep his bearings as Jimmy led them in and out, between piles of broken concrete walls and heaped-up slabs of stone, roughly cemented.

'That's the church up there,' whispered Jimmy. 'I could show you a way of getting into it. If you climb up the side, there, you can get into the cupboard where they keep the cleaning things. You wouldn't have to pay a penny and you needn't go to the Shawlies' place, neither. You could sit with all the toffs and no one would know that you hadn't put your sixpence in the plate.'

Patrick winced. His own mother, despite his pleas, still wore a shawl and still went to the same side chapel in St Finbar's Church where no collection was taken. The Shawlies' Place, as it was known. No wonder the Republicans were angry with the Catholic Church who were very keen on people knowing their place. Priests like Father Dominic were the exception. But that was not important now. So that was one way in getting into the Holy Trinity Church without being seen.

Jimmy, however, did not seem to find that so interesting. He had turned direction. Now he would be going towards the South Mall, thought Patrick. A rat peered out at them and then disappeared. There was a scamper of dozens of tiny feet. A wooden floor over their heads. Another warehouse. He shone the beam of the torch over their heads and saw the boards. And heard more frenzied scampering.

Rat poison, he thought, that's interesting.

And it was. Jimmy and his cousins were unlikely to have put that there. There was an empty cardboard box on the ground and Patrick turned the light upon it. 'Rough on Rats' it said and there was a picture on it of a rat lying on its back with its paws in the air.

'Don't touch it; that stuff would kill you as well as a rat,' he hissed as Jimmy, pausing to put another sweet into his mouth, bent to pick it up.

'I'm tough; I don't kill easily,' said Jimmy. 'I just thought that there might be some left. My aunt wants rat poison, but she says it's awful dear in the shops. She's asked us to try and get some for her. Look, inspector. See that turn up there. We're coming to the treasure now.'

Patrick followed the direction of the finger. More rat poison, he noticed as they rounded the corner. Some people, other than Jimmy and his cousins, were in on the secret of these underground passageways of Morrison's Island. And they didn't like rats.

And then he saw why when they rounded another substantial pier.

A floor of broad planks had been laid above the rough concrete. Tarpaulins hung from the boards over their heads, forming walls, and a ceiling and creating a room of about twenty square feet. It was Jimmy's treasure house. Some cheap trestle tables had been set up and they were loaded with gold watches, silver candlesticks, silver tea and coffee sets, teaspoons, silver boxes of all sizes and shapes, trays, women's jewellery, gold tiepins, and two small owls with amber eyes. Against one stone pier leaned a stack of oil paintings, half covered with a rough woollen blanket. There was more rat poison here and Patrick kept a sharp eye on Jimmy. He had seen enough, though. The list of valuables that the Reverend Mother had given him was in his mind. He inspected the items on the tables. The silver and cobalt potato rings, were, he thought, quite distinctive and she had described that blue very well.

Jimmy nudged him and pointed. One stone pier bore the signs of being recently plastered with a coat of well-laid, rather professional-looking cement. Bolted to it was a sturdy iron ladder, its wide steps and a handrail ensuring that there would be no falls for people carrying valuable goods down to this hidden storeroom. More of a staircase, than a ladder. And above it was a square hatch cut into the wooden ceiling. As they stood there just below it, he could hear Jonathon's voice calling some command.

'Let's go,' whispered Patrick. This was not the moment to burst dramatically upon those overhead. He would come back with a police van and a few Civic Guards, armed with truncheons. Now that he knew of the existence of this place, it should be easy to find the entrance to it. And easy to find how Peter Doyle and his assailant had left the antiques shop that night and ended up in a warehouse across the road. Patrick bent down until he was level with Jimmy's face.

'What's the quickest way out?' he asked and Jimmy nodded. Unhesitant and silent, he went towards one of the tarpaulins and slipped through it. Just as silently, Patrick followed him, squeezing past another rough pier, and emerged into a passageway. The air was better here. Jimmy was going quite fast across the rough ground strewn with stones and broken lumps of concrete. They were, Patrick thought, going slightly downhill. They rounded another corner. And then stopped before a massive pier oblong in shape, made from stone slabs, covered with concrete, but showing the stone by the squared-off shape and the actual stone in one place, near the ground where the outside layer had crumbled from damp. Again, there were signs of new work, good workmanship; the pier was covered in a smooth cement, well finished off at the corners.

And, once again, it had an iron staircase with a handrail bolted to it, and a strongly made wooden hatch above it.

Jimmy looked at Patrick with a smile that showed a missing front tooth. Without saying anything, he sprinted up the steps. The hatch was only a foot above the top step. An adult would be able to lift it from the security of the second or third highest step and then could proceed easily and safely.

Patrick followed Jimmy. It was a very neat garden shed. A fork, a shovel and an English spade were hanging from one wall. There was a trestle table with a row of pots and some small gardening tools. It had been placed so that it would screen the hatch, without blocking it in anyway. A scythe leaned against one corner and a smart, new-looking lawnmower was in another. Patrick carefully replaced the hatch and took Jimmy by the hand. Patrick went cautiously to the door, opened it, just a crack, and put his eye to the space.

There was a well-kept small garden, a lawn in the centre, fruit trees and rose bushes on either side.

And a back view of a three-storey-high Georgian house.

Jimmy let go of the hand holding him back, pushed past Patrick and slipped behind an enormous bush. Patrick gently closed the door before following him. By the time he saw him again, Jimmy had opened a garden gate leading to a narrow lane, lined with dustbins. No one said anything until they reached the South Mall and then Jimmy was the first to speak.

'That's Judge Gamble's house, sir,' he said.

Patrick turned and looked up at the house. For a moment he thought that he saw a figure at the window. He hesitated for a moment. After all, what would be the harm in asking the judge to explain why there was a staircase leading from an underground store beneath the antiques shop and right up into his own garden shed? But then there was no law against constructing an underground passageway. Patrick thought back to something that the Reverend Mother had said about Morrison's Island. Once the entire island had been owned by the Gambles, big traders in their time. Perhaps the passageway was constructed originally more than a hundred years ago, perhaps kept in repair for the convenience of the people in the antiques shop. There would be no law, either against Tom Gamble, his father, or even his sister, holding shares in that profitable business, or even perhaps financing it. He decided to do nothing for the moment.

'Come on, Garda Jimmy. Let's get you back to the Reverend Mother,' he said. He said no more. Jimmy, unless addressed with a question, would be a silent companion and for now Patrick just wanted to think. He had two murders on his hands. He was fairly certain that Peter Doyle had murdered Father Dominic, but who murdered Peter Doyle? One of the gang – and by now he had the evidence that the antiques shop owners and their friends were criminals, involved in the lucrative business of stealing antiques from burning houses. It would, he thought as he stood back to allow a Beamish horse-pulled dray to get ahead of them, be easy enough to get the cook to identify the men involved in the raids. After all, she had seen them twice and, according to the Reverend Mother, had identified the raiders of Abernethy House as the same men who had burned down the Wood's house last year.

SEVENTEEN

1917-18 session of the Cork Municipal School of
Commerce, Lecture on the "General Principles
of Housing and Town Planning", delivered by the
Principal, D.J. Coakley.

*'Some (houses) are so old and dilapidated, and so
structurally bad, that repairing them is out of the
question. As a consequence, 38 to 40 houses were
closed some years previously as being unfit for human
habitation. There were several instances of where the
father and mother, and sons and daughters over 20
years of age, all slept in the same apartment. Of
12,850 houses in Cork, 1,300 were unprovided with
back yards, nearly half of which were situated in the
city centre. Coakley noted that if the Corporation of
Cork were to demolish all the houses in the city which
are absolutely unfit for human habitation and those on
the border line, it would mean dispossessing 16,000
people, or one fifth of the population.*

The rain had stopped, but the fog was so thick that the streets were dark as night. Here and there gas lamps were lit but they made little impact on the dense fog. People stumbled over each other and cars slowed to walking pace.

Only the horses were undisturbed by the lack of vision. The Beamish beer dray was making a terrible rumbling sound as they followed it down Parliament Street. There were no pavements here and Patrick was glad to feel Jimmy's hand firmly clasping on to the flap of his pocket. Each one of these wheels was about three foot high and was capable of cutting through a man's body.

Normally the drays went down the South Mall, but this one, perhaps because of the fog, had turned into the short narrow length of Parliament Street. It could cross over Parliament Bridge and go down the quays until it reached where the ferry waited to depart in the morning for Wales. In a week's time, London Irish, homesick for their native country, could be drinking the 'Black Cork'.

And then, suddenly, the rumbling from the iron wheels, rolling over the cobbles seemed suddenly to grow to deafening proportions with a dull booming noise. It sounded as though the street was hollow and Patrick recalled the words of the Reverend Mother when she was telling his class how the city of Cork had been built over river channels – perhaps there was a culvert under the short, narrow length of Parliament Street.

Then there was a roaring sound, almost the sound of thunder. The team of horses tossed their heads and one of the leader horses gave a high-pitched squeal – quickly picked up by others. Patrick hesitated, clasped Jimmy's wrist firmly, ready to drag him aside if a panic-stricken horse broke his trace and stampeded through the crowd that was streaming along Parliament Street, avoiding the floods in South Mall. There was a rumbling sound, a deafeningly loud crack, a confused sound of shouting voices, a woman's scream, echoed and drowned by the high pitch of the horses' squeals. Car drivers revved up their engines and began to reverse. The rumbling grew louder; Patrick pulled Jimmy back and clamped the frail body to his side. Terrifying screams and roars of a crowd mad with panic, a sudden smell of strong beer, a thud of running feet from behind them. The roaring of a car engine from behind them. The lights on the back of the dray moved and tilted, the press of people in front of Patrick parted and flowed back on either side of his square, resolute body.

And then he could see what had happened. Jimmy gave a terrified scream and buried his face in the wool of Patrick's overcoat. It was like a scene from hell. In front of them, a huge hole had opened up in the road. The team of four horses were on the other side and so were the first two sets of the wheels of the dray, but the end two wheels still dangled precariously over the edge of the enormous jagged hole that had opened up in the road. Cars were backing away, on both sides, reversing rapidly in case they too fell into the hole.

All the layers of tarmac laid on the road during recent years had broken up and the stones beneath it had slipped into the river. And now for the first time in his life Patrick could see what lay beneath. There had been a culvert, enclosing and containing a stream and it had been arched over by blocks of the rose-red sandstone of the area. It was, he knew well, a hard stone, far, far harder than brick or even the local lime-stone. But the constant wearing by the force of the floodwaters had found the weak spots in the joins and now the arched roof that had imprisoned the water had broken away. And the rushing waves of the incoming tide could be seen thundering along, just as though a portal had been opened into a watery hell.

'Hold the horses' heads!' A great roar went up from the crowd. Patrick was jostled and knocked as a crowd of men squeezed past him and edged their way along the narrow pathway by the side of the small houses and shops that fringed Parliament Street. Patrick stayed where he was. He had little Jimmy to keep safe. He longed to shout out to the draymen to cut the traces – let the barrels and the wagon fall into the hole, but keep the living horses and men safe, but he knew that was a decision that was theirs to make. He could not be responsible for them losing their jobs from the brewery.

The noise was deafening. Men shouting, horses screaming, but the next sound made everyone spring back.

From beneath their feet came another rumbling sound, the sound of the water-loosened stones churning against the archway under where they stood. The tide was turning, sucking back instead of leaping forward.

And then there was a great cheer. By a tremendous effort, the mighty horses managed to pull the last set of wheels free of the broken mass of tarmac and stone. A few more barrels rolled off and bobbed below in the water, but that would not matter. The owners of Beamish's Brewery would be thankful that the dray and the horses were safe. The men would be rewarded and there would be plenty of onlookers rushing off to the quaysides to try to secure an unbroken barrel of the porter. Patrick smiled to himself at the thought of the excite-ment as the predications of the eventual landing places flew from one to another. Probably, he thought, some of those casks now bobbing in the dark waters below them had been made by his grandfather who had been a cooper. The old man had worked for most of the breweries in the city from time to time. He bent over the hole and peered down into it. There was the sound of cars revving their engines, reversing out of danger. Jimmy grabbed his arm tightly and said something in an alarmed voice.

And at that very moment Patrick felt a blow in the middle of his back as though he had been struck by a sledgehammer. He pitched forward, seeing with absolute clarity as he fell downwards, the whole scene below lit up by the lanterns that were angled down. For a moment he felt a weight on his left arm but then it was free and a small shape was ahead of him falling, head first, while the boy frantically flailed his arms in circles.

'Jimmy!' he screamed but knew that his voice was lost in the roar of the water and the rumble of the stones.

And then he hit the water. The shock was stunning; the cold was paralysing. For a moment his wits deserted him, but then he began to kick feebly with his legs, to claw at the water with his hands. Even at that moment he was conscious of the stench from the river.

'Jimmy!' He screamed the boy's name again, but this time a mouthful of water choked him and he spluttered. He felt himself sinking. He could do nothing. The water had captured him and there would be no help for him. He felt the weight of his heavy leather boots pull him down. He had never learned to swim and did not know what he should do. He tried to kick, but his legs felt as though weighted with lead. His woollen great coat, his uniform, his shining boots, all of the things that his mother was so proud of would now be the means of killing him.

The thought of his mother, though, roused him. He roared the name of Jimmy again and thought, through the water that bubbled in his ear canal, that he caught a faint roar of sound from the crowds above. This encouraged him and he tried to kick again.

But the movement filled his boots with water. His legs pulled

him down, down underneath the stinking green slime. He
struggled desperately, frantically, flailing his arms, trying to
force them upwards as though the river was solid and he could
grasp its strings of water weed and pull himself free by hauling
on them.

Once again he sank.

Three times, he said as he surfaced once more. Someone
had told him that once. A man can only sink three times
and after that he drowns. Or did he drown on the third
sinking? He tilted his chin and tried to breathe, a spout of
water gushed from his mouth. His boots were pulling him
back down. They felt as though they were filled with lead
instead of just water.

He would give up, he thought. He had a vague feeling of
sorrow about his mother left all alone and about little Jimmy
whom he had failed to save. He should have sent him home
by himself. The boy would have been safer without him. He
had done everything wrong. It was easy to let go and to drown
there in the river water. He turned his face towards the spire
of the Holy Trinity Church, reaching high above the river and
breathed a last prayer that his mother would be all right
without him, that the God to whom she prayed every day
would comfort her and would send friends to her. He sank
below the river again, trying to remember the words for a last
act of contrition.

But then he rose again. That would be the third time. But
as the thought crossed his mind he saw something bobbing
up from the murky waters of the river.

Suddenly he was invigorated. Suddenly he knew what he
should do. How could he not have thought of it? A barrel, he
thought, will float.

There was one not far from him. He could see it now,
bobbing drunkenly on the water. It would have struck the
overhanging stone parapet as it fell. The Beamish porter would
be leaking out, would leave the barrel buoyant. Ideas floated
mistily through his head and he prayed, watching the barrel,
knowing that only minutes of life were left to him.

The tide had turned and the drag of the water was drawing
the barrel towards him. Frantically he beat his hands on the

surface of the river, clawed it to him with splayed fingers and strained every muscle to lift up the heavy lead-filled boots.

And the frenetic splashing somehow kept him afloat, kept him alive and waiting, his eyes straining towards the rounded shape of the barrel rolling and bobbing in the fetid waters. He was calm now, no longer filled with agonies of remorse for the past or fears for the future; just calm and concentrated, awaiting his chance, awaiting the one opportunity that God had offered to him.

And the barrel rolled towards him, lurching from side to side like a drunken man. He risked that his left hand would keep him afloat while he clawed at the smooth wood. There was nothing to grab hold of on it. Each of the staves was securely grooved into its companions on either side, the outside laboriously shaved and planed, smooth as glass.

The croze! The word just jumped into his head, pronounced in his grandfather's husky voice and his frantic fingers felt for the groove at the top of the barrel. And found it. He dug his nails into it, holding on for his life. The other hand clasped the barrel to his chest.

Now his two arms were around the barrel, hanging on desperately. Now he just had to hold it and allow the river to take him where it wanted.

But no; there was no safety in that. The circle of light ahead of him told which way deliverance lay. If he surrendered to the outgoing tide then he would be dragged down under the long length of South Mall until he emerged at Albert's Quay. By then he would probably be dead – dead from lack of air, dead from inhaling the stinking gasses from the city's sewers, dead from a blow on the head as the tide tossed his helpless body against the stone sarcophagus which enclosed the water where once Cork's eighteenth-century ships had sailed.

Hang on, he told himself. *Hang on to the barrel*. And this is what he did. Trying feebly, from time to time, to kick his heavy legs, he hung onto the barrel, now edging his fingers under the iron rim of the lid and finding the spot where the spigot would be inserted.

Now he dared to look up; to make out the figures looming ghost-like through the fog, standing precariously on the edge of the broken roads. The word 'peeler' was being shouted from mouth to mouth.

And then a figure, gleaming white in the glow from the lanterns, launched itself over the edge, arms together, well over his head, hands joined, fingers pointed, it dived down and landed so close to Patrick that a great splash made the barrel rock and his nails broke from their precarious grasp on it. For a moment he panicked and then he realized that he had been seen. His hair was seized in a painful grasp and he was held still for a moment, gulping and spluttering.

'Come on, old fellow. Keep your chin up. Let's be having you. Don't struggle whatever you do. Let's get your arms into the noose.'

'Mr Beamish!' gasped Patrick.

'I should get a medal for this.' Robert Beamish seemed at his ease in the water, kicking efficiently, his bare feet gleaming white through the green water and one hand stirring the surface while the other pulled taut the rope under Patrick's arms.

'That's it, lads,' he shouted. 'Pull away now like good fellows. And someone run for a doctor from the Mercy Hospital.'

'A peeler on the end of a rope,' shouted someone and there was a shout of laughter. Patrick did not grudge the joke or the amusement. Already the rope under his arms was taking his weight, was holding his mouth and nose well above the surface of the water.

'On the count of three,' yelled another voice. And then: 'One, two, three . . .'

The last word was roared and suddenly the rope tightened almost unbearably making Patrick think that he would be split in half. He rose from the water slowly. There was a heart-stopping moment when he just seemed to dangle there, a dead weight of body, saturated wool clothing and leather boots, filled to the knees with water.

It was at that moment that he remembered the broken edge of stone and realized the danger that he was in. He was a dead weight and the slow haul of the rope against the sharp edges of the stone would fray the strands and cause them to split and part.

'On the count of three,' came the voice again. And then the numbers: 'One, two, three . . .'

But on the third numeral, Patrick felt the energy flow back into his arms and legs. He could not swim, but every Barrack Street boy could 'wax a gazza', that particular rite of passage in Cork City when, with bare knees and clutching hands, a seven-, eight-, or nine-year-old managed for the first time to climb from the pavement up the slippery pole of the gas lamp. And then proceeded to do it again, and again and again and again, queuing up behind friends and enemies, through the long days of the summer holidays and the fog-filled evenings until some butcher took pity on them and gave them an empty cow's bladder to play football with.

The muscles were still there. Patrick took a firmer grip on the rope, lifted his knees with a huge effort, clamped them around the thickly corded tarry surface – from a moored ship, he thought, and proceeded to make a slow progress up the rope. There was a great cheer. People shouted excited commands to him and from the corner of his eye he could see that Joe was standing on the quayside. He began to exert every muscle.

Now the tug-a-war team's task was easier. He was no longer a dead weight but was actively helping. The peering faces came nearer; there were shouts of 'keep back' and then another cheer.

Perhaps they have found Jimmy, he thought and his heart was filled with thankfulness, but then he heard them say something about the doctor. He switched his mind back into survival mode and went on monotonously placing hand over hand and inching, little by little, up the rope with the sodden cloth of his trousers forming a good barrier between the rope and his legs.

'And one more pull. On the count of three – a one . . . and a two . . . and a three.'

The last word was almost completely drowned in a great burst of cheering. His head had reached the surface of the road. Hands reached out and grabbed him under the arms and then he was sprawled on the road while someone turned him over and started to pump vigorously at his back.

'There you'll do now. Lucky man. Don't you worry, now! I've seen plenty of people hauled up from the river. Soon as they get rid of the water, they do fine.' A large pair of hands were holding him up. He had been sick three times, had vomited up the river water and was held propped up by someone who was holding a bottle to his lips. It was Robert Beamish who had produced the pocket-sized bottle. Dr Scher was in front of him, his finger on the pulse in the wrist. Patrick choked over the whiskey but it warmed him and he looked around feebly, but there was no sign of little Jimmy. An apprehensive silence had fallen over the crowd. Not even Dr Scher was looking at him and the doctor's finger on his wrist tensed. Everyone's eyes were on the river. Something was coming up on the end of the rope. The men pulled, but there was no strain, no counts of three, no shouts of encouragement; they pulled steadily and silently.

Several constables, Joe with them, had arrived on the scene and they stood around the edge of the hole, shining lanterns down into the broken culvert below. The lights focussed steadily on the rope that was being pulled up – and on the burden that it bore, attached to a hook. Patrick sat up and looked. Could that be the child? There were a pair of child's wellington boots on the road.

'I had Jimmy, the Reverend Mother's boy, I had him with me,' he said to Dr Scher and felt the hand which held his wrist stiffen suddenly and then relax.

'Just an ould shawl,' shouted someone.

'Knotted up so that it didn't float,' said Joe in his ear and Patrick tried vaguely to remember why a shawl might be important.

'Jimmy,' he said again and Joe was silent.

'No sign of him,' said Dr Scher. There was a slight catch in his voice.

'Let's get you back to the barracks and out of those wet clothes,' said Joe. 'Can you stand?'

Patrick tried to get up. He had an agonising pain in his back. There was an odd, metallic taste in his mouth. He put his hand to it, spat and brought it back before his eyes. There was a pinkish-red smear.

'I have a terrible pain here,' he said, putting his hand on his abdomen. And then with a sudden recollection. 'A car hit me. I remember now. A car hit me. It knocked me forwards. I fell. I had Jimmy by the hand.' He tried to remember what had happened next. 'Perhaps I let go,' he said and tried to look around. Suddenly he vomited again and this time the colour of it was a dark red.

'Stay still,' said Dr Scher urgently. 'Don't try to move. We'll get an ambulance.'

Patrick thankfully gave up the effort. He was beginning to feel faint and quite ill. Everything was hazy and he leaned against Robert Beamish's shoulder. Joe was already blowing his police whistle urgently. 'Jimmy . . .' Patrick mumbled. And then, with a great effort: 'Tell Joe . . .' But he could say no more. There was a smell of river fog in his nostrils. It made him sick and dizzy. His face felt cold and damp. Joe's whistle seemed to blend into an ambulance siren. He could do no more for the moment . . .

EIGHTEEN

W.B. Yeats:
'Things fall apart; the centre cannot hold
Mere anarchy is loosed upon the world,
The blood-dimmed tide is loosed, and everywhere
The ceremony of innocence is drowned;
The best lack all conviction, while the worst
Are full of passionate intensity.'

Eileen was having fun with Jimmy's book.

'Take the day over it, you and Jack,' said the boss. 'There's nothing urgent to do. And, who knows, if you get good at it, we might print a few children's books, teach the younger generation their Gaelic past and stop them turning into little West Britons. You could write them. Would be a piece of cake for you, wouldn't it? You could write them and Jack could do the illustrations. Keep it all in-house.'

'That should take about five minutes,' said Jack reading through Jimmy's story. 'Only about twenty sentences there. That's not a book; it's a leaflet.'

'It can be a twenty-page book,' said Eileen. 'One sentence for each page. The child has a problem with reading. We should make it a picture book. You can do the pictures when you've printed out the sentences. You're really good at drawing. Remember those caricatures you did.'

'I'll need my pay doubled if I'm going to be an artist as well as a compositor,' grumbled Jack, but he carefully read through the little story again and a meditative slight smile curved his lips as he set up the type. When he had finished he folded the sheet into twenty-four small pages and handed it to Eileen. Some of the sentences were at the bottom of their small section, some were at the top, others in the middle, and twice, the sentence slanted across the middle of the page, sloping down from the left-hand top corner to the right-hand bottom corner. He had even remembered to put a page number on each page.

'Just you trim these like a good girl while I work on the cover. What's the name of this book? Yes, I see, UNDERGROUND, hmm, let me think . . .'

Eileen hated trimming, but she did not complain. She watched as Jack glued the last two pages together with a piece of cardboard between them. This would be the cover. Working quickly and skilfully, he outlined eleven seated rats scattered down the page, each holding up, etched onto a banner, one of the letters from the word 'Underground'.

'That's wonderful; that would teach any child his letters,' she said enthusiastically as he went over the pencil lines with a lettering pen and black ink. With a deft line here and there, perky or drooping whiskers, different tails or a slight twist of the ear, he managed to give each little rat a personality. 'You're a genius,' she finished.

The book was finished by noon. Most of the pictures were black ink drawings, but Jack had uncovered some coloured inks in a cupboard so that tongues of orange fire reached to ceiling height in the warehouse pictures and piles of gold and silver nuggets glittered on the page where the treasure was found. And then, last of all, the planks on the rat's boat were etched in red ink.

'Leave it all to dry while you grab a bit of lunch,' advised Jack. 'When you come back you can sew it together and then you can take it over to the convent. Nice for the little fellow to see it before he goes home. Don't worry. I'll fix it with Robert.'

Perhaps I might be a teacher instead of a lawyer or a doctor; it must be a great thrill when you teach a child to read, thought Eileen, as she set off for the convent with the little book carefully wrapped in brown paper and lying inside her handbag. She walked out onto the South Terrace, lost in her usual daydreams of what she would do when Ireland was a republic and education was free to all who wanted it, and took a shortcut through the back streets towards St Mary's Isle. Normally she would have waited for the evening, but she was impatient to show the little book to the Reverend Mother, and perhaps, have the opportunity to see Jimmy's face light up when it was read to him.

But there was no sign of Jimmy in the playground where the children were lined up until the Reverend Mother could see that they were going home with a parent, or a neighbour or at least in a group with one of the older girls in charge. Eileen waited patiently, remembering how her mother used to collect her from school and how she would tell her everything she had learned that day as they walked back together towards Barrack Street. They would sing the songs and recite the poems, make up stories about what they would buy if they had a shilling. Her mother had the gift to make learning such fun for her daughter. What a shame that Maureen had never been able to fulfil her early ambition to be a teaching assistant and then a teacher. Pregnancy must have been a dreadful shock for a fourteen-year-old girl, but Eileen had never felt unwanted. She owed her mother a lot. Once again, she thought of how excited and animated her mother had been on the night when Maurice the lawyer from Mayo, now holed up in Ballinhassig with Eamonn and the others, had visited them and had brought a present of a cake. She resolved to buy a cake for her mother with her Friday pay packet on her way home and then turned her attention to the Reverend Mother who had just handed over the last child and signalled to Sister Bernadette to lock the gate to the school playground. The elderly nun looked very white and her eyes were worried.

'Are you well, Reverend Mother?' Eileen asked anxiously

'Come into my room, Eileen.' The question was ignored and nothing more was said until the door was closed and both were seated.

'There's been an accident, Eileen. There was a landslide in Parliament Street. The road there covers a stream and the blocks of stone slipped. Patrick, Inspector Cashman, was knocked into the river. First of all, they thought that he had fallen, stumbled over the broken tarmac, but now they think that a car hit him hard on the back. He is in hospital with terrible bruising to his back and damage to his liver. He is

very ill. The postman told Sister Bernadette all about it.
I'm very worried about Patrick.' The Reverend Mother paused
for a moment. 'And Jimmy, who was with him, has completely
disappeared. They've dragged the river twice and there was
no sign of him, nothing was found except his pair of too large
wellington boots which perhaps floated from his legs.' The
Reverend Mother's voice broke and she got up swiftly from
her chair and walked across to the window.

Quietly, Eileen replaced the brown paper package back
within her handbag. The Reverend Mother still stared through
the window and Eileen did not know what to say. Eventually
she cleared her throat.

'Has the story about the underground passageways anything
to do with the attempt to murder Patrick?' she asked. She
could not trust her voice to pronounce Jimmy's name.

'You're a clever girl, Eileen,' said the Reverend Mother
turning around. 'Yes, we must concentrate on that. No more
lives must be put in danger. There must be no more deaths.
It appears that the superintendent has taken over the case.'
There was a bleak note in her voice. And then, after a minute,
she said with an effort at briskness, 'Jimmy could swim, you
know. One of the older girls told me when I asked for prayers
for him. He and his cousins used to swim off Morrison's
Island.'

'And his mother?' Eileen made the query timidly.

'Is in Liverpool, apparently. I never knew. He didn't want
me to know in case he couldn't keep coming here to this
school, but he's been dossing down in Morrison's Island,
according to my informant.'

'I see. Well, he may have gone there. He would have been
frightened if he saw the car. If he could swim, he might have
gone down river a little and got out on the quay.'

'There is another possibility,' said the Reverend Mother. A
little colour came back into her cheeks. 'Jimmy told me that
Robert Beamish has a place for his boat, just at the height of
the river, on St Matthew's Quay, not far from the bridge. It
leads back to Jimmy's underground passageway. It seems
almost too much to hope for, but I pray that he might have
found safety. He would, of course, be very scared if he thinks

that a car deliberately hit him. He's a sharp little lad. He may well have seen who was driving that car. He may be hiding in that underground passageway. But, if so, well, he is in grave danger.'

'I'll go and look for him.'

'Yes, do,' said the Reverend Mother, 'but before you go, Eileen, there is something that I want to ask you. It's about confession. What do you think about confession?'

'Confession?' Eileen felt alarmed. She had not been to confession for years. The Bishop of Cork had issued an edict against the Republican activists in 1920, banning them from the sacraments and few that she knew had ever returned to the church despite the efforts of certain priests like Father Dominic.

'I was wondering about your feelings when you were here at school. I used to notice that none of the older girls went to confess to the convent chaplain.'

Eileen giggled a little at the memory. 'People used to pretend that he would tell everything to Sister Mary Immaculate as they were such great friends,' she confessed. 'But no one really believed that. That was when we were little. We knew really that no priest would ever break the sacred seal of confession. I think it was just that we felt more grown up going to confession in the town and it was a good excuse to get out and go around the shops,' she added in an embarrassed fashion.

'I see,' said the Reverend Mother. 'That's interesting. Telling secrets is a human frailty so it would not be surprising if priests could be suspected of human frailties and yet, somehow no Catholic, no adult, does ever fear that will happen.' She seemed to brooding about something and Eileen looked at her with curiosity.

'You're thinking of the murder of Father Dominic, Reverend Mother, aren't you?'

The Reverend Mother sighed. 'It's amazing how stupid I've been,' she said. 'To paraphrase George Bernard Shaw, "Ireland is a country divided by their belief in a common Deity." The one half believes that the other half must understand. But, of course, they don't really comprehend the secret rules and understandings, the rituals, the set procedures. So when you think back to the murder of Father Dominic, and the consequential murder of Peter Doyle, well, in the end, the answer is quite simple. It couldn't be otherwise.'

Sounds very cryptic, thought Eileen, but she did not feel that she could ask the Reverend Mother to explain herself. She sat very quietly, turning over matters in her mind.

'The key to the secret is confession; that's what you're thinking, isn't it?' she hazarded after a minute. 'A fear . . .' She considered the people whose lives had become entwined with hers during the last few weeks, considered the Protestants and the Catholics – two people divided by their belief in a common God or Deity, as the Reverend Mother had put it. 'Someone went to confession,' she went on. She was beginning to understand. 'They went to confession. And there was another person who went, not to confess, but in consequence of that confession.'

'And this person was armed with a hat pin,' said the Reverend Mother. She brooded for a moment and then added, 'And knowledge.'

'Knowledge?' Eileen had no sooner uttered the query when the solution came to her. Of course, she thought. Knowledge had been needed.

'They say that confession is good for the soul,' said the Reverend Mother meditatively, 'but, of course, as you so rightly say, it can bring a fear of betrayal. And, of course, betrayal could affect others as well as the sinner.'

Eileen thought back to that night when she sorted the roses and the pins for the wigs in the costume cupboard of the Father Matthew Hall. She had heard a secret then.

'A secret shared . . .' she said aloud.

The Reverend Mother bowed her head. 'Yes, it can bring relief, but can leave fear in its wake,' she said. 'Fear for oneself, or for someone else. And fear can provoke violence, or even death.'

Eileen jumped to her feet. 'I'd better go,' she said urgently. 'I think that I should go now. I must find Jimmy. If he saw something he will be in danger. I will come back, Reverend Mother. One way or other I will come back.'

Standing inside the gate of the convent was a delivery boy's bicycle, labelled 'Murphy's Poultry' on a broad metal strip, attached to its cross bar. Eileen grabbed the handlebars, wheeled it through the gate and, blessing her very short skirt, threw her leg over the crossbar and began to cycle as fast as she could, her cropped hair clinging to her head like a black helmet as she sped through the streets. She would risk the flooding on North Main Street and approach the South Mall from the Grand Parade, she decided, as her legs flew around, pushing the pedals as hard as she could. And from the South Mall, she could enter Morrison's Island. She had a car in mind and she kept a sharp look-out for it. It shouldn't be too hard to find the one that she wanted if she scrutinized every driver that she met. After all, the majority of cars were driven by men.

NINETEEN

St Thomas Aquinas:
'*Medicus autem abscindit membrum putridum bene et*
utiliter, si per ipsum immineat corruptio corporis.
Iuste igitur et absque peccato rector civitatis homines
pestiferos occidit, ne pax civitatis turbetur.'
(Nevertheless, a physician quite properly and
beneficially cuts off a diseased organ if the corruption
of the body is threatened because of it. Therefore,
justly and without sin, the ruler of a state executes
dangerous men in order that the peace of the state
may not be disrupted.)

The Reverend Mother took a sheet of quarto paper from
her desk. Meditatively and with slow deliberation she
wrote a series of numbers down her margin and then
dipped her steel pen again into the inkwell. Now she wrote
quickly and without pause. By the time that she had finished
there were ten neatly written questions filling the page.

She read the list through, twice, and then put it down. She
knew the answer to every one of those questions.

But now what would she do?

If only there was a way of making sure that this person
did not kill again, she thought. A cornered rat is very
dangerous. Little Jimmy had told her that. A rat, of course,
had only his teeth. But a person could make use of all sorts
of weapons. She thought of Jimmy for a moment. Even if he
had escaped the river – and Eileen had given her hope for
that – even if he were still alive, he was now in deadly danger.
Already there had been two murders and an attempt at two
more on this very day. Would more people lose their lives
because of her hesitation? She rose to her feet. The telephone
was only a three-minute walk from her room. She would
ask for the police barracks, request politely a visit from the

superintendent on an urgent matter. Tell him what she knew, what she had guessed.

And then the matter would be out of her hands.

She stood very still. Steadily she forced herself to contemplate a gibbet. A human being hanging from it. Deliberately she pictured the person in her mind and deliberately she tried to imagine the terror, the anguish, the physical torture, the wild despair, the agony of the nearest and dearest. And that last, final strangulation. She took a long moment over that. Could she do it? What if she were wrong? Only God is infallible, she reminded herself. Why not leave it in the hands of the superintendent. He would undoubtedly assign the guilt to the Sinn Féin.

But what if there were another murder? What about Jimmy and Eileen? And Patrick? Or even Dr Scher? Or even perhaps one of the friars from the church?

She could wait until Eileen returned, she could wait to make sure that Jimmy was safe. And then she would keep him safe. Sister Bernadette would find him a bed within the convent and she would forbid him to leave the premises.

But safe for how long?

Would someone who killed the gentle priest, Father Dominic, hesitate to kill a little boy from the slums?

She thought not.

Restlessly she paced up and down, and looked at the clock. She had mechanically dealt with Eileen's theft of the messenger boy's bicycle. Murphy the Poultry Merchant had been telephoned. No doubt Sister Bernadette had poured out apologies, sympathy and reassurances, the messenger boy had been given a meal in the kitchen. Now the Reverend Mother tried to calculate how quickly a bicycle ridden by a determined young lady in a short skirt would take to reach Morrison's Island. Perhaps she should wait a little while longer. The appearance of police there might force the guilty person into a panic-stricken action against a boy who may have been a witness. She told herself those things but at the same time despised herself for being a moral coward.

The Reverend Mother folded the sheet of paper, placed it within an envelope. She hesitated for a moment, then took it out again, unfolded it and made another copy. Then both were returned to the envelope. She did not seal it or write upon it. Time enough for that when Eileen returned. Carefully she locked it inside the bottom drawer of her desk.

And then she went to the chapel. She could pray for Jimmy. It was the only thing left for her to do after so stupidly sending him into such danger.

And she could pray for herself, also, for enlightenment. And for courage. If a decision was right, then she would have to find the courage to take it.

Her patron saint, Thomas Aquinas, had said that one should not shirk to rid the world of a murderer, but he had also said that humans were given reasoning powers and should act according to them. The Reverend Mother pushed open the door of the chapel, walked up to the altar, sank to her knees and prayed to the Holy Spirit for enlightenment.

TWENTY

Michael Collins:
'Give us the future. We've had enough of the past.
Give us back our country. To live in.
To grow in. To love.'

There was a small group of young boys around when Eileen skidded to a halt on the quayside. Just back from school, she guessed, as the bells of the Holy Trinity Church chimed the hour of four o'clock. They immediately gathered around her, overawed by this apparition, a well-dressed young lady scooting along on top of one of Murphy's Poultry bikes.

'Janey Mack, did you hobble that?' said one.

Eileen saw her opportunity. 'Where can I hide it? The peelers are after me. Quick!'

They didn't hesitate. With sidelong glances and sliding along very close to walls they led her down a back laneway, between rows of dangerously derelict warehouses, most of them leaning at odd angles.

'In there,' said one.

Eileen looked in. The whole place still smelled strongly of smoke. Jimmy, she thought, if he had escaped from the river, might well use this place to hide. She remembered the page with the leaping flames and the underground passageways leading to the treasure and to the boat where the dog ate the giant rat.

'Go and keep guard,' she hissed to the boys. 'Whistle loudly if you see one of the peelers.'

It was quite a jump down to the lower level. Eileen hesitated for a moment, but then took a chance on it.

She was driven by a feeling of terrible anxiety. Speeding down the streets on the saddle of the poultry merchant's bike, she had been feeling hopeful. Jimmy was a street kid. She had seen him one day, with some other boys, playing the game of hanging on to a lorry and being raced across Parliament Bridge, dropping neatly off once it had reached the other side. He would react faster to a speeding car than Patrick, a careful but slow man.

But now she began to feel apprehensive. This murdering monster was ruthless, was determined to destroy all threats. Softly and then more loudly, she called 'Jimmy' and the name echoed back. Something stirred directly above her. A gun? No, this murderer did not deal in guns. But a heavy stone could knock her unconscious and then there would be the deadly hat pin through the ear. She heard the sound again. This time it was louder and now she recognized it. She shuddered and picked up a broken piece of wood, banging it loudly on one of the piers. She hated rats; hated, loathed them and was frightened by them, but not as much as the thought of that deadly hat pin stealing in through her ear and piercing her brain. Where was the little boy? She would have to call again. Jimmy was in far more danger than she. She, unlike Father Dominic, and unlike Peter Doyle, was armed with knowledge. She knew who to look for. She flexed her arms and clenched a fist.

But it was getting very dark. The light that had come in through the broken and burned floorboards had almost faded away and there was a heap of fallen masonry in front of her where a wall had collapsed. The passageway seemed to lead off to the side, but it was black as night, far more impenetrable darkness than any night under a clouded sky.

And then the toe of her rubber shoe touched something on the ground, something soft. She heard a cry that was half a sob and realized that it was her own. She clenched her fists, thought of her mother, but forced herself to bend down and to touch.

Fur. Fur and a scaly tail. It was a dead rat. Not just one of them, a whole heap of them. She shuddered with disgust. Once more she tried calling Jimmy's name, but the echoes just came back to her and over her head there was a panic-driven scrabble of claws and the thud of running feet.

She would have to go back. Go back and buy some matches

and a candle. And perhaps ask those boys if they knew Jimmy. And perhaps they could direct her to Jimmy's aunt and his cousins. She followed the patch of light back. There had been a rope tied to a pier. She was weak with relief when she came to it. There were boys shouting so she was not alone.

'Patch, Patch, Patch!'

And then they saw her.

'Catch him, miss, catch him. There's loads of dead rats down there. If he eats one, he'll be a goner.'

Quickly she grabbed the small black and white terrier by his short, curly tail and held on firmly, glad of her gloves as he twisted around and tried to bite her.

'Thanks, miss.' The biggest boy was beside her, knotting a piece of twine to the dog's collar.

'I've seen a dog die of eating a poisoned rat. It's terrible.' A younger boy bent down and stroked the little dog.

'You must be Jimmy's cousin. He told me all about Patch. Is Jimmy at your house?' She found herself surreptitiously crossing her fingers, but he shook his head.

'Nah, haven't seen him?'

'I'm looking for him.' She looked at them with desperation. 'Perhaps he's hiding.' They didn't seem to be too interested so she tried again. 'He's in danger. Someone's after him, please help me to find him. I'll give you sixpence if you find him for me.'

The boys looked at each other with interest.

'You can guess where he's hiding, Bob, can't you?' One boy addressed the eldest.

'That'll be it,' said the other with a nod.

'He hides there,' said a third boy to Eileen. 'When a lady gave him half a chocolate bar one day, he went scooting down so that he didn't have to share it with us.'

'And when we caught up with him, there he was, sitting on a velvet chair like a lord, and swallowing the last bit of it.'

'I'll buy you each a chocolate bar if you show me the place,' said Eileen recklessly.

'Benjy, you stay with her,' ordered the biggest boy. 'Take this candle. We'll go on ahead in case there's a gang of rats charging down.'

The boys were already running down the passageway, Bob in the lead and his younger brothers behind him, Patch, held on a stranglehold by a short leash, but still managing a few hoarse barks. Benjy stayed with her, holding the stump of a candle impaled on a large rusty nail.

'Mind where you walk, miss,' he said. 'You don't want to trip over a dead rat.'

She shuddered, but continued to look in every corner and at the broken ceiling above her.

'Don't you worry, miss,' said Benjy. 'He'll be there. Bob's right.'

'Be careful' she called out to the boys ahead. Perhaps someone would be there ahead of them, someone carrying a deadly weapon. For a moment Eileen half-hesitated and then the thought of Jimmy drove her on. The weapons so far had been a hat pin and a car. No car could get down here, but the boys might not be on alert for a hat pin.

'Wait for me, or no chocolate,' she screamed, hearing her voice echo again and again against the concrete piers that surrounded them. She had lost sight of them. She began to run, almost tripping over another dead body. This time she did not even pause. There was a faint light ahead.

'Wait,' she screamed again. 'Or no chocolate.'

This time they stopped instantly. And her heartbeat slowed. 'Let me go first, Bob,' she ordered. 'You go behind me.'

Eileen slipped through the gap in the tarpaulin. She looked all around. It was not as Jimmy had described it, but she could see how the silver dishes and candlesticks and the gold watches glinted in the candlelight. That would have taken his attention, sparked off some memory of a story about treasure. There was no little boy there, though. Her heart skipped a beat as she saw something rolled up in the corner of the storage space. She snatched the makeshift candle from Benjy and went across with her heart thumping.

It was a small rug, rolled up. She felt it carefully, her heart thumping, but the centre was hollow. There was no body concealed within it. Rapidly she searched behind the tarpaulin and then stiffened. As quietly as a swarm of rats, the boys were moving away from her. She opened her mouth to say something, but Bob had snatched up Patch and held his hand clamped over the little dog's small short muzzle. In a moment he had seemed to melt from the storeroom. His brothers followed him, their bare feet making no sound on the wooden planks laid on the rough cement.

'I'll just put it in the storeroom. It can stay there.' There was a clip of heels on the floor above and the click of a key in a lock. Marjorie Gamble was upstairs in the showroom. It was her voice.

'That's too heavy for you, Marjorie.' It was Jonathon Power. Tense. Harsh. Unlike Jonathon. Would he help Marjorie? Could she be a match for both? Was she even a match for Marjorie? The woman was short, but sturdy.

'Miss!' It was Benjy's whisper. She had left him without his candle. Silently on her rubber soles, she joined him, handing over the candle. He moved away. His instincts would lead him to avoid discovery. She allowed him to go. Her heart was thumping inside her chest. She had to know. But the sound of Jonathon's voice had alerted her to danger. If Marjorie screamed he would be down in a flash.

There were footsteps thumping on the stairway. Slow, careful footsteps, someone feeling their way, vision barred by a load held in the arms. Once she slightly stumbled and Jonathon called out, 'You all right, Marjorie?'

'I'm fine.' She sounded impatient, tense. Unlike the usual calm even-tempered Miss Gamble. Eileen held her breath. Three more careful steps, a slight shuffle as the woman's feet checked the floor surface, a thump and then instantly the sound of feet running back up to the shop above. A slight slam of the door, a click in the lock and now there was nothing, no sounds, no words.

Moving slowly and carefully, judging her pathway by the crack of light coming from the doorway above, Eileen shuffled her way over to the bottom of the stairs, waiting until her hand was on the wooden rail before kneeling down. Marjorie had dropped her burden almost as soon as she had stepped off the last stair.

It gave her a shock when she touched it. It was quite warm. Rough to the touch, wool, she thought. Rough, harsh wool, not one of those beautiful rugs, Aubusson, she thought, not one of these that she had seen in the shop.

'Miss!' There was a faint gleam from the darkness that surrounded her. Benjy had come back. Getting to her feet, she crossed over the planks and took the candle from him. 'Keep hidden!' She breathed the words into his ear and then returned to the bundle. Jonathon and Marjorie Gamble were just above her head and she hoped that they were not going to re-open the door. She had to know, though. The roll of carpeting was tied tightly with a string and her shaking fingers could not undo the knot. Without hesitation she took the feeble flame from the candle stump and held it to the twine. The flame flickered and she watched intently, smashing down her fist on it the moment the twine parted. Trembling she opened the roll.

Inside was just a pair of ornate silver candlesticks, heavily tarnished. Eileen sighed with relief. She found that her legs were trembling as she got to her feet. She bent to roll the rug back, but one candlestick escaped, falling with a soft thud on the boards.

'What's that?' A sharp exclamation from above. The light streamed down again as the hatch was opened.

'Jonathon!' There was a note of fear in Marjorie's voice. 'Jonathon, listen.'

Eileen cupped her hands over the flame. Could they see the pinprick of light? She thought of blowing it out. Then thought of going back down that passageway without her candle. She held her breath, stretched out her hand towards an ornately engraved silver tray and with her longest fingernail scratched rhythmically.

'A rat! Bother! I'd better buy some more of that poison. I thought I'd got rid of them all.' Marjorie's voice was loud with relief. Eileen heard the hatch door slam shut again and this time the rim of light disappeared. They had gone back into the shop.

There was no sign of Benjy. He had fled when he heard the voices, she reckoned. Eileen held the stump of the candle and made her way along the passageway, doing her best to avoid the corpses of the dead rats. She had an uneasy feeling that she was not going back the way she had come, but sooner or later there would be a hole in one of the boards over her head and she could scramble up it. The concrete shuttering was falling apart in places, large crumbling lumps of it strewn around and the roadway, itself, was broken in places. Eileen wanted to run, or at least to hurry, but caution slowed her steps as she picked her way among the obstacles. There was a cool dampness around her, a strong smell in her nostril. A sudden scream almost made her drop the little candle but it was followed by another and another. Her heat thumped violently. Those boys! She bit her lip, bit hard down to stop the scream that rose in her throat. The candle in her hand trembled. And then the scream came again, but now she knew what it was. Seagulls. She was coming back by a different route. There would be a sewage outfall quite close to her. The seagulls fed from these. Should she return?

And then she remembered Jimmy's story. The little dog had chased a rat and they had found it in a boat. A boat meant mooring ropes. She was strong and a good climber, as good as any of the boys in Barrack Street, she told herself. And she could not bear to turn back. Desperately she wanted to get out of this place. The draught was blowing the flame of the candle and the wax was melting rapidly. A second later it flickered and then went out. Eileen forced herself to keep moving, her hand on the damp, crumbling cement of the wall. The smell of the river, of sewage was getting stronger, the shrieks of the seagulls almost unendurable. 'Jimmy!' she screamed and the seagulls screamed back at her. Stupid! The boy could not be still in the river. By now he had run home. The light was getting stronger and so were the river sounds: the suck of the tide, the churning of an engine, the cranking of the unloading cranes, the shouts of the dockworkers. She quickened, and then slowed, forcing herself to go carefully and to find a safe footing with each step that she took.

She was out of the darkness and into the mist and fog. Seagulls whirred around her head, raucous and menacing. She flung the candle stump at them; the wood and the large nail gave it weight and the birds rose in a screaming white mass of beating wings and viciously opened jaws. The boat was there; Robert Beamish's boat, well secured at both ends to the mooring rings in the wall, but no sign of Jimmy. The fog was very thick; she could see little of the river, but she could hear the sound of a motorized trawler coming upstream; coming very fast, in the centre of the river, she thought, but the wash lifted the boat below her and it swung on its ropes, bumping against the wall as the wave caught it.

And then the fog seemed to lift. She could look down into the murky water. Horribly something emerged from it: a hand, a child's hand, waving, the small wrist bending over.

The force of her jump rocked the boat dangerously. For a moment she thought it was going to tip her into the river but the ropes held it in position. She knelt down, reached into the water and lifted out the small body.

TWENTY-ONE

Sean M O'Duffy, Lieutenant IV Dublin, 1916;
Registrar and Organizer of Republican Courts,
1920-1921

*'The Republican Courts are of the most vital
importance and they must be kept going at all costs.
Should hostilities be resumed between this country and
England, the Courts, for reasons which it is yet
premature to disclose, will be called upon to play a
mighty part in the struggle and it may reasonably be
anticipated that the enemy will redouble all previous
efforts to destroy them. Therefore if you wish that the
Courts in your area should be ready for the fight, you
must be up and doing without a moment's delay.
Otherwise your Courts will be hopelessly inefficient
and shamefully inactive at a time when the Courts in
other parts of the country will be bidding dauntless
defiance at all efforts to suppress them. This is the
golden hour. Therefore be prepared.'*

She was very old, of course, thought Eileen. She remembered how the Reverend Mother had told her once about how she had worn a crinoline, so that meant she was as old as the girls in Dickens' novels. Perhaps that was why she did not shed a tear. She talked with the sergeant, Joe Duggan, arranged for the child's body to be brought to the convent chapel once the police and the doctor had finished with it. The convent would pay all burial costs, a white coffin, she told him. They would have a requiem mass next week. The whole school would attend and the older girls' choir would sing. Jimmy's aunt and his cousins would be invited. The little boy would be buried in the convent garden, under the flowering magnolia tree. Eileen looked at the composed face and made a great effort to hold back her own tears. She didn't think that she could ever forget that small body, tangled up in a mooring rope, his neck twisted at an odd angle, his eyes dead and staring. It had taken all her strength to lift him from the river, with the help of Bob, while the other boys ran for the police. She blinked hard and went over to the window.

And then when the sergeant, Joe Duggan, had gone, the Reverend Mother beckoned to Eileen to follow her to her room. She selected a key, unlocked a drawer, took from it a sheet of paper and handed it to Eileen.

'I know the answer to each one of those questions, Eileen,' was all that she said. And then she sank down very heavily upon a chair, almost as though her legs could no longer support her.

Eileen read rapidly down the page, and then read the questions aloud.

'I'm beginning to see,' she said and after a quick look at the Reverend Mother, she returned her gaze to the sheet of paper.

Arguments and pieces of evidence jostled in her mind. Of course the use of the confessional, so familiar to some and so strange to others, was central to the case. It was quite a while since she had been to confession, but the whole details of the cramped space and of the iron grid between confessor and penitent immediately flashed through her mind. And the choice of weapon. That was so significant. Knowledge, once learned, is not easily lost. The means of death depended on that knowledge.

The second murder, like the first, was motivated by fear, fear of discovery, and of disgrace, and fear of losing a comfortable income. And, of course, she knew how the murderer could approach a man without giving alarm. She opened her mouth, ready to articulate her reasons, to argue the case, to put forward justifications and last of all to tell the Reverend Mother all about the Republican, or Sinn Féin court which had been set up and was all ready to hear the case. She would lay emphasis on the two experienced and well-qualified barristers, one acting as prosecutor and the other for the defence. And on the bench, she would say, there would be an experienced and well-qualified solicitor who had acted as a judge in many such trials. She would reassure the elderly woman that the evidence would be as carefully weighed as it would in the Cork City Court House. And that sentence would be carried out rapidly and would be quick and relatively painless.

Unlike the agonized death that poor little Jimmy had suffered when the life had been throttled out of him. Eileen rehearsed all of those arguments.

But she looked into the tired elderly face before her and knew that it would be unkind to transfer any responsibility, so all that she said, as she put the sheet of paper carefully into her pocket, was, 'Give it forty-eight hours, Reverend Mother.'

And then she left. She would mourn Jimmy adequately some time in the future, but now she had to ensure that his murderer would kill no more. The faces of the boys, Jimmy's cousins, came to her and she knew that they, too, might now be in danger. She began to run. She would have to get a train to Ballinhassig and find Maurice the lawyer as soon as possible.

TWENTY-TWO

St Thomas Aquinas:
Quidem iusta esse potest et a Deo et ab homine
inflicta, unde ipsa poena non est effectus peccati
directe, sed solum dispositive. Sed peccatum facit
hominem esse reum poenae, quod est malum,
dicit enim Dionysius . . . quod puniri non est malum,
sed fieri poena dignum. Unde reatus poenae directe
ponitur effectus peccati.
(Further, a just punishment may be inflicted either by
God or by man: wherefore the punishment itself is the
effect of sin, not directly, but to settle the matter. Sin,
however, makes man deserving of punishment, and
that is an evil: for Dionysius says . . . that punishment
is not an evil, but to deserve punishment is.
Consequently the debt of punishment is considered to
be directly the effect of sin.)

The Reverend Mother read the article on the *Cork Examiner* through again, folded the paper carefully and looked across at Dr Scher. He looked puzzled. He would be waiting for some reaction from her. After all, he had rushed around to the convent at eight o'clock in the morning, the *Cork Examiner* under his arm and probably leaving his breakfast untouched. She considered the matter thoughtfully.

'And Patrick, how is Patrick?' she asked, putting the paper aside.

His face changed and she waited, tucking her hands into her sleeves and sensing the hard knot of tense knuckles against the soft veins of her wrists. He was, she knew, trying to find words of hope, but she felt her heart skip a beat and a sharp knife of pain in her left side. A wave of nausea swept over her, leaving her trembling and the starched linen wimple was cold and damp against the skin of her forehead.

'Not good,' he said eventually. 'Initially it was a matter of stopping the bleeding, you see. Of tying up arteries, but now . . . The liver, of course, was damaged by the massive blow in the lumber region from the car, and, of course . . . However, you don't want a medical lecture, Reverend Mother. Pray for him. He's in the hands of God now.'

The Reverend Mother received this in silence. Dr Scher and two other doctors had worked on Patrick's inert body for six hours in the operating theatre of the Mercy Hospital. That had been told to her. She thought of the young policeman, thought of him as the earnest child in her school, the hard-working schoolboy, the policeman, guardian of the peace. And she thought of Jimmy's little body and knew that Dr Scher was thinking of it also. 'Strangled, not drowned; very professionally done', had been his verdict. Once again she felt that sharp pain and another wave of nausea swept over her. She sat very still and willed it to pass. She had too much to do. She could not afford to give in.

Dr Scher was lost in thought, reviewing all the medical procedures and his attention was not on her. She could rest for a few minutes, but then she would have to share the knowledge. That pain in her left side made it a matter of urgency. The facts needed to be known by someone other than herself, someone who would be respected by the police. She had hopes that Patrick, young, strong, toughened by early hardships, would survive and when he was well enough, someone would have to tell him the truth about these killings.

She, at her age, might not be there to serve that purpose.

But if she were not, then Dr Scher had to take her place. And so she had to convince him. There should be no grain of suspicion left to attach itself to innocent people. Sooner or later the real facts about those three murders would have to be known. She felt a certain measure of energy come back into her veins and straightened herself unobtrusively, her eyes on the clock, pacing herself, hoping that her time-worn heart would last for yet another few weeks, months, or, if God was good, perhaps even years. When the large hand reached the third numeral, then she would speak. In the meantime, she rested, watched the doctor's pensive face and thought about Eileen.

As soon as the clock hand reached the quarter mark, she got briskly to her feet and unlocked the bottom drawer of her desk.

'I wrote this last Friday, Dr Scher,' she said 'and I gave a copy of it to Eileen.' She did not hand the paper to him, but held it, still folded, in a hand that was now quite steady.

He roused himself from his inner thoughts, his review of medical procedures.

'How is Eileen?' he asked, trying to smile.

'Well,' said the Reverend Mother. 'She has changed her mind about being a doctor. When Utopia will reign in Ireland; when university education is free to all who can avail of it. Eileen,' she said deliberately, watching his face as she spoke, 'has now decided to be a lawyer. She met a man, by the name of Maurice, who acts as a judge, or prosecutor or defending lawyer in the Sinn Féin courts. I think he has impressed her and now she feels that as a lawyer she can do more for the cause in which she believes. I gave her a copy of this list and she said that she knew the answer to each one of my questions. And so,' said the Reverend Mother, hearing her voice now strengthening to a note which was firm and ringing. And so,' she repeated, 'I allowed her to take the list away in the name of justice.'

He was staring at her and somehow his air of unease made her feel more confident.

'A list,' he repeated.

'A list. And the first question on it was to query the reason for Father Dominic's visit to the antiques shop. It seemed to me,' she went on, choosing her words with care, 'that as Father Dominic spent most of his time in the confessional that it might have something to do with a confession, that he might have gone there to endeavour to prevent a crime.

'So you think that it was a confession to Father Dominic that triggered the killing.' Dr Scher's face was thoughtful. 'Well, that must mean that James O'Reilly, the only Catholic in the group, confessed to Father Dominic that the Merrymen were not just a nice, lively group of young people, putting on Gilbert and Sullivan plays for the their own enjoyment and in order to entertain the citizens of Cork, but were, in fact, a gang of thieves and arsonists who had taken advantage of the Sinn Féin attacks on those lovely old houses, owned by Protestants, and were stripping valuable antiques from these houses and reselling them in the shop on Morrison's Island.'

'That's right.' The Reverend Mother gave him a nod of approval. 'I don't know that I could ever prove this, but I think that in some way, Tom and Marjorie Gamble encountered Peter Doyle and Jonathon Power in London and between them this scheme was hatched. The Gambles, who had once owned all of Morrison's Island, would know that there were plenty of underground places where stolen goods could be hidden, until the memory of them had begun to fade. It was a clever plan. Jonathon, I'd say, already worked in antique restoration. Peter Doyle, his friend since the army days, was passing himself off as the grandson of landed Anglo-Irish gentry and was an enterprising man of business. I can imagine the plan being hatched in some smart hotel in London, the sort of place where Marjorie Gamble, and her brother, enjoyed a holiday.'

'And once they got going, it proved to be immensely lucrative,' said Dr Scher.

'Yes, of course,' said the Reverend Mother. 'We never realized it when we were young, but these houses were filled with treasure. They were probably cautious in the beginning, opened the shop. The Gambles, between them – and perhaps Judge Gamble may have been in the enterprise also – financed the fitting out of the warehouse. Then, bit by bit, they recruited members. They told Patrick that it was a barman who suggested they set up a singing group. Well, that's as maybe. In any case, they recruited Robert Beamish, a young man with plenty of brawn, few scruples and a great desire for easily earned cash.'

'And James O'Reilly?' queried Dr Scher.

The Reverend Mother's face grew grave. 'James O'Reilly was a victim,' she said. 'Eileen told me that he was a drug addict and I would be surprised if that were not a deliberate act on the part of his new friends. He was useful to the group because he could manage the bank accounts, could prevent any questions being asked about a business account which had no outgoings and a continual stream of income.'

'And James O'Reilly was the only Catholic in the group, was the only one who would know that there was an iron mesh between penitent and priest, the only one who would know how small the space was. But somehow, he seems to me to be an unlikely murderer. I saw him in the bank one day a few weeks before all this happened and I thought that the man was a bag of nerves. But you think that he was the murderer, do you? You think that he thought Father Dominic betrayed him.'

The Reverend Mother suppressed an impatient movement. She remembered her words to Eileen: a country divided by their belief in a common Deity. The one half believes that the other half must understand.

'No Catholic would fear that a priest would betray him, Dr Scher.'

'I'm sure that you are right. I'm a bit outside these sacred mysteries.'

'"*Odi profanum vulgus*". If you remember your Horace, Dr Scher, you will know that our English word "profane" means being outside the inner circle of worship. But of course there is another inner circle, another sanctity and that is marriage. Both of us are outside of that circle, but one can imagine that information is continually exchanged. Very easy for a wife to ask a husband questions.'

'A wife!' Dr Scher looked startled and incredulous. His eye went to the folded newspaper.

The Reverend Mother nodded. 'It seems to me,' she said in a conversational tone, 'that this country does a grave injustice to the female sex when it forbids married women to practise their profession, such as teaching or nursing, as soon as the wedding ring is on their finger. Rose O'Reilly was an excellent nurse with a thirst for medical knowledge; I have spoken to a sister in our Mercy Hospital and she made that remark. But as soon as she married she had nothing to do. No children arrived, and after four years of marriage, would be unlikely. So because she was bored, she took a job in the antiques shop.'

'I saw her there myself.'

The Reverend Mother nodded. 'Yes, you told me that she was there on the fatal day when poor Dominic visited the shop and saw the ceramic hawk. That day when he tried, without breaking the seal of confession, to avert any more raids, any more deaths.'

'And James O'Reilly came to hear of it. Rose must have told him. He must have got a fright when Patrick went to see him in the bank, went to question him. Do you think that he had already told his wife that he had been to confess to Father Dominic?'

'Of course! It is impossible to know all the secrets of a marriage, but I would guess that he did tell her.'

'And that frightened her.'

'Being a Protestant, she did not realize how sacred the seal of confession would be and immediately feared that her husband would be arrested, and perhaps executed for his part in the arson and murder of that poor gardener who worked for the Wood family.'

Dr Scher frowned. 'If she were a Protestant – and I bow to your knowledge of the ins and outs of families of Cork – but if she were a Protestant, how did she know what the confessional was like? How would she know about the grid?'

'I imagine that her husband told her – she may have asked him what it was like. Protestants, I find, are fascinated by the idea of confession,' said the Reverend Mother. 'And, of course, being a Protestant she might not have known how Father Dominic was so dearly loved by all Republicans, how his defiance of the bishop when he ministered to the dying hunger strikers had touched their hearts. In this distressful city of ours, sudden violent deaths are usually laid at the door of the Sinn Féin movement. She would assume that the Republicans would be blamed. But there is a more important question about the means of murder which I would expect someone like you to fasten upon?'

'The hat pin?'

'Yes, of course. I would never have thought of a hat pin

being able to inflict death though I and my sisters handle them every day. But the murderer knew. And, that I found to be significant. Who knows but some teacher, some professor, standing in front of a class of trainee nurses, might have pointed to a picture of the brain and showed how near it was to the ear. Once I thought of that, my suspicions began to be roused. Rose was the only one among those connected with Morrison's Island Antiques, who had medical knowledge. And the murder itself had to be swift, efficient and carried out by someone who had been trained to know that hesitation could be fatal.'

'And why Peter Doyle? Why kill him?' Dr Scher, she thought, was not wholly convinced by her reasoning. To a medical man, she supposed, it would seem obvious that the brain was so near to the ear, obvious that a person who would set out to jab through the ear could carry out the action swiftly and efficiently. She set herself to convince him. The right person had been executed. She was certain of that. The killing had to be stopped. But justice must be seen to be done. Eileen had come to see her yesterday. Together they had prayed before the small coffin, and laid the little book within it, resting it on the child's heart.

'Because Peter Doyle guessed what she had done,' she said. 'Remember, Dr Scher, Peter Doyle was the only one who knew for certain that he himself had not been in the church before the Novena prayers began. You will recollect that Patrick told us – "a small man, wearing a black suit and a moustache" had been witnessed in the church. The description was given by a man who owned a garage on Morrison's Island and who filled the lorry with petrol for Peter Doyle and Jonathon Power.'

Dr Scher nodded slowly. 'So when Patrick questions him, Peter Doyle knows it was not he, and starts to guess who it was. She dressed up, I suppose that you are going to say, but would that have been easy?'

'Well, Eileen told me that there was only one female part in Gilbert and Sullivan's *Trial by Jury* and that was taken by Anne Morgan – she was the plaintiff. So the other two women, Marjorie Gamble and Rose O'Reilly must have been dressed up as men – probably members of the jury, if I remember the play correctly. Peter Doyle donated a few old suits to the dressing-up cupboard; so Eileen told me; no doubt there were false moustaches in there as well. I imagine that Rose, having seen you in the shop that day when Father Dominic asked to see the manager, wanted to throw suspicion onto someone other than her husband or herself. And, of course, like a lot of young women these days, she wears her hair shingled, as short as any man's hair. And she had dark hair.'

'I would never have thought of her,' said Dr Scher. 'Though, I suppose, a hat pin is a woman's weapon.'

'Peter Doyle, of course, was a more difficult subject than Father Dominic.' The Reverend Mother was conscious that the slight nausea was hovering over her again and she resolutely quelled it, focussing on the problem of conveying days of thought in a compact and comprehensible way. 'Nevertheless, he was, according to Eileen, a great flirt, a ladies' man and had flirted with all of the girls. I suspect that Rose invited him out to sit in his car, she probably pretended she had something to show him, a present for him, or something like that, and then once they were in the warehouse, probably him ahead and she behind, she threw her arms about his neck, as though to embrace and then throttled him.'

'Again using her medical knowledge,' said Dr Scher.

The Reverend Mother nodded. 'I would imagine that it would be easy for her to use just enough force to render him unconscious. She inserted the hat pin – there were, of course, a large supply of them in the costumes' cupboard, very necessary to pin the roses to the girls' wigs – so the hat pin was neatly and quickly slipped in through the ear, while she held him. She laid the body down, added the prepared card, and she went back the way she came.'

'Without anyone seeing anything?'

'You forget my stories about Morrison's Island,' said the Reverend Mother. 'Flooding destroyed the original foundations of the Holy Trinity Church and of the early warehouses. The whole of the present day island is a platform built on piers of stone and concrete. There are underground passages everywhere.

Rose O'Reilly would have known all about this. My little Jimmy . . .' She stopped for a moment, stared across at the raindrops running down the window. With an effort, she steadied her voice. 'My little Jimmy told me about these passageways and that he had found an underground room full of treasure, all the silver and gold . . .' She stopped again, unable to go on.

'Don't distress yourself,' said Dr Scher. 'I'm a stupid old man, but I understand what you are saying. They could all come and go underground. The murderer could probably get from the shop to the church with no bother, could have found the shawl, concealed it in a broom cupboard, come back . . . in fact, if you are right, and I begin to see that you must be, then this murdering nurse could have made the journey between the shop and the church by an underground passageway and somewhere like a broom cupboard would have been an obvious place to emerge. A woman with short hair and glued-on moustache might have passed for a man in the dark at the back of the church. Harder out of doors, I'd say.'

The Reverend Mother recovered herself. 'When I was thinking about it originally, I found it hard to work out why the murder of Father Dominic and the murder of Peter Doyle were not carried out by the usual method in this city, where there is a gun in eight out of ten households, or at least they know where to get hold of one. And remember that all of those connected with the nefarious traffic in Morrison's Island Antiques, and I do believe that all must be connected – all of the men, anyway, Peter Doyle, Jonathon Power, Tom Gamble, Robert Beamish and James O'Reilly, remember all of these men had guns. The evidence for that is undeniable. Every raid was carried out by masked men holding rifles.'

'And, of course, the Gamble and Beamish families would be out shooting unfortunate birds as soon as the boys emerged from their nursery,' put in Dr Scher.

'And the two young Englishmen had served together in the war. They would be able to handle a gun. Remember someone shot the Woods' gardener. Why not shoot Father Dominic?

He went everywhere, all over the city. He would have been an easy target. And Peter Doyle, also, if the necessity arose. Morrison's Island is full of derelict warehouses. Why not shoot him from an upper storey as he walked out towards his car. People in Cork tend to close their doors and windows when they hear gunfire.'

'But the women would not have guns. Would not be used to handling them, would be unlikely to be able to be accurate enough to kill a man.'

'That's right,' said the Reverend Mother. 'And of the women, only one had medical knowledge, had the training that would make her fast and accurate at piercing the eardrum, rendering a man unconscious, and . . .' Her voice faltered again, but she took in a deep breath and added, 'And would be able to strangle a young boy. She has been tried and found guilty by the Sinn Féin court.'

The Reverend Mother sat back, re-opened the newspaper and read through the article again.

The Cork Examiner
Monday July 2, 1923:
ANOTHER APPALLING ATROCITY!

The body of twenty-five-year-old Mrs James O'Reilly, whose husband is an employee of the Cork Savings Bank, has been found shot, outside her home in Pope's Quay. Republican involvement is suspected. Superintendent Hayes tells us he is hoping that a card left beside the body will lead the Civic Guards to her murderers.

Mrs O'Reilly was the daughter of Mr and Mrs John Burke, retired manager in the Queen's Old Castle, and was an only child. She trained as a nurse when she left school and worked in the Mercy Hospital until her marriage four years ago. She was a talented actress who took part in the much acclaimed Gilbert and Sullivan operas in the Father Matthew Hall, including the recent performance of *The Mikado*.

Messages of sympathy are pouring in for the grieving husband and the parents of the lovely young woman whose life has been cut short by dastardly scoundrels.

The *Cork Examiner* would like to extend their deepest condolences to the family.

And then she put the newspaper aside. *Noli respicere post tergum*, she said to herself as she picked up her time-worn copy of *St Thomas Aquinas*.

ACKNOWLEDGEMENTS

Many thanks to all who have helped me with 'Beyond Absolution'. First, as always, my agent Peter Buckman who is such a source of inspiration, encouragement, and practical help to me. My editor, Anna Telfer, who spots any weaknesses and is liberal with praise. My publisher, Edwin Buckhalter, who shows a keen interest in the books and all of his staff for their hard work on my publications. Sister Anne Cahill who investigated the confessional stalls in the Holy Trinity Church on my behalf. Last, but not least, my daughter Ruth, who was of great assistance in a redraft of the first half of this book.

Lightning Source UK Ltd.
Milton Keynes UK
UKHW01f0945051018

330010UK00001B/2/P